ELIZABETH'S STAR

BOOK 1 - WE'LL MEET AGAIN SERIES

RHONDA FORREST

Valeena Press

ELIZABETH'S STAR 2021

BOOK 1- We'll Meet Again Series

Published by Valeena Press 2021

Published by Valeena Press (Feb 9 2026)

Book Cover Design and formatting by Ethel Beckett and Rhonda Forrest

ASIN 978-0-9945356-8-9

❉ Created with Vellum

WE'LL MEET AGAIN TRILOGY

Elizabeth's Star is Book 1 in a series of 3

You can continue the story of *Elizabeth's Star* by reading, *Until We Meet* and *We'll Meet Again*.

***There are also sample chapters in the back of this book for your enjoyment - from the bestselling novel - 'Silkworm Secrets'.

HAPPY READING!

AUTHOR'S NOTE

In January 1941, my grandfather, James McGowan, enlisted for service at Kelvin Grove, Brisbane. His unit was the Australian Army Ordnance Corps, which would later become part of Lark Force. On the 10th of March that same year, he was 'marched out to duty – Rabaul, New Britain', leaving behind a young wife and five children. At the time, my mother, Margaret, was twelve years old; her father used a school atlas to show her and the rest of the family where he was going. They weren't allowed to tell anyone. He was going to build observation structures and do maintenance work—he would be back home in six months.

When the Japanese forces invaded New Britain on 23 January 1942, the small garrison of Lark Force was supposed to defend Rabaul against overwhelming odds. Australian women and children had been evacuated in the weeks prior, but others had not been given the option to leave.

The ill-equipped Australian force of 1500 soldiers fought gallantly in an attempt to turn the tide of the advancing Japanese, who completed well-coordinated attacks with their navy, air force and army. With no sign of backup or support from the Australian government, the assessment of the situation by the head of the unit, Lieutenant-Colonel John Scanlan, was that the situation was hopeless. His subsequent orders were, 'Every man for himself'. Members of Lark Force and the civilians of Rabaul retreated into the jungle, scattering in every direction as they searched for an escape route through the thick rainforest and treacherous terrain. Struggling with malaria, dysentery, malnutrition and exhaustion, some made their way to points where they could escape on small boats to the New Guinea mainland. Others perished in the jungles of New Britain.

One hundred and seventy men made their way to Tol Plantation, hoping to be rescued. However, Japanese forces were waiting for them, and the Australians had no choice but to surrender. Only six of those 170 men survived the surrender at Tol; the rest of the Australians were shot, bayoneted or beheaded.

In the occupied township of Rabaul, 1053 Australian troops, along with other residents of Rabaul and the nurses who remained, were held as prisoners of war. On 22 June 1942, 845 military personnel and 209 civilians were marched down to the wharf at Rabaul and loaded into the holds of the Japanese ship, *Montevideo Maru*. The ship was unmarked and—en route to Hainan Island, off the coast of southern China—was torpedoed and sunk by an American submarine, the *USS Sturgeon*. All on board perished. This tragedy remains the greatest loss of Australian lives at sea.

Margaret was seventeen when the war ended. She remembers all those years her father was away, and the telegram that arrived in 1942 announcing he was 'missing in action'. Every night she would listen to the radio for the names of current prisoners of war. Perhaps she would hear her father's name, and know he was alive and where he was. In October 1945, more than a month after the war ended, the family finally received a telegram announcing their father, James McGowan, QX64913, had been on board the Japanese prisoner-of-war ship, the *Montevideo Maru*, which was torpedoed by an American submarine. There were no survivors.

For many years there was confusion around the plight of those left in Rabaul. The ship's list was missing, and the families given either varied versions or no further information about where the ship and the bodies of their loved ones lay. Today, families can look at the ship's roll, written in Japanese and transcribed into English. It is moving to read the names of those who were on board, the names of men who were, as many say, left behind as 'hostages to freedom', disregarded by an Australian government who made no plans to either evacuate them or to send any reinforcements or rescue crews after the invasion.

Like so many other families, my mother and her siblings may never really know what happened to their father, who they thought would only be gone for a matter of months. The following story is a work of fiction and is not James' story. It does however, feature actual events and a depiction of what life was like for those who were in Rabaul, those who escaped, and those who waited to learn the plight of their loved ones.

Lest We Forget

ELIZABETH'S STAR

BOOK 1 - WE'LL MEET AGAIN SERIES

'A dingo howls. A star falls.
Don't worry for me. I'll be home soon.'

Map of New Guinea, Australia and South-East Asia

Map of Papua New Guinea and New Britain - Rabaul

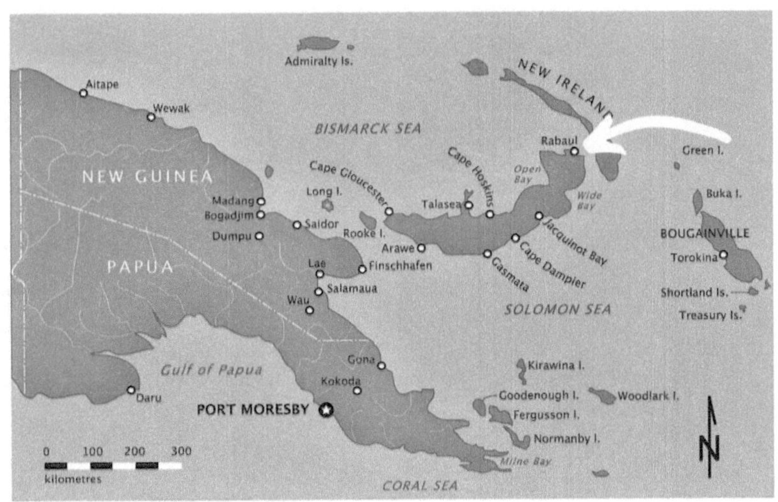

CHAPTER 1

Bundeen Station – Channel Country, Queensland
1929

Michael sat at the kitchen table, running his fingers across the five names carved into the well-worn timber top. His name was in the middle: Michael McTavish, 1916. Two names were written above his; his twin brother, Dan, and elder brother, Rory. Below Michael's name was a star and the year 1918.

'That was the year the Great War ended,' Michael's father, Hamish, said. 'It was the war to end all wars, and Australian men from all over the nation signed up, with sixty thousand never coming back.'

'How many died altogether in the whole world?' Michael asked.

'Millions. Millions and millions. Fifteen, sixteen million they say, but probably more than that.' Hamish grimaced. 'They wouldn't take me because of this bung leg. Let's hope there'll never be anything like it again.'

'Surely, with so many people dying, they've learnt not to start wars.' Anxiety tugged at Michael—the thought of going off to war and dying, never seeing his mother again, stopped him from eating his dinner, just for a moment.

'Let's hope so.' Hamish turned to his wife, Edith. 'Your mother and I are blessed you five boys were born after the war, so we didn't have to suffer the loss of sons like so many others.'

Michael returned to the carvings in the table. Below the star and year 1918 were the names of his two younger brothers, Frank and Lachie. He ran his fingers over the star, the shape familiar, the edges smoothed by the hands that had touched it over the years.

His mother never talked about it, but there had been a baby girl born before he and Dan turned two. Michael often sensed there was something that bothered his mum. Sometimes her eyes dulled, or she stared vacantly across the paddock at nothing in particular. Often, when she sang a lullaby or sat resting in the evening, tears moistened her cheeks. When he asked what she was looking at, she would wipe her face and turn away. 'It's nothing, Mickey. Just something in my eye. Nothing for you to worry about.'

Michael had quizzed his father, but it wasn't until he was older that he found out why his mother was sometimes a bit distant, or sad without reason. Michael would always remember the night their father told the story. It was the night after his and Dan's thirteenth birthday, and they were camped out on the long paddock, the stars filling the night sky above.

* * *

Earlier in the afternoon, Michael had ridden ahead to pick the best campsite for the night; by the time the others arrived, the spare horses were hobbled and the damper on the fire. By dusk the cattle were settled, the sun dropping quickly below the low scrub lining the horizon. There were no fences to hold the mob, and Michael chose the camp and fire area carefully, so the smell of preparing dinner wouldn't drift near them. The cattle hated the smell of cooking meat. Even the water used for cooking and drinking was carefully poured out so they wouldn't get wind of it and become unsettled. Camps needed to be tidy and well ordered, with nothing left lying around to be kicked during the night, spooking the cattle and causing a stampede.

The three brothers sat around the fire with their father, the silence of the night settling in. Michael wrapped his heavy coat tighter, warding off the winter chill as he repositioned the billy in the dancing sparks. He watched the fire flicker brightly as slivers of flames licked the dry logs, the branches and twigs crackling in the still of the evening.

Dan placed more logs on the blaze and looked up at the night sky. 'That star to the west is always the brightest and the first one to come out in the evening.'

'That's Elizabeth's star,' Hamish said, casting his eyes upwards.

The three boys waited, looking at each other silently. Michael knew better than to ask questions. His father always thought and paused before he spoke. When he did talk, his Scottish brogue was like music, lilting on the night air.

'You know, your mother and I came here from the home country with only a suitcase each and that old bugle my brother brought back from the Boer War. All the way from Glasgow to Sydney, the two of us, your mother a young lass. We found our way here to Bundeen and it was a lucky day for us, and all of ye, that Bill and Charlotte gave me work and offered for us to buy the hut and block.'

Dan stoked the fire. 'You were going to tell us about Elizabeth.'

'Ah, I was, wasn't I? She was born after you boys.' Hamish nodded towards Michael and Dan. He picked up a stick and stirred the embers of the fire, pausing for a long while before continuing with the story. 'The healthiest chubbiest bairn, with eyes as blue as the sky above Loch Lomond on a clear summer's day.'

The silence hummed with tension as they waited for him to continue. The silhouettes of the cattle in the distance remained motionless, not a swing of a head or bellow of a calf. The dogs lying next to the boys were also silent, two of them lifting their heads and watching Hamish, as if they too were listening to the story. Rory got up and took the billy from the fire, his father holding out his tin mug for a refill.

'Thanks, son.' He took a long sip, his stare fixed on the fire's embers. The glow lit up the boys' faces, the flames throwing flickering shadows across their coats. 'Aye, she was the bonniest baby you ever saw. At six weeks old she was already smiling and reaching up to my face.' Hamish's voice shook, and he pulled his hat lower over his face. 'She'd grab my beard and make those sweet sounds babies make. A wee noise that pulls at ye heartstrings.'

Their father sat upright, wiping his eyes with the back of his leathery hands. 'There's something about a wee girl that affects a man; it's a softness, a love different from that of a son. She held my heart from the moment she was born.'

Michael waited while his father took a deep breath.

'Your mother would never talk about it, not to you boys. Sometimes she and I talked, when it first happened, but after a while she couldn't bear it. I think she always blamed herself.'

'What happened, Dad?' Dan asked.

'It was the middle of winter. You three boys slept in the wee bed together, out near the fireplace to keep you warm. Elizabeth slept right up next to your mother's side of the bed in a crib.' He looked up at the evening star for a long time before continuing, struggling with his words.

'She went to get her from the cot in the morning. I remember lying in bed waiting, because your mother always passed Elizabeth to me after she fed her. It was a morning ritual and it kept us all warm. You know, a special time for the three of us.' A tear rolled down his face and the boys looked at each other, unused to such a show of emotion and unsure what to say.

He placed his cup of tea on the ground, his voice barely audible. 'The wee baby had died. She was dead in your mother's arms.' His hands ran through his hair. 'Your mother screamed my name, yelling at me to wake Elizabeth up. But there was nothing to be done. She was gone.'

Dan's voice was a whisper. 'What made her die, Dad?'

'We never knew. The doctor said sometimes it happens. Babies go to bed healthy and don't ever wake up. Your mother blamed herself. But the bairn had plenty of warmth and it was nobody's fault. Just the will of God, maybe.'

'If that's the will of God, then I don't want anything to do with him!' Michael declared. The thought of his parents' suffering was too much for him to bear.

'I remember her.' Rory spoke up. 'I have a memory of holding a baby in front of the fire. I remember the smell, a soft baby smell.'

'That would be her. You were about four and you used to nurse her. You were only a wee fella yourself.' Hamish's voice broke again. 'She smiled when you talked to her.'

Michael sat by the fire for a long time after his father and Rory turned in for the night. Not far away, Dan played a wistful tune on his harmonica, his silhouette and that of the horse he sat on visible as he rode around the mob. Dan was the night watchman and in charge of the cattle, the tune letting the mob know where he was so they didn't startle. The music, as usual, settled the cattle and, before long, lullabied Hamish and Rory to sleep, their snoring accompanying Dan's tune. Michael's gaze turned towards the evening star, a vivid, winking diamond pointing directly down at him. He stared hard, imagining what his baby sister would have looked like, how her voice might have sounded. A shooting star blazed across the sky. A streak of light, in slow motion, its sparkle fading before it reached the ground.

CHAPTER 2

Bundeen Station – 1929

undeen Station was situated in the Channel Country of far Western Queensland, the nearest town, Windorah, over one hundred miles to the north. The Diamantina River and several of its tributaries ran through the forty thousand square miles of mostly flat, arid land. In times of high water, the tentacles of braided channels cut through and over the floodplains, leaving in their wake nutritious grasses that were excellent for grazing cattle. The shallow waters, sometimes stretching fifty miles wide, brought moisture and nutrients to the soil, heralding the beginning of plentiful seasons to come.

Michael barely remembered what the plains looked like in flood. The baked, cracked earth and dying trees were a familiar landscape, no matter which direction he travelled, the wet years a distant memory. Bundeen Station was owned by Bill and Charlotte Roberts, who had many years ago sold a one-hundred-acre block to the McTavish family, the small hut on it providing a starting point for the family, who increased its size as their own numbers grew.

It was a harsh environment, but the five boys thrived, all of them loving the lifestyle of working and living among cattle and horses. By the time Michael and Dan were thirteen, and Rory fifteen, they were already skilled stockman. Along with Hamish, who was known as the best ringer in the area, they made a reliable team for moving mobs of cattle.

Bill Roberts was full of praise for them. 'You boys are as good as any of my men. You two,' he nodded towards Dan and Michael, 'you've got different skills from one another and you make a solid team.'

'Dad says we're like chalk and cheese, both the way we look and the way we are,' Michael said, stretching up tall to look Dan in the eye.

Dan continually reminded Michael, or 'Mickey', as he called him, that he was the eldest. 'Don't forget, I'm older than you by ten minutes—and *way* taller.'

Dan had always been taller, making him an ideal kitchen helper who could reach the tins on top of the hutch. Michael was easy to spot, with a mop of unruly blond hair, unlike Dan's straight, brown hair, always combed back or hidden under a hat. Their facial features were similar: the broad cheeks of their father, the long eyelashes and deep-set eyes of their mother, and a mixture of the two in their full lips and straight white teeth. The fact that the boys all had good teeth was put down to the fact that their pet goats supplied them with plenty of milk, particularly when the boys were little.

Their mother often caught them drinking from the goat or hiding some other stray animal they'd found. 'Lachie, get yourself out from under that goat. You're covered in dust, and not much of that milk is going in your mouth. And Dan, you're squeezing the poor goat dry.' Her eyes missed nothing. 'Mickey, I wasn't born yesterday. What have you got in that box? If it's another lizard or baby bird, you'll have to find food for it—and make sure you use those old rags to keep it warm.'

Lachie and Frank always wanted to help look after the animals, and they followed Michael everywhere, their cries of *'Mickey!'* echoing across the paddocks as they tried to keep up with him. Even the pet parrot had picked up on his name, screeching *'Mickey!'* every afternoon when it wanted feeding.

Michael always made sure to take care with his chores, because although Edith was short in stature, she was in charge of the household. Their father told them that when she first came to Australia at the age of twenty, her waist was tiny, her arms and legs thin and short like a child's. Now, although she had gained a little weight and her face was tanned, she still looked like a youngster, her dark brown eyes and deep dimples an attractive sight.

Edith's wavy hair intrigued Michael, the long blonde tresses hanging down the middle of her back, the colour the same as his and his younger brothers'. At night she sat patiently as Michael plaited it, her eyes closed, talking to him while he braided.

'It's the best feeling in the world, having you boys all together with me.'

Dan often interrupted the tranquillity. 'Ha, Mum, look at Mickey's hair. I plaited it while he was doing yours. He looks like a girl.'

'That's the worst plait I've ever seen.' Rory joined in. 'There's more sticking out than in.'

'Look, everyone, I've tied a pretty ribbon in it. Now he'd pass for a young lass.' Dan tugged hard on the plait, pulling a silly face as he jigged around Michael.

Michael's mother turned around and patted him on the arm. 'Leave him alone, Dan. If only you were all as easy-going. Not through all the years has Michael ever given me a second of grief, unlike the rest of you.'

'What about when he puts the fear of God into you with the

tumbles and jumps he does on the horses? You always say the twins give you grey hairs and wrinkles,' Rory said.

'Aw, Mum, you love us.' Dan wrapped his strong arms around her, lifting her off the ground. The boys huddled, hugging her tight, not letting her move, even when she started yelling out to their dad. 'Cheeky bairns, the lot of you. Get out of my way and let me do my work! You're nothing but a bunch of troublemakers and a terrible example to those younger two.'

'Ah, the spoilt ones', Rory said, 'they're the real trouble. Only yesterday Mickey rescued them from the big house. Stealing fruit from right under the nose of Ah Lee. Poor old gardener, with his one ancient tree in the dusty dry paddock and barely a piece of fruit on it. Those two were up it and ready to take what they could.'

* * *

Michael's favourite times were when they moved large mobs of cattle across the plains. The days were long and hot, but at night they sat around a campfire, listening to Hamish as he reminisced about life in the old country. It was hard to imagine a country where the landscape was covered in snow for more than half the year and cattle had shaggy coats and long wide horns.

It was a stark contrast to the vast plains of outback Queensland and the robust, short-haired cattle that spent their lives flicking away swarms of flies.

'Was your house like the one we live in?' Michael asked his father.

His father shook his head and wiped the sweat from his forehead. 'Nothing the same at all. It was a thatch-roofed blackhouse, with stone walls on the outside, lined with earth on the inside. The roof was made from rye grass, keeping out the rain and warming your mother and me through the long winter months when the sun hardly shone.'

'Our walls are thick slabs of bark,' Rory said. 'The roof is tin, and Mum says it's hot enough to fry an egg on in summer.'

'Aye, it's a different life. It's hard for ye to believe, but back in the old country our animals slept inside. Us down one end, them down the other. Now we're working with hardened cattle and horses, as well as with men who can tell stories about tracks that are drier and wilder than ours here on Bundeen Station.'

Michael hung on Hamish's every word, his father conjuring exotic images of a different world. 'Are you glad you came here, Dad?'

'Aye, at first it was foreign territory and I had to work hard to earn my place among the cattlemen. Men back home were tough and could withstand the harsh winters and the bleak mountain countryside. But the men here,' he shook his head and stoked the fire, 'when I first arrived, I was in awe of how they'd kill a black snake as thick as your arm, or wrestle with cattle as wild as the devil himself.' He paused for a long while, casting his eyes out into the blackness surrounding them. 'Here the distances are huge, the people are rugged and,' he looked back to the boys, 'this country has everything a man could ever want or need.' He sniffed the air. 'There's nothing better than smelling the cattle nearby, the burning wood there in front of ye, and feeling the isolation that comes from being surrounded by thousands of miles of scrub and desert. Aye, it's a rare country, and it was the best day of our lives when we arrived here.'

* * *

Although the hut Hamish bought from Bill was small to start with, over the years—as the family grew—several rooms and a long sleepout had been added down one side, and the iron roof extended accordingly.

A new floor with timber boards was a welcome comfort after years of dampening down a dirt floor. The houseproud Edith had turned the hut into a cosy retreat that not only kept them out of the weather, but also had some tender touches of the old country. Straggly sweet peas grew over an arch, welcoming visitors to the house, and there was always a vase full of whatever wildflowers or foliage Edith could lay her hands on.

It was a difficult time in Australia. The Great Depression had begun, and throughout the country—in city and rural areas alike—regions of men were unemployed, having to survive on handouts.

Occasionally a swagman stopped by their hut, his face gaunt, a small bag of belongings hanging from a stick resting on his shoulder. These men were down and out, moving from property to property in search of work. Edith would always find something for them to eat and let them spend a night in one of the sheds, sleeping on the feed bags, or send them on their way with a full belly and perhaps the possibility of work over at the main homestead.

The men were grateful for anything they received, and their gratitude was a reminder that not everyone had food in their belly, or somewhere safe to sleep at night. Michael never wanted to be lonely like they were. Their faces came to him at night when he closed his eyes, and he promised himself to never be in a position where he needed to beg for food or with no family around him.

CHAPTER 3

Bundeen Station – Winter, 1932

ichael sat warming his hands at the wood-fired stove. He watched the younger two as they helped set the table in readiness for the special dinner tonight for his and Dan's sixteenth birthday. A large pot bubbled and boiled on the stovetop, a delicious aroma filling the room. The availability of sheep on a nearby property catered for the family's traditional meal of haggis, and Michael's mouth watered in anticipation.

'Sit down, the lot of you.' Edith's quiet voice was commanding, and immediately the five boys sat around the table, waiting for their father to join them.

Hamish was a quietly spoken man. He rarely raised his voice but had a canny way of making sure the boys all toed the line. He only needed to tap his finger on the table and someone would be up and getting the milk out of the cold box, or filling the water jug for their mother. Out in the paddocks, a nod of his head or a wave of his hand was enough to command not only his own sons, but any man who was working for him, to ride in the direction he indicated.

Edith was adamant Hamish was the boss and every idea had to be run past him, but Michael and his brothers all knew that the backbone of the family, and the one they needed to heed, was their mother.

For many years, Hamish's work had been out on the stock routes, the droving taking him away from the family for months at a time. He covered countless miles with thousands of head of cattle, mixed with tough men and endured isolation and hardships while battling the heat and cold of the outback. Back at the station, Edith persevered without complaint, continuing to carve out a life for her family. It was a sweet day for the family when Bill offered Hamish the position of homestead stockman, in charge of the activities of the nearby cattle and horses.

'When cattle go astray or I need someone to find water, I can rely on your sons,' Bill said. 'Your boy Michael has an extraordinary gift for finding water. He can track down a steer and find those hidden waterholes that only the Aborigines know about. It's uncanny, like he's one with the land.'

'Maybe he learnt from the Aboriginal kids he played with. They were always out yonder together,' Hamish replied. The two men leaned on the fence, looking over the latest mob of cattle they had brought into the yard.

'I can tell you, that boy would survive in the middle of the desert. His sense of direction is unerring, and his mind is as quick as any.' Bill shook his head. 'Your other boys work as good as any of my older men, but Michael, he's going to be a big asset for you in the future.'

'Aye, he's a grand lad with a heart of gold,' Hamish replied.

Bill chuckled. 'I saw your two boys in the home paddock the other week. It was the day after they brought that big mob in. They were letting off a bit of steam and having a wonderful time doing tricks on their horses.'

Hamish grunted. 'It'll be the death of my poor Edith, watching those two on the horses. I've never seen anyone do what they can.'

'I counted the tumbles in the air and then every time, they landed back squarely on the horse's back. The amazing thing was, the horse never faltered either.'

'They've had their share of falls, but nothing too serious. They've been doing those tricks since they were wee lads.'

'You should be proud of them—and all your boys.'

'Aye, we've been blessed alright. I hope they never have to go through war like our generation did.'

Bill shook his head. 'They say never again will there be a war like that one. It's good times ahead for all of us, once these Depression years roll by. And they will.'

Hamish smiled as he gazed out across the vast expanse stretching in front of them. '*Aye khoi*, never again. They are indeed a lucky generation.'

CHAPTER 4

Bundeen Station – Spring, 1933

Working with stock in the paddocks was what Michael loved most. The land swarmed with life, and he never tired of watching the many creatures that shared the area where he rode. His keen eyes followed trails of spiky dragon lizards that scuttled through the red dust, their short legs moving at a million miles an hour, seeking safety away from the hooves of horses and cattle. The ambling echidnas were not as fast. Michael would stop and loosen the reins, giving his horse a sniff of the spiked animal that had decided its safest bet was to roll up in a ball and wait until the stock moved on.

The sky was also alive. Enormous flocks of corellas soared overhead, their white bodies stark against the vivid blue sky, their screeches echoing across an emptiness as they flew eastward in search of water. Black kites glided high above, wings spread wide, eyes cast downwards in pursuit of prey. And every so often, thousands of striking blue and yellow budgerigars flicked across the heavens, also seeking to quench their thirst.

At sunset, huge mobs of kangaroos bounded effortlessly in front of the cattle, their bodies partially hidden by clouds of dust stirred up by movement, hazy particles dancing in the glare of the sun. As the sun sank lower, brilliant golds, pinks and reds filled the sky, a few low distant hills the only break in an otherwise flat land. The burning colours of the sky cast their reflected glow back onto land and, for a short while, rich hues of gold and red covered the earth, the cattle and the men who moved across it.

As the sun dipped below the horizon, its last, lingering rays cast long shadows. This signalled the end of the working day, and time to head home and clean up for dinner.

* * *

The lounge room was a cosy after-dinner retreat, a place and time to reflect on the day now past and what tomorrow might bring. Michael stretched his body out on the long lounge chair, stretching his neck from side to side to relieve the aching and stiffness that had built up during the day. The muscles in his arms were tight, and he rubbed them hard, noticing the hairs on them getting thicker and his once-gangly forearms starting to thicken and look more like a man's. He enjoyed the sight of his body developing, maturing, his limbs now thicker, stronger—no longer those of a boy.

He glanced at Rory and Dan, who lay on cowhide rugs, a serious game of draughts in play. The two younger brothers lay next to them, propped on their elbows, while Hamish watched from his armchair in the corner, a pipe tucked into his mouth, the sweet smell of tobacco wafting through the room.

Edith usually had mending to do, and the golden light from the lamp next to her cast a warm glow over the family as they enjoyed the quiet of the evening. Michael lay on his back, looking at the pictures hanging on the walls. His mother had hung gilded frames, filled with paintings of green pastures and babbling brooks – rural idylls from the old country. There was a carved wooden frame with a photo of Hamish's brother before he went to fight in the Boer War. On the shelf next to the pictures, taking pride of place, was the 'good luck' bugle, brought back from that same war.

Sometimes his father took it down and passed it to Dan, who was the only one of the boys with any musical ability. Dan had inherited his mother's gift for music—he could also play a lively harmonica.

An old drover had given the harmonica to Dan when he was a kid. Edith had invited the drover, who brought a mob of cattle down from way up north, to have a meal with the family. The wiry stockman entertained them for hours on the small verandah, his Scottish tunes a melancholic sound across the plains. For the first time Michael could remember, his mother cried, the music bringing back memories of the people and places that had once been her life.

Hamish passed her a handkerchief and, once she'd composed herself, she sang along, her voice a melodious accompaniment to the drover's music. As the drover was leaving the next day, he gave the small harmonica to Dan, who sat mesmerised at his feet the entire time he played. 'This old tin sandwich belonged to Sid Kidman himself,' he told Dan. 'I'm running out of puff to play, so you learn it now. Your mother knows the tunes. It'll calm the cattle and horses when you're out on the track.'

Dan drove them crazy, the tinny notes shrill to their ears, until he learned to play in tune. His determination paid off and within a few months he mastered every tune his mother could remember. At night Edith's strong voice filled the hut, with the boys joining in, their deep voices blending harmoniously as they sang the haunting lyrics of her favourite songs.

***

Not long after Michael turned sixteen, a mystery load arrived at the hut. Not only was there equipment and supplies for the main house, but hidden behind a cover was a surprise delivery for Edith. It was an upright wooden piano that had made its way on the back of the supply cart all the way from Brisbane.

Hamish grinned like a mischievous boy, laughing loudly when Edith threw herself into his arms. He swung her around like a doll, and his arm stayed around her shoulders as the precious piano was lifted down. The boys manoeuvred it through the front door and positioned it in pride of place in the lounge room, directly below the bugle on the shelf.

After the piano arrived, every night was spent in the lounge, with Edith often playing for hours on end. Her singing was accompanied by the boys, filling the house with music and love. Hamish told them that no man was as lucky as he. Sometimes, he'd lean back in his chair and close his eyes, the only sign that he was awake the smoke that continued to puff from his pipe. Michael knew he was thinking of the tiny baby, Elizabeth. He moved closer to his father and sat on the rug next to him.

'She'll always be with us, Mickey. With us in spirit.' Hamish ruffled Michael's hair. 'Life can be harsh and full of ups and downs. The best day of my life was when I met your mother. Treat a woman well and you'll have a friend for life.'

CHAPTER 5

The Channel Country – 1933

It was the first night of the New Year, 1933. Edith gazed around the table as the five boys and Hamish devoured every last scrap of the hearty stew she had cooked. She closed her eyes and tried to hold the moment in her heart. The boys were all getting older—sooner or later they'd be wanting to spread their wings.

Only last week she overheard Hamish talking to one of the station managers from further south. The McTavish family had known John O'Donnell for years, and he was well aware of the stockman capabilities of their three older boys.

'You should send those older boys down to work for me at Durham Station,' he told Hamish. 'I'd give them different work and it would do them good. They could see a bit of town life and mix with other folk in the area. Bill won't mind; it was him who suggested it.'

'I'm not sure my Edith will be wanting to part with any of them.' Hamish pushed tobacco down into the funnel of his pipe, puffing heavily to ensure it caught. He dragged on the pipe, holding it like a treasured friend as he drew it away from his mouth. 'You're right, though. Sometimes they don't talk to anyone outside the family for months.'

'With us being a Kidman property, they'll get to move from one station to the other,' John said. 'There are runs into town for supplies and a special job coming up. I'd be interested in Michael. I'd pay him well.'

'I thought you'd be after my older son, Rory. He's more settled. Michael's only young; he's just turned seventeen.'

'I'll take him and his twin brother, or him and Rory. You're a lucky man, Hamish, having five sons.'

***

Hamish had discussed John's idea with Edith and now she nodded, indicating tonight was a good time for a discussion on the matter. No-one would leave while there was still food on the table or left-overs to be scraped from the big pot, warming on the wood fire stove. Besides, no boy or man, would be game to leave the table until she excused them.

Hamish's voice caused them all to stop chattering. The only sounds were his Scottish brogue and the clinking of cutlery on plates.

'John O'Donnell from Durham Downs came to see me.'

'Aye,' answered Dan. 'That's one in a line of Kidman properties on the Cooper Creek. In full season it can carry more cattle than anywhere else in the area.'

Rory chipped in. 'I've talked to men from there. When it floods, they say the water is like an ocean and deeper than a man is tall.'

'When they had the last big dry, they lost ten thousand head of cattle.' Dan added. 'They also have trouble with wild horses—they eat the good pickings.'

Michael listened with interest. He'd travelled long distances with the cattle, but there were thousands of miles to the south and north he'd never seen. With a trusty horse and a swag, a man could ride the length of the country stretching endlessly in every direction, with ranges to the north, green pastures to the south and, in the east, oceans that rose and fell with the pull of the moon.

He'd only ever seen pictures of the ocean in the geography and history books his mother used for their lessons. She'd tried to be strict with their education, but it was only ever him and the two younger ones left after the first hour passed.

Michael was drawn in by the black-and-white pictures showing cities and villages in other parts of the world, as well as oceans with waves that were high and curled at the top. He plied his mother with questions, his finger running over a page showing mountains covered in snow.

'Life can't stay the same forever. One day you boys will move on, maybe marry and build a life somewhere for yourselves.' Edith patted Michael's hair down, flattening the unruly curls and pushing a few stray strands from his face. He looked up from the book, the dark brown of her eyes similar to his own.

'The younger two will be around for a while,' Michael said. 'Frank told me he wants to get married and have ten children, and Lachie said he's going build a house for himself right next to you and Dad.'

Edith laughed. 'Wouldn't that be grand. All those little ones running around and you boys close by. Mind you, you'll all have to become a bit more social for any of that to happen.'

'I want to see other places, Mum, but I'll always come back here to you and Dad. This is my home and where I belong.'

'There's a big world out there, Mickey, but we'll always be here for ye to come back to.'

* * *

Now Michael waited for his father to continue. He looked to his mother for clues, but she shook her head, not giving anything away.

Hamish sat back in his chair, his arms crossed as he looked at the boys. 'John O'Donnell has asked if ye would like to go and work for him. He's willing to pay good money, and you'd be on the properties as well as droving cattle to stockyards further south.'

Frank and Lachie sat upright, their faces taut, their eyes wide, as if they were soldiers at attention in the army.

'He is, of course, only after ye older boys.'

The younger boys' faces fell. They scowled at each other across the table.

Rory was the first to break the silence. He lay his knife and fork down and pushed his plate to the side. 'I'm not wanting to leave this place. I'm happy here.'

'I'm not forcing any of you to go, but your mother and I have talked about it and it would be good to see what's on the other side of these paddocks.'

Michael looked out the window. Out there were places and people he could only imagine.

He looked towards his mother. 'What do you think?'

She hesitated then spoke softly. 'You'd learn new things, and John O'Donnell is a good man.'

Michael held his mother's gaze. 'I wouldn't want to leave this place or any of you,' he cast his eyes around the table, his hands clasped and resting on his lap, 'but if it's for a short while, it would be fine.' He paused and looked at Dan. 'But I understand if Dan is the one to go.'

Dan sat upright. 'I've wanted to do something different for a while and,' he grinned at Michael, 'there aren't too many girls around here.'

Edith smiled. 'It's okay, Dan, to admit missing the company of women your own age. You're young men now.'

Michael's shoulders slouched. He may have to wait his turn. Dan was bigger and stronger, and full of confidence.

* * *

Edith listened with interest as she poured Hamish a cup of tea, the steam wisping up in spirals before disappearing into the rafters of the hut. Silence drew down upon them again as Hamish methodically placed three teaspoons of sugar into his cup and began to stir. It was a habit of his, and no one would dare hurry him when he was stirring his tea. He stirred it for what seemed an eternity before tapping the spoon on the side of the cup. Initially this was to rid the spoon of any drops of tea threatening to blot Edith's clean tablecloth. But they all knew that the number of times he tapped the spoon signified the seriousness of whatever conversation was taking place.

The tapping went on and on as Hamish concentrated, his eyes fixed on the spoon. After a while it was too much for Edith, who leaned over and gently stilled his hand. He lay the spoon down on the table.

'John said he'd take two of you. Are ye sure, Rory, you don't want to go?'

'I'm sure, Father. I'm nineteen, but I want another couple of years here. I want to teach these youngest boys a thing or two.'

It would be a different stage for the family without the twins, but it had to happen sooner or later. Dan needed to spread his wings, he was restless, itching for adventure. Edith's gaze lingered on Michael; her kindred spirit, the most soft-hearted, caring and kind son a mother could ever wish for. She would miss them, but they weren't boys any longer, rather two young men on the cusp of a new adventure.

Far to the west a dingo howled; another, nearer the small hut, took up the mournful cry. Edith looked around the table in the golden glow of the kerosene lantern. The dingoes howled again, and a shiver ran down her spine.

A spider running over my grave, she thought. Was this a premonition of what lay ahead, or was it normal anxiety for a mother experiencing the impending separation of her family for the first time? It would take her a long time to find out and, when she did, she would think back to this night so many years earlier, when they had all sat together as a family, looking forward to a bright future.

CHAPTER 6

Road to adventure, 1933

As the ferocity of summer bore down on the outback plains of Western Queensland, Michael revelled in his new job at Durham Downs. The landscape was similar to home, with dusty red plains stretching wide in every direction, the regularity occasionally broken by tufts of brittle yellow grass dotting the ground. Tendril roots of straggly bushes hung precariously to the loose soil, the winds that threatened to tear them from their anchors swirling across the plains, spiralling whirly-birds into the air.

Durham Downs was a much larger property than Bundeen and came with different challenges. The Cooper Creek ran through the property, a hundred-mile vein of precious water that could cover seventy miles of flats when in flood, or be reduced to vast sand beds in the dry. Droughts and floods were an accepted part of life, hardened stockman coming and going, their lives and stories entwined in the history of the property.

Now Dan and Michael were part of that story too, their names written in the huge wage book, their few belongings finding a place in the living quarters on the property.

* * *

Tonight, the two boys were camped out on their own, sent to look for strays that had eluded an earlier muster. Michael served up the night's dinner of stew, a concoction of salted meat and bush tomatoes, with chunks of damper. Dan sat cross-legged on the ground, slurping the tasty stew, the steam from his tin bowl rising into the air. Michael's eyes followed the steam. His mother had said to look to the south and think of the family sitting around the table eating their dinner. He looked along the path where the Southern Cross threw its pointer, and could almost feel the warmth of the kitchen and see his mother serving up dinner, firstly to Rory and then to Frank and Lachie. Hamish would be at the head of the table and, as was his rule, the last to be served.

Dan stirred the embers of the fire, the well-picked bones from the night's feed scattered in amongst the coals of the fire. 'Do you think about them much, Mickey?'

'Aye,' Michael said, 'those wee two will have grown taller in the six months we've been gone. I wouldn't mind trying to get back there before summer sets in.'

'I don't think John would let you take the time off. It's busier now he's picked up those extra head of cattle. He's talking about you and I helping to drive them south through the Kidman properties to the stockyards for sale. He wants us to go with the cattle to Maree. Once we finish there, the two of us are to push on with some horses for a special delivery.'

Michael sighed. He wasn't as enthusiastic as Dan. 'I know you're keen to see what's happening to the south, but it's been months since we left and the more miles we travel, the further we are from home. It could be a year or more before we see the family. It hurts my chest every time I think of them.'

Dan pummelled Michael's arm good-naturedly. 'I know, Mickey. I miss them too.'

Michael looked up at the stars again, feeling more at ease as he located the one he sought. 'I'd like to meet a girl one day.'

Dan laughed loudly. The dogs lying nearby woken from their slumber, looked up. 'You might get your chance. John wants us to stay down there and work with the buyers of the horses.'

'We've never seen those big places.'

'I know. It's exciting. The other fellas tell me the yards are not far from the centre of town and sometimes there are travelling shows with pretty dancing girls. They called it a burlesque show.'

'What's burlesque?'

'It's all those dancing girls. The ones who kick up their legs and show their knickers.'

'They can't be very nice girls if they go around doing that.'

'C'mon, Michael, we can't stay boys forever. Think of our ancestors, off to war, sailing around the world and kicking up their heels with beautiful girls. What have we ever done? Moved up and down the dusty length of these Kidman properties, that's all.'

'Most of those men never came back.' Michael frowned, always sceptical of Dan's plans, which often saw Dan, or both of them, embroiled in trouble.

'They say the girls in those shows are after a good time.' Dan grinned and raised his eyebrows.

'I don't want a good time. I want to find a girl who'll love me forever and give me a house full of kids.'

'Gawd, what would you want kids for?'

'I like kids. I'll have some one day.' He sighed, the dream so far off and the possibilities of meeting anyone out here in the outback so distant that he wondered if the two of them would be bachelors until the day they died.

'I can tell you right now, I'm not waiting any longer. When you and I go into town, we're going to let our hair down. And we'll each get ourselves a girl. Maybe you'll find yourself a wife.' Dan threw a small rock at Michael, who leant back against his swag, pulling his hat over his face to show he'd had enough of the conversation.

He sat upright, the rock bouncing off his arm and landing next to him. Michael picked it up and threw it as far as he could into the dark. The sound of it bouncing across the rocky ground echoed back to them, causing a flock of birds nestled down for the night to flap and squawk.

Dan laughed. 'You're lucky we've no cattle with us.'

'I wouldn't have thrown it if we had. I'm not stupid, and I want you and me to stay out of trouble. You always seem to get us into tricky situations.'

Dan sighed. 'There'll be no problems. You'll thank me afterwards. I can assure you.'

Michael pulled his hat over his face again, settling down into his swag, pulling it tight around him against the cool of the desert night air. 'We'll see,' he said, 'we'll see.'

CHAPTER 7

Durham Downs – 1934

Dan and Michael walked towards the main homestead, a rocky path leading them to the front verandah, a cool spot out of the heat of the sun. Dust swirled around the yard, the withered remains of small shrubs clustered in a garden, testament to the dry conditions that had plagued the property for several years.

Durham Downs homestead was impressive compared to the hut at Bundeen, its exterior timber walls protected by the wide verandah that wrapped around the entire building, a shimmering corrugated roof sloping down low like a tin hat. Quarters for the stockmen and a long workshop nearby added to the cluster of other structures: a meat house, saddle shed and stockyards. To the rear of the house a patch of green stood out, the main source of fresh foods, a vegetable patch surrounded by a sturdy fence made from branches tied together with heavy wire.

John O'Donnell stood in the front doorway, nodding a greeting as they neared.

Michael pushed his shoulders back and walked tall, stopping to remove his hat and wipe his boots on a mat before stepping up onto the verandah. He nodded his head politely to John's wife, Nessie, who sat in a wicker chair, a paper fan in her hand swaying back and forth in long, elegant sweeps. A blue cattle dog growled possessively at her feet, its head lifting as the boys neared, looking for all the world like it was ready to leap into action if required.

The boards of the verandah creaked under Michael's feet and the dog growled louder, the hackles rising on the back of its neck.

'Oh hush, Barney.' Nessie patted the dog. 'Don't worry, boys, she won't go for you unless I tell her to.'

Mrs O'Donnell was a tall woman who always wore her hair in a tight bun. She came across sweet and friendly, but Michael knew this was not always the case.

John's large frame filled the doorway. 'I want to go over the details for the drive,' he said. 'I'm putting a lot of trust in you two, but I know you're capable and able to manage those wild bush cattle.'

The brothers replied together, 'Yes, sir.'

'Michael, I want you as the horse tailer. They tell me you're the best at finding water. You can also help the cook.'

'Yes, sir.'

'Dan, you're to work with the mob. If you're half as good a stockman as your father, then we'll be right.'

'Yes, sir.'

Michael stood tall, almost at attention, taking in every detail of the instructions.

'Once you drive the mob and those horses down to the cattle yards at Maree, there'll be more work for you. It'll last a couple of months and you'll work for a man called Boss. He's a fair man, but don't cross him, and don't go near him when he's got the rum in him. The last fella who upset him was sent to where it was so dusty that even the crows fly backwards.'

'Is Mr Boss your partner, sir?' Michael asked, intrigued why John would get them to work for someone else.

'His name is just Boss, there's no mister about it. He's my brother-in-law. He stays down in town away from me and I supply him with livestock and workers when he needs them.'

Dan nodded. 'There's no-one as good as Michael and me.'

'Keep your heads down and work hard. I want you back here by the droving season. I'll need you to go with the mob up through the centre.'

Mrs O'Donnell stood up, pushing strands of loose grey hair back behind her ears. 'I've got some extra clothes for you and I've also made a couple of coats.' She passed the boys a hessian bag full of clothes.

'Thank you, Mrs O'Donnell. We are indebted,' Michael said.

'Oh, don't thank me.' Her voice was stern. 'Just do what you've been asked to do and stay out of trouble.' Her stare moved to Dan, whose face reddened. He was always up for a bit of fun and had sometimes incurred the wrath of some of the older stockmen when he played a prank or two.

'We won't let you down, ma'am,' Dan replied.

'Make sure to look after each other,' John said as he walked them back down the path and out of earshot of his wife. 'And,' he added, giving them both a firm look, 'stay away from the women and the grog.'

'Yes, sir,' they said in unison.

CHAPTER 8

The Track to Maree – 1934

The men Michael and Dan rode with were hardened drovers who had travelled the track many times. They talked about wild mobs of cattle, relentless droughts continuing for years, and men and camels from faraway countries that roamed up and down the trails of Central Australia.

Fortunately, the southern areas they moved through on this trip had experienced good seasons and floods the year before had left a trail of grass that fattened the livestock.

The plentiful fodder and water pleased the head drover. Jericho was a tall man who sat upright in the saddle all day, his eyes constantly roving over the cattle as he whistled, signalling the dogs and men in the direction he wanted them to go. At night, when they sat around the fire, Jericho told stories about the men and cattle he'd worked with over the years.

'It's either feast or famine in the Channel Country,' he told the boys. 'Now I mainly work on the Kidman properties.' Michael was familiar with the story of Kidman, who at one stage had owned more land than anyone else in Australia.

Jericho took his hat off and banged it on his leg, dust puffing up. He ran a leathery hand through his thick white hair before putting his hat back on then turned to Michael, who sat beside him. 'Sid Kidman was smart,' Jericho said. 'He bought properties from the bottom of Australia to the top. When it was dry in one region, he'd move the cattle to the next property and then again on to the next one. That's what you have to do in this country—you can't just rely on your own area because it might not rain for years on end.'

'Is it true he left home when he was only young?' Dan asked.

'It is indeed,' Jericho said as he placed a cigarette paper on his lip. 'Left Kapunda, way down south here, on a one-eyed horse called Cyclops when he was only thirteen. Ended up owning a large part of Australia and got knighted by the king.'

Jericho finished rolling his cigarette and bent down to light it, using a small stick from the fire. Soon the strong aroma of tobacco added to the smell from the burning logs, the smoke puffing up and disappearing into the blackness of the night. Eventually he leant back against a stump and pulled his hat over his eyes, the cigarette positioned to the side of his mouth.

Michael stared out into the darkness. The story of the man known as *The Cattle King* was one of his favourites. Perhaps his life, like Kidman's, would be spent in the long paddocks, surrounded by land with no boundaries to hem him in. His thoughts turned to his family, the distance from them increasing every day. By the time he and Dan arrived in Maree and did the job for this fella called 'Boss', another three or four months would have passed. It would be many months before they travelled back up the track to Durham Downs and then drove north, up through the Kidman properties for John.

Michael's hat hung low as he lay back in his swag, listening to the tune Dan played on his harmonica. The music made him think about the hut at Bundeen Station. He pulled the hat to the side a little and looked straight up at the evening star. Perhaps his mother was doing the same and thinking about family.

Pulling his hat back down, he again counted the months this job and the next would take. His breathing evened and he relaxed, his thoughts focused on returning home. Soon he drifted off into a deep sleep, the stars shimmering above him as the cool of the night air closed over the men and cattle.

CHAPTER 9

Working with Boss – 1934

The town of Maree was a welcome sight after the long track. Both men and cattle picked up their pace, sensing the end of the journey. Dan and Michael were the only ones staying on, and the next morning they watched as the others gathered their belongings, readying themselves for another drove with a different mob.

'I hope we meet again,' Michael said as he shook hands with the men they had lived with over the last weeks.

'We will,' Jericho said. 'It's a big country, but we travel the same tracks.'

* * *

The first couple of days at the new place were spent sorting the cattle and horses for Boss, who limited himself to grunts and loud obscenities when directing his workers. The third day after they arrived, he beckoned Michael and Dan. The boys looked at each other, straightened their shoulders, brushed off their shirts, and walked quickly to him.

Boss was a huge man. He leaned back against the wooden rails of the stockyards; their timbers smoothed by the men who had gripped them over the years. Today, stocky bush horses clustered in the enclosure, hooves stomping and heads flicking at the flies that continually landed on them. Boss squinted, looking the two young men up and down.

His voice was deep and gruff. 'You done good with those horses.'

'Thank you.' Dan was quick to answer.

'I got a job for youse.' He drew on the stump of a cigarette as he talked; Michael stared at the butt glowing in the corner of his mouth. 'I want you to take twenty of those horses along the track and on to Broken Hill. You're to stay there for a month or more and help the buyers train them up. I'll pay ya for the days getting there, and they'll pay you for your time with them.'

He spat the butt onto the ground, grinding it into the dust with his boot. 'Youse can continue then, back up to where you came from.'

'Is it a big station we'll be going to?' Dan asked.

Boss laughed, his wide smile revealing yellowed teeth, crooked between his lips. 'It's a different kind of customer. You're going to be working for the circus, Wirth's Circus. They're in town for the month and they need extra stock. I'm sending them twenty.' He gestured to the animals behind them. 'And you two, to train them.'

Michael and Dan stood speechless. They had never been to a circus.

'I want you to have those horses ready to go by morning. There're twenty in the yard ready for you. They're the pick of your bunch, plus you've got your own horses to ride.'

'Thank you, Boss,' they said in unison.

* * *

The morning sun was hidden under the eastern horizon when Michael and Dan began the four-hundred-mile journey from Maree to Broken Hill. It was dim in the yard and the horses were flighty, sensing they were moving out. The brothers had ten horses each, tied like a camel train to their own trusty horses.

Some of the other workers watched as they prepared to leave, laughing at the sight. 'Off to the circus, gawd knows what wonders you'll see there,' one of them yelled. 'Watch they don't feed you to the lions!'

Boss also came to see them off. He shook their hands and passed Dan a scrap of paper with a map drawn on it. 'It's been a good season, so you'll be right,' he said. 'Plus, if this boy,' he nodded towards Michael, 'if he's as good as what everyone tells me, then it should be a quick and easy way for you to go. There's nothing out there in the middle, mind you, just a big old lake as white as the salt on your plate and a few mountains easy enough to go over or around. But apart from that, there's not much, so take heed of this map and look after those horses.'

The boys dipped their hats and thanked him. Michael pushed his heels into the side of his horse, leading the way for Dan and the other horses as they set off on their new adventure.

* * *

As they rode away from the small town of Maree, the lights of the houses faded into the background and the wistful tune of Dan's harmonica filtered through the air.

Michael moved his shoulders back and forth, bones cracking as he stretched his neck from side to side. His body was strong and fit, and shirts that were comfortable a month ago were now tight around his arms, his trousers firm around his legs.

His thoughts drifted to home, his mood pensive as he imagined his mother in the kitchen, stoking the fire for the kettle. The younger two would be curled up in bed, drawing out the last minutes of sleep, while Rory would be bringing in wood or helping his father move cattle. It was over a year since he'd seen them; pangs of homesickness washed over him. He took deep breaths, sitting as one with his horse, the cool, crisp air refreshing on his face.

It would be cold back home, too. The faded lounge chairs would be warm to curl up in, and the piano and his mother's singing soothing to the ear.

Dan rode behind him, the music of his harmonica in tune with the horses' hooves and the clinking of their harnesses. Dan took the mouth harp everywhere with him, and now the melody of the old Scottish song 'Maggie' accompanied the orange and red hues of dawn.

The horses quietened. Earlier they had tossed their heads, some of them kicking and shying, disturbing the others they were tied to. Now calm descended. The rumps of the horses became an even line, their pace a steady rhythm. Their ears pricked up, alert, but no longer agitated and flighty.

Michael guided his horse with his knees as they moved past the outer reaches of the town. He looked up for a last glimpse of the evening star, still visible in the early morning light. It was, like he and Dan, a tiny speck in the vastness, one of many moving across the space stretching out infinitely in every direction.

The darkness lifted and the caravan of horses plodded methodically along the dusty course in the direction of the lightening sky. As they passed the last of the small huts clustered on the outskirts of town, streaks of pink and orange shone across the horizon, topped by a vivid blanket of blue.

Michael stopped for a moment, gazing at the grandeur of the sky before scanning the countryside. 'We'll turn up here,' he said, pressing his heels into the horse's side and steering it with his knees. The horse moved with him, leading the others up through a narrow rocky gully between two hills.

'It's amazing how you know exactly where to go.' Dan shook his head. 'You're like the Aborigines, as if you're one with the land.'

Michael turned in the saddle to look back at Dan and the following horses. 'No-one is as good as them. They read the land like a book and follow their songs and the spirits of their ancestors. Even in the middle of the desert they can find water. I just have a few directions on this map Boss gave me.'

Michael stopped again, the horses behind him coming to a halt as he surveyed the land in front of them. They had reached a low hummock and they stood on its highest part, surveying the lands below. 'She's a flat old country,' he said, his eyes drawn to a trail of dust in the distance. The horses behind him shuffled, their bridles jangling as they tossed their heads, impatient to move on. Michael pointed far across the plains. 'That'll be one of those Afghan camel trains. They're definitely not horses.'

Both boys shielded their eyes, looking at the train of animals and men making its way northwards. Michael stood in his stirrups to get a better view. 'They'll be men from that section of town on the outskirts of Maree.'

'They say camels are better suited to our land than these horses.' Dan also stood up in his stirrups, riveted by the sight of the camel train snaking through the dust.

'You can see their turbans from here. They've come all the way from Afghanistan, so many miles across the sea.' Michael squinted against the low sun. 'Those gravestones we passed earlier with the strange writing must be for their people. It would be their language.'

Dan replied, 'I'd like to wear one of those turbans.'

'I learnt about their religion. It's called Islam and their god is Mohammed. The country they're from can be as barren as what it is here, but in other places it's freezing cold and snows. They also have to pray each day. They kneel down and face a certain way.'

'How do you know that?' Dan frowned and sat back down in the saddle.

'While you were out doing tumbles and tricks on the horses, I studied those geography and history books with Mum.'

'Ha.' Dan kicked his horse into action, his gaze still drawn to the line of animals and men snaking across the expanse. 'If your geography is so good, you should know exactly which track to take. Onward bound, Michael. Take me to the circus!'

'We need to head due east and then southeast until we cross the border into New South Wales. Broken Hill's not much further down the track. Surely a circus will be easy to spot once we're there.'

'The boys at the yards told me the circus has a boxing tent,' Dan said. 'I'm keen to give it a go.'

'Don't forget, we're only there to train the horses and then go back to Durham Downs in a month's time.'

'We'll see,' Dan replied. 'I feel there's something bigger in the wind for us – well, for me anyway.'

CHAPTER 10

As the boys descended from the low hills, the camel train disappeared into the dust. Below them, the flats of South Australia stretched out, an orange-tinged ground broken intermittently by craggy outcrops of rocks. A hazy horizon showed a ridge of mountains, a range as rugged and dry as the lands they now moved across; grey and brown clumps of grass dotting the rust-coloured plains. The boys picked up their pace, looking forward to the trek ending.

The landscape changed slightly over the next two weeks: the further south they travelled, the easier it was to find patches of grass to feed the horses. Michael was usually able to find a small waterhole or a creek bed where water was trapped. The mud map was handy, but at times he deviated from it, going on a hunch that water was in a different location than where the map showed. So far he had been proven right, and every night there was grass for the horses and enough water for all.

On the last night, they came across a cluster of buildings made of stone bricks piled neatly one on top of the other, their roofs long lost to the harsh elements. Openings that had once been windows and doors gaped wide. It was a perfect place to stop so the boys tethered the horses nearby and set up camp in one of the buildings.

'It's a strange feeling, camping in someone's home,' Michael said. 'It's a harsh land when you build a house like ours and then have to leave it.'

'You're always thinking about home.' Dan lay his head down in his swag.

'Aye, I think about them at night. I see them all, one at a time. Lachie and Frank first, and then Rory. When I think about Dad, he's sitting in the lounge chair smoking his pipe. Sometimes I think I can smell the smoke from here. And then last is Mum.' Michael sighed, pulling his hat over his eyes.

Dan sighed. 'I think about Mum too, usually her flicking the drying cloth at me or yelling at those two to get down from the roof. When I think of Dad, it's him playing the lucky bugle.'

Silence descended on the camp. Michael wriggled his body inside the swag, the ground rocky beneath. He closed his eyes and visualised his father's rough hands, always gripping a rein or stroking a horse's neck. A night owl sounded its eerie call. Michael looked up at the sky, a million stars flickering brightly, with no moonlight for distraction. He thought at length of his mother and the sound of her sweet voice singing 'Maggie', her favourite tune. Smiling to himself, he remembered the way she'd stand in the kitchen doorway, watching as they did tricks on their horses. She'd frown, and her hands would twist her apron in an agitated state until the boys had landed, either on the ground or back on the horse. She worried too much about all of them; they could do bare-back tricks with their eyes closed.

One day, when Michael and Dan put the drying cloth over their eyes and did tumbles on the horses blindfolded, she yelled at them, telling them they were idiots, they didn't have a brain in their heads, and they would be the death of her. Michael tried to assure her nothing was going to happen, and she'd still be cooking and baking for them all when she was a hundred years old. Maybe when they were older, they'd have their own children and she'd have grandkids to look after. His lips curled into a smile. Maybe one of them would have little girls, and Edith could sew pretty dresses for them and braid their hair. Michael looked up at the sky again. It must have been hard for her, losing baby Elizabeth. The thought of it made his heart heavy and he reminded himself that, once he got home, he'd never leave again.

Dan rolled on to his side. 'You're such a homebody,' he said, as if he could read Michael's thoughts. 'Now go to sleep. Tomorrow's a big day and we need to look our best in a big town like Broken Hill.'

'Night, Dan.'

'Night, Mickey.'

CHAPTER 11

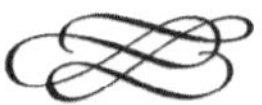

Wirth's Circus, Broken Hill

Michael and Dan made their way along the last stretch of the track to Broken Hill. They compared stories as they rode. 'I heard there's a man who has two heads and four legs,' Michael said as he looked eastwards, searching for the first sign of the town.

Dan sat tall, shading his eyes with his hand and peering into the distance. 'The fellas at the sale yards told me there's a girl who does somersaults on a pony while it's moving around the ring. They said she can flip backwards, five times in a row and never lose her footing.'

'Do you think the owner will want us to hang around for a while with these horses?' Michael asked.

'Yeah, I reckon. Boss said the circus workers are laid up for a while because of the flooding further south. It's a perfect time for them to get new horses and extra hands to help train until they move on.'

'We'll find out soon enough.' Michael stood up in his stirrups, his tattered hat low on his face. 'That has to be Broken Hill, out there on the northern flats.'

Dan stood in his stirrups too, the horses hitched behind them coming to a halt. In front of them a well-worn trail wound its way down a small hill towards the biggest town they had ever seen. Wide streets separated straight rows of houses, their tin roofs forming a mis-match of flat and sloping lids. Brick chimneystacks, sometimes three side-by-side, poked up above the roofs, their tops blackened by smoke and soot.

'That'll be the main street, the business houses and government buildings,' Dan said, eyeing the southern end of town. The buildings were close together, a collection of houses with tiny verandahs jutting out in front. Their small yards were defined by fences of tin or timber, the backyards neat and desolate, with only a few small bushes or a rickety clothesline here and there. The horses stomped and snorted impatiently, eager to move on, perhaps sensing the change in scenery.

Dan pointed westward. 'There's a mine over yonder. See the piles of tailings? That's the rocks they dig out. They lower horses down in lifts, over a thousand feet down, all powered by electricity.'

'What? Why would they do that?' The mere thought of being so far underground sent a shiver through Michael.

'The horses pull the carts down there, saves the men hauling them.'

'Jeez, I can't imagine that, horses under the ground.'

'They say there're good jobs for young men like us. The more I think about it, the more I want something different from life on the track.'

'We're horsemen and there's no way you're going to get me underground. Don't think we're going to do anything other than what we've been sent to do.' Michael was often sceptical of the 'wisdom' behind his brother's decisions.

Dan made a clicking sound with his mouth, prompting his horse to move. He steered it gently with his reins, guiding it down the side of the hill towards the town. The horses picked their way steadily through the rubble, both boys leaning back in their saddles, pressing their heels into the horses' ribs to keep them moving down the steep, windy track.

* * *

The circus and its array of wagons, cages and tents was easy to locate. Wirth's Circus was one of the largest and best-known in the country. Not even the isolation of growing up in the Channel Country had stopped the boys hearing of the incredible feats of the circus performers. They were known for their amazing acts and exotic animals, and for decades they had travelled across Australia, providing entertainment to thousands of people who gathered in small towns as well as the bigger cities on the coast.

'There she blows!' Dan yelled. 'I can see the flag on top of the tent.' Beyond Broken Hill's practical buildings and sparse, dusty streets, large red and green tents alongside brightly painted wagons were conspicuous, the ornate structures devoted to enter-tainment and pleasure contrasting with the hard-working, tough nature of the mining town.

Before long they were staring up at the largest tent, its peaks adorned with blue and yellow flags fluttering in the breeze. A smaller tent provided an entrance for circus-goers, the sign above the entrance announcing, 'Wirth Bros Grand Circus'.

'It's a big set-up.' Dan adjusted his hat. 'They put it up and down every few days. Now dust yourself off and look smart. We don't want them to think we've never seen a circus before.'

Although Dan advised Michael not to look awestruck, he was the one who was spellbound when they came to the first wagon. A large, gypsy-style wagon with red sides had one side folded open, forming a platform about four feet off the ground. On the edge of the platform sat a young woman, legs crossed, toes pointed towards the ground like a dancer. A clown stood in front of her, his eyes closed as the girl applied colourful make-up to his face. Michael stared open-mouthed at her bare, porcelain legs, the tiny shorts barely covering the top of her thighs. The girl's arms and shoulders were uncovered and a tight-fitting bodice showed off her curvy figure. Large, diamond-shaped earrings dangled from her ears, and she laughed as she drew dark lines across the clown's eyebrows.

Michael and Dan stopped in their tracks, the horses behind them also coming to an abrupt halt.

The girl noticed them and sat up straighter, her legs dangling, toes in high-heeled sandals still pointing gracefully to the ground. A picture of beauty, she beamed at the boys as she swung her body around towards them.

The clown raised thickly painted eyebrows. 'What have we here? Two young fellas who look like they've collected all the dust from here to Bourke,' he said, putting down a dish of make-up before approaching them. 'These must be the horses Boss sent.' He ran his eye over the line of horses.

For once it was Michael who did the talking. He glared at Dan, who didn't speak and couldn't tear his eyes away from the most beautiful girl either of them had ever seen. 'We've driven them from the north, to Maree and then on to here,' he said.

'Tally's my name. And this here is Audrey, our top-notch bareback rider and somersaulting queen of the arena.' The clown placed his hands around Audrey's tiny waist and lifted her gently to the ground. She smiled warmly at them, nodding her head in greeting. Her eyes moved over the horses, who seemed to sense they were being inspected and stood still, with only an occasional stomping leg or flickering tail when a fly annoyed them. They pricked their ears forward when Audrey spoke.

'Welcome, beautiful horses. You're dusty and matted.' She ran her hand over one of them, her fingers untangling the burrs and mud knotting its coat. 'But beneath the dirt,' she looked back along the line, 'I see plenty of potential. Welcome to Broken Hill.'

'Welcome to Wirth's Circus,' Tally said to the boys. 'You've come to the greatest show on earth, with acts and animals like nothing youse have ever seen before.'

'We've never been to a circus before,' Michael said.

Audrey looked surprised. 'We're the best in the country. People travel for miles to come and see the show.' She moved along the line of horses, her hand stroking the shoulder of Dan's horse. The young circus girl had mischievous eyes and a cheeky smile, and she grinned at the boys, her gaze resting on Dan, who still hadn't spoken. He loosened the hold on his reins as his horse bent its head down and pushed its nose into Audrey's hand. Audrey stroked the horse's shoulder, her finger scratching roughly across its coat as its eyes closed.

'Looks like I've made a friend,' she said, moving her hand across the horse's face, stroking behind its ears. 'These are in good condition considering how far they've come.'

Michael looked at Dan, waiting for him to say something. Michael spoke again. 'The two we're riding are ours. They're not staying because we'll be riding them back. The rest are for the circus.'

'That's a shame. This one's a beauty. Nice broad back and a good eye.' She turned to Dan, watching him dismount.

Dan took his hat off, brushing the dust from it before placing it back on his head. He waved his hand, shooing the flies away before smiling at Audrey, who stood still as his horse rubbed its head up and down on her back. His words came out slowly. 'Her name's Bonny.'

Tally chuckled. 'Audrey has a way with horses. Now, if you'd like to come with me, I can show youse where we've set up the yards for these horses and where youse can bed down. We could use you boys here until we move on, which going by reports of the weather down south, won't be for some weeks.'

The boys followed Tally as they led the horses away, Michael glaring hard at his brother. 'Blimey, Dan, close your mouth and stop goggling. Remember what you said, act like we've done all this before.'

Dan rubbed his eyes, still lost for words. His gaze followed Audrey, who gave him a quick wave and a wink before disappearing into one of the wagons set up behind the big tent.

Tally helped them settle the horses before leading Dan and Michael over to an older wagon. 'This is where you can stay while youse are here. It's not as flash as some, but it's comfy.'

'It's comfortable compared to what we're used to.' Dan seemed to have found his voice. They followed Tally to another tent, where he untied a section and pulled a flap back for them to enter. This tent was set up as a washroom, a deep bathtub set in the middle of the room. The boys stared at it.

Tally laughed. 'Looks like you haven't seen one of them for a while. The sign's outside. You turn it around to show you're 'ere then back the other way when ya leave.'

'A bath will be something special,' Michael said.

'When you're ready this afternoon, come to the food tent and I'll introduce ya to everyone. Tomorrow we'll put the new horses in with the old. Here –' Tally threw a couple of threadbare towels and a bar of soap to them.

'We've been working them blindfolded and getting them to run around a ring at Boss's for a couple of days before we left,' Dan said.

'Once we put them next to some of the older ones, they soon learn. Boss tells me you two are experts when it comes to trainin' 'em.'

'It's what we know best,' Michael said, but his eyes were focused on the deep bathtub that would remove weeks of dust and grime from his body.

* * *

The boys scrubbed up and changed into clean clothes before making their way to the dining tent. Long wooden tables with bench seats were already full of workers who talked and laughed loudly, voraciously devouring the piles of food the cook had prepared. Tally guided them to a table where others moved over to make space for them. Michael tried to remember the names and faces as they were introduced.

They shook hands with Philip, the manager, a towering man with hands the size of dinner plates that gripped their own hands like a vice when he greeted them.

'He gives the orders around here,' Tally told them, 'and he's who we answer to first. He's under Garth, the owner. We call Garth the big boss; a few of us here are related to him. I'm his cousin and Audrey's his niece. Are you going to stay for a while?'

Dan had again gone mute, and the only movement was in his eyes. He blinked rapidly as Audrey sat down opposite him at the narrow table, her stunning smile scattering all reason from him. Michael nudged him before answering Tally's question. 'When you're ready to move on, we'll go back. We've got a bit of time up our sleeve before we work up north.'

Michael took his seat and smiled warmly back at Audrey.

A deep voice behind the boys caused them both to turn around. 'You'll have to serve yourself next time. Just this once I'm serving you, seeing you got those horses to us in good nick.' A stocky man placed two plates of roast beef and vegetables covered in delicious, thick gravy in front of them. He introduced himself as Sammy. 'Cook by trade, Sammy by name, and sometimes trainer by game.'

'He's Jack of all trades,' Philip said, smiling broadly. 'But best in the kitchen. There ain't a cook this side of the range who can serve up a meal like our Sammy.'

Audrey moved over, making room on the bench seat for another young lady, who wiggled in beside her. The attractive, dark-haired lass gave the boys a seductive smile as she sat down opposite Michael, her tight red shirt matching her lipstick, baggy blue trousers drawn in tight at her waist.

Audrey introduced them to the young woman, whose name was Layla. 'Dan and Michael are brothers and from the bush. They've never seen a big town, or a circus.'

Layla threw her head back, a sarcastic laugh causing some of the men to turn around and stare at her. 'Are you joking, you call this a town? It doesn't even show movies every night.'

'Layla's from the city,' Audrey said. 'You miss those city comforts, don't you?'

'I sure do. I wasn't born in one of your dusty wagons. I'm of theatre and burlesque heritage.' Her eyes locked on Michael, and she fluttered her eyelashes at him. 'I've been on grand stages and entertained bigger audiences than this circus will ever see.'

'She blew in with the last lot of musicians. They left; she stayed,' Philip added, his voice tinged with disdain. 'We had bands and all sorts of musicians and dancers once, but now we use recordings.' He grimaced. 'It ain't the same but it's a lot cheaper.'

'Maybe it would be cheaper to have monkeys ride and jump between the horses instead of men,' Layla's tone was cutting, and it was obvious there was animosity between her and Philip. 'Maybe the monkeys could train the horses ...'

Audrey nudged Layla. 'Remember, we have guests here today, let's leave the squabbles for another time.'

Philip picked up his plate. 'Once you boys finish here, Audrey can show you around. Come to the wagon later and we'll talk about your wages.'

Michael fidgeted in his seat, his reply stuttered. 'Thank, thank . . . you Philip, we, we . . . we . . . we appreciate the opportunity.' He moved awkwardly, focussing on his plate as he tried to sit up straighter. Philip sent one last glare in Layla's direction, then pushed his hat down hard on his head as he left them to finish their lunch. Layla giggled, leaning over the narrow table, her eyes fixed on Michael as she spoke.

'He has it in for me, wants me gone. But at the moment I'm the sixth person in the pyramid act, so maybe they'll go for a tumble if I'm not here.'

'We're looking forward to seeing the acts. Where we come from there's nothing but flies, cattle and horses,' Dan said.

'So why do you stay there?' Layla asked.

'It's sounds dreary but it's the most wonderful place,' Michael said. 'The colours and the open spaces. It's a sight to see.'

'Sounds like someone's missing home,' Tally said as he sat down beside the two girls.

'Dan and I are keen to get back and once we're finished here. We've got another mob to take back up along the track.'

Michael jumped and moved in his seat again. His face burned and he gritted his teeth, ignoring the glare Dan sent his way. Layla giggled again, her silver bracelets jiggling. The top button on her blouse was undone and, when she bent over to pass Michael a glass of water, he couldn't avert his eyes from the deep cleavage between her large breasts.

'I think you have somewhere to be, don't you Layla?' Tally growled. 'The others are down there in the tent ready to practise.'

Layla stood up, an unhappy look on her face. 'You Wirth people are always out to spoil any fun. Why is it always about work?'

'They're waiting for you.' Tally's voice was stern. He turned away and began talking to some of the other men who had arrived for their meal.

'See ya round.' Layla gave Michael and Dan a quick wave and blew them a kiss before flouncing off.

CHAPTER 12

Once Layla had gone, Tally appeared to relax. He introduced some of the other men. A tall, thin man sat down next to Michael.

'Meet the Great Pribyl!' Tally exclaimed, patting the man on the back. 'Direct from Europe. You boys will not believe it, but we have the largest barrel of any cannon in Australia and we fire this man from it, out into space!'

The Great Pribyl grinned. 'Don't worry,' he said, his foreign accent and long droopy moustache presenting an air of exotic mystery. 'They catch me in a net. Men have been killed doing the same, but the Great Pribyl never fails.'

'Tell you what, you'd be safer getting fired out of a cannon than taking your luck with that Layla,' one of the other men joked.

'Now, now,' Audrey interjected. 'Let the boys make their own judgements.'

Tally shook his head. 'She's burnt too many bridges here and even upset people in town.'

The chatter around the table picked up and there was a buzz of excitement as the workers talked about the months ahead, the loud conversation and clanging dishes a noisy background din. These men were different from those Michael had spent most of his life with. The talk wasn't about the drought, waterholes or cattle, but rather light-hearted banter and jokes about new tricks that had gone wrong, the excitement of being in one place for more than a couple of days, and what was happening in the weeks ahead. There was talk of a creative twisting somersault, debates on different rope methods and suggestions of alternative ways to erect the tents. The route for the coming year needed to be worked out, repairs had to be completed, and costumes sewn.

In the corner of a room, a very large lady with short red hair sat behind a Singer sewing machine, her bare foot pumping the pedal up and down, her thick hands manoeuvring a shiny green fabric under the needle, which rose and fell in unison with her foot.

A solid man no taller than the table sang loudly as he worked next to her, pulling glittery costumes, bright capes and oddly shaped hats out of a cane basket. He stood on a chair to reach the outfits, shaking them free of dust before draping them carefully on wooden hangers on a solid wooden rack. The pair worked quickly, chatting together and calling out to other workers who passed.

Audrey stood up, signalling for the boys to follow.

Michael hid a smile when he noticed Dan walking quickly to be next to her, mustering every polite gesture he knew, jumping in front to hold the canvas flap open for her and rushing to unlatch gates once they were outside.

Audrey showed them around, explaining the purpose of each section of the circus and laughing at their excited reaction to the various animals pacing up and down in their cages. 'We have fourteen cages of exotic animals. They come from all over the world and have their own names and different roles to perform.'

'Imagine training a huge cat instead of a horse,' Dan said as Audrey guided them to the big tent. They stood in the shade of the canvas, the voice of a trainer working with a tiger echoing across the otherwise empty area. The trainer moved calmly, cracking a whip in the air as he signalled the direction he wanted the animal to move in. The huge tiger's paws thumped solidly on the drums on to which it leapt, its attentive eyes following the path of the whip.

Out in the yards behind the tents were donkeys and camels as well as seven huge elephants, swaying where they stood shackled, waiting to be fed.

Audrey waited patiently as Michael and Dan stood mesmerised, their eyes wide at the sight of creatures they had only ever seen in pictures. Michael sniffed the air, the musky smell from the big cats' cages mixed with the smell of animal manure filling his nostrils. Small clouds of dust puffed up from the bed of dry grass where the elephants stood, their huge feet stomping every so often. Shouts from some workers sounded behind them and a camel bellowed loudly in the background. It was a foreign workplace. Michael stared hard at the elephants, their huge forms towering above him.

'They look at you like they know what you're thinking,' Dan said, following Audrey as she led them closer.

'Here.' Audrey took Dan's hand and stroked it up and down on the leathery skin on the chest of the largest elephant. 'This is Patricia, she's been with us the longest. She's our star performer and my favourite.'

Patricia's tiny eyes rested on Dan, and he struggled to remain still as her wrinkled trunk sniffed up and down his arm before coming to rest on his shoulder. The elephant held his stare before giving a little snort and moving her trunk to his cheek. Audrey laughed and scratched the underside of Patricia's trunk, telling her what a good girl she was. 'She's given you the sign of approval. Normally she ignores newcomers.'

Michael screwed his face up and squeezed his eyes tight as Patricia's attention turned to him. The elephant closed her eyes, resting her trunk on his shoulder.

'Open your eyes, Mickey,' Dan said. 'She winked at you.' Michael slowly opened his eyes and, just as Dan said, the elephant was indeed winking at him, at the same time nuzzling the end of its trunk into his neck.

'Wow.' Audrey shook her head. 'I've never seen that before. She really likes both of you. It usually takes months for her to interact with new arrivals.'

Michael stroked the elephant's trunk, scratching it underneath as she lifted it higher. 'Not much different to a horse,' he said with a nervous laugh, relieved when the elephant dropped her trunk and turned back to the feed.

Audrey gave Patricia one final pat before leading them to the yards where their horses and other circus ponies were corralled. Michael climbed through the fence, locating some of the horses they had brought with them. The familiar connection soothed his rising anxiety about being somewhere alien and a long way from home.

***

Once they were alone, Dan questioned Michael about his behaviour during lunch. 'What the heck happened to you, Mickey? Did the cat get your tongue? Don't leave me to do all the talking and what was with the twitching and jumping in your chair, and for God's sake since when have you stuttered?'

Michael concentrated on picking burrs from a horse. 'It was the girl, that Layla girl.'

'I know, they're beautiful girls, but we have to get used to it.'

'You're drooling over Audrey. I've never seen you act like that or be lost for what to say. Your eyes are popping out of your head every time she looks your way. Jesus, we've only been here a day and you're already making eyes at her.'

'I feel a connection. It was instant from the moment I saw her.

56

But now, no more jumping or twitching. It's embarrassing, they'll think we're real country hicks.'

'We are, you idiot!' Michael laughed.

He failed to tell Dan how, when Layla sat opposite him, she wasted no time in running her foot up and down his leg. His face had burned as she moved over his groin, and it took all of his self-control to remain still. It was lucky he hadn't overturned the table when her toes found their way to their intended destination.

CHAPTER 13

*W*ith something new to learn every day, Michael slipped easily into the circus lifestyle. Philip checked on him and Dan after a couple of days, reminding them they were now working for the most famous circus in Australia.

The horses they had brought with them had shed their scruffy, dusty coats and now looked like well-groomed show animals. It had only taken a couple days of solid training for them to be cantering gracefully next to one of the circus horses, their heads arched and tails held high. Philip nodded his head in approval, a look of satisfaction on his face as he watched Michael and Dan work with the horses under the big tent.

Dan and Philip were in deep conversation when Michael left them and made his way to the ring. He concentrated on the horses as they went around again, marking his position as they came close. He timed their strides, running alongside before leaping onto the bare back of a brown pony. It was an easy landing and he sat comfortably on one of the mares, Tinker, who didn't flinch or change pace.

Tinker had always been a reliable steed when they had worked with the cattle – he had often used her for tricks in their back yard. If he leaned slightly to the side or touched her neck with the reins, she would respond accordingly.

His balance, as always, was solid, and he moved first into a crouching, then a standing position, his arms stretched out to the sides. The mare cantered obediently, Michael's feet firm on her back as she paced herself in time with the other horse at her side. Eventually she completed a full circle of the ring. Michael returned to a crouch and then straddled her once again. He used the reins to slow her, pulling both horses up until they were standing still in front of Philip and Dan. Tinker flung her head up and down, her coat glistening with sweat.

'You've done well, my friend,' Michael said quietly to the mare as he scratched her forehead.

Philip came and stood beside him. 'You're a bloody natural. You boys are two of the best horsemen I've ever seen. There's always plenty of work for fellas like you. Why don't you consider staying on and working with us.'

Michael untied the horses and passed the ropes to a young boy, who led the horses away for a rubdown and a hosing. 'We're born into it, Philip. We've both been in the saddle since before we could walk. Doing tricks is just a bit of fun.'

Dan had been listening. 'Your offer sounds interesting,' he said to Philip.

'I'm serious. There could be work here for both of you if you're keen.'

'I'm happy with droving,' Michael said, sending a glare Dan's way. 'Don't get me wrong; circus work looks exciting, but I'm only here to do what we were asked. My heart is on the track.'

'You could do a season with us, just to see if you like it?' Philip suggested. 'Wirth's is after riders and innovative acts. We need to keep pace with other large circuses and the shows being imported from America.'

'Thanks for the offer, but we're taking a mob back north and also there's our family. We haven't seen them since we left nearly a year ago.' Michael's answer was firm.

Dan crossed his arms. Michael sent another glare his way, but his brother was oblivious, his eyes fixed on Audrey who was beginning her warm-up routine.

'I'd like to stick around to see this tent when it's full of people,' Dan said to Philip.

Philip smiled, perhaps sensing the excitement of his offer for Dan. 'This tent we're standing in is one of the largest in the business. It stretches over one hundred and seventy feet across and, when it's set up for performances, it'll have a stage as well as the ring.' He winked at Dan. 'It seats up to three thousand people.'

'I can't imagine it!' Dan said. 'I'd give anything to see that and be working here.'

'You won't see it full of people until we take to the road. We cover thousands of miles of track. Once we start, we don't stop. The wind and rain down south will need to be gone and hopefully the waters from the north won't trap us in. This six weeks of lay-up is a good opportunity to see what you think.'

Audrey had begun riding around the ring. Her short training skirt revealed solid, muscled legs, the sign of a well-trained acrobat and tumbler. Dan grinned from ear to ear when she finally stopped in front of them. She sat sideways, swinging around on the pony as if it were a lounge chair.

'Can you stand on a horse like your brother?' She directed her question to Dan as she slid gracefully to the ground.

'We've been standing and sitting on horses since we were kids. We invented our own circus acts. It was a game for us,' Dan replied.

Michael shook his head. Here we go, he thought. Dan took the ropes from her hands and sent a cheeky wink her way before jumping up on the pony's back. He touched his heels to its ribs, balancing with his knees as the dappled pony arched its neck and broke into a smooth, rolling canter around the ring. Once he had his balance and the motion fixed, Dan jumped up into a crouching position, before standing straight and tall, his arms stretched out—as Michael's had been—to either side.

It was a trick the two boys had perfected before they could write their names. Now there was an audience, including the beautiful Audrey.

Michael chuckled to himself thinking of his mother and her reactions to their tricks. There had been many a fall , but never anything warranting more than a splash of the yellow iodine she used to fix every scrape or cut. Now someone else held Dan's attention, and he was out to impress.

Dan balanced easily, a surge of excitement tingling in his body as the pony he rode cantered gracefully around the ring. He slowed down as he neared where Audrey stood, her arms crossed as she watched. The pony stopped in front of her, and Dan returned to a sitting position.

A small audience had formed behind where Philip and Michael stood. Dan noticed the big boss standing discreetly at the back of the tent. An older lady stood with him; Dan suspected this was his wife, Matilda. Audrey had told him how her aunty had been a renowned performer in her youth and had taught Audrey tricks she used in her performances.

Dan leaned down and spoke to Audrey, who nodded as she listened. He moved further back along the pony before pulling her up by her hand. She swung into a seated position in front of him. The pony moved off slowly to begin with, before breaking into a rhythmic trot. Dan gripped the pony's back with his knees. His bare feet flexed as he tried hard to concentrate as Audrey's body pushed back against him, her arms rubbing up against his as she hung tight to the pony's mane. He took a deep breath before asking if she was ready.

'Let's give it a go,' she replied, turning her head to look at him. Her face was close to his and the excitement in her eyes made his heart thump. Hopefully she couldn't feel the pounding in his chest as she leaned back, their knees gripping tight as the pony broke into a smooth canter. Once they gained their point of balance, Dan stood up, guiding Audrey to stand in front of him. She turned slowly until she faced him, their eyes meeting.

The pony maintained a regular continuous movement. Dan steadied himself. He held Audrey firmly around her waist, his arms strong and steady. 'Ready?' he asked.

She nodded and placed her arms on his shoulder. Dan lifted her high above his head, his arms straight and taut as her body straightened out. Her arms stretched out wide and her legs pointed out behind her. Now she was horizontal above his head, and he steeled his arms, holding her balanced and steady. His legs ached and he concentrated hard, aware one wrong move would send them both tumbling to the ground. Before long, Audrey tucked her legs in under her body, signalling him to lower her.

She sat back down in front of him and they laughed loudly together. The pony continued to canter around the ring, the spell of the moment broken by the cheering and clapping of the small audience assembled.

Dan was so focussed on the stunt that he had forgotten there were people watching. He had held his younger brothers high in the air like that many times, but this was a young woman whose poise and balance had not wavered. Never before had he moved in such harmony with another person. They hadn't spoken a word to each other once their synchronised movements began. Their bodies simply moved in unison.

Dan knew what he wanted to do next. It was a trick he and Michael had practised a thousand times, often landing on the rocky ground. On other occasions they had perfected the trick, much to the relief of their mother.

He crouched behind Audrey.

'Keep her going for me.' Dan said. 'This could go well or end badly.' He gave Audrey a cheeky grin before kneeling and then standing upright. It was a difficult job to train a horse to go in a circular motion around the ring. It was natural for them to move in a straight line, but the training with blindfolds and being in the ring with the experienced horses had prompted the new ones to learn fast.

Dan straightened up, his arms stretched high, his gaze directed forward. The balance felt right so he didn't wait long before bending his knees and then coiling his body as he launched himself backwards, high into the air. He held his knees, his body tucked in tight as he spun in the air, his eyes focussing on where he was going to finish. Landing on the ground in an upright position, he straightened up, his arms out to the sides.

He took deep breaths, waiting for Audrey to come back past him. The pony slowed a little as she neared, and he reached for her hand before propelling himself upwards, back on to the pony's rump behind her.

The rhythm of the canter picked up pace and they completed another circle of the ring before pulling up directly in front of the small audience. Dan jumped down and turned to Audrey, her face flushed with excitement.

'Perfect landing! Your balance is amazing!' she exclaimed. She swung her legs around and Dan lifted her down, his hands circling her waist as their eyes locked. He wanted so badly to kiss her, but not here in front of everyone. He didn't want to get kicked out when he may have just won himself a job.

The small crowd clapped. Michael came over and took the reins, leading the pony away to the other side of the ring. Dan had wanted Michael to join him – together they could show off other stunts. They had some amazing tricks, and if Audrey thought what he had just done was good, she should see what he and Michael could do as a team.

Deep down, though, he knew circus life wasn't for his twin brother. This was going to be a turning point for them, a fork in the track. His body tingled with the exhilaration of performing in a real circus ring on a pony he'd trained. If it was this good without a proper audience, he could only imagine how it would feel with the tent packed with excited circus-goers. And there was Audrey, the feeling of her waist in his hands still tingling through his body.

Philip came and thumped him on the back. 'Bloody fantastic! I haven't seen someone do that with such sure footing. You never faltered. God only knows what else you have up your sleeve.'

'I have plenty. They're the easier tricks.'

'You'd better think about what other tricks you can do because the big boss was watching and he wants to see you in his wagon. His wife's there, too. She's the one who does the bookwork and wages. He's got an offer for you and your brother. You'd better get up there straight away before he changes his mind.'

'Thanks, Philip, but it will only be me. Michael is adamant, and once his mind is made up there's no changing it. He's hankering after the bush and home.'

CHAPTER 14

The big boss's grand wagon stood out from the others. The paintwork was new, and ornate metal awnings gave shade and protection to the windows and doors.

Garth opened the door before Dan had a chance to knock, beckoning him inside. Matilda greeted him, her hand outstretched for a welcoming handshake. They were dressed like city folk, as if ready for a day out on the town; Dan was fascinated by the crisp, white shirt and long, thin tie Garth wore. Matilda wore a long dress, the front of it draped with colourful beads and chains. Her hair was shoulder-length and dark red, and together they made a striking couple. Garth pulled out a chair for him to sit down.

'We're pleased to finally meet you properly, young man. We've heard much about you and your brother since your arrival,' Garth said.

'Thank you, sir, we're enjoying our work here.'

'You have fine capabilities with those horses. Seems to be a mutual respect between you and the animals.'

'It's our life. Michael and I are twins, and we were brought up with horses and droving. My father is one of the most respected horsemen in our part of the country.'

'And what would he think of either or both of you staying?'

'I've two younger brothers, and an older one, so he has plenty of help on the property.'

'Your brother is not interested?' Garth cut straight to the point.

'No, sir. He's a drover and he's pining for family and working with the stock. There'll be nothing stopping him from going back.'

'How old are you, Dan?' Matilda's voice was polished and she spoke clearly, her speech articulate.'

'I'm eighteen.'

She looked over to her husband, waiting for him to talk.

'We'd like to make you an offer of work. Stay with us for six weeks of training and then come on the road with us for the season. We've lost good riders going to other circuses for a few extra dollars. We're a reputable family circus and the biggest and the best in Australia. We only want you to join us if you give us your word you'll stay for the entire season.'

Dan hesitated.

'Is there something wrong?' Garth frowned, his eyes narrowing.

Dan looked towards Matilda. 'I was hoping for something more than one season. If I commit, I want to become the best trick rider there is and stay around for many years.'

Matilda and Garth's laughter echoed in the small van. 'You've got plenty of confidence for a young man,' Garth said. 'I like that.' He put out his hand for Michael to shake, his palms rough, much like the men who rode out on the plains.

'Matilda will work out your wages and living arrangements, and you still have six weeks with your brother here. But we'd like you to start training with Audrey and Philip straight away. Matilda and I want you and Audrey to be our star act when we start next season. I've got some new ideas I saw in America on our last visit.

By God, it will bring the house down if you can perfect what they're doing over there.'

Dan's reply came out as a stutter. He felt his face redden. 'You mean I get to work with Audrey? Thank you, sir – and, um, ma'am. She's a great rider.'

They both stood to see him out. Garth came up close to him, his hand clenched on Dan's shoulder. 'She is a good rider, young man, but she's also our niece. If you want to pursue anything other than circus work, I suggest you talk to me first. Audrey is a very respectable young lady who thinks she's all grown up, but she's only young. We don't put up with any shenanigans around here. Do you understand?'

'Yes, sir. I have nothing but the utmost respect for Audrey and I give you my word, you won't ever regret hiring me.'

* * *

Michael lay motionless on his back in the wagon he shared with Dan. He stared at the colourful ceiling above his bunk. Someone had painted it to resemble the posters that hung in town advertising Wirth's Circus. The painting directly above him was of three men and four women standing on different-coloured horses, arms high in the air as they balanced, posing in perfect unison. A large tent filled the background, colourful flags flapping against a blue sky. Another scene adjoined it, depicting trapeze artists swinging through the air, their legs hooked around swings and their arms out, ready to catch their fellow trapezist swinging from the other end of the painting. There was an image of a young lady with her head in a lion's mouth, looking at the viewer, her smile captured forever on the roof of the wagon.

He swivelled his neck to decipher the most colourful picture on the ceiling. It must have been a talented artist who had created the collage, because the people and animals looked real. It was as if he was among them, not lying on his back staring up. He peered at the elephants, painted with intricate detail. They perched on top of cylindrical drums, their trunks held high, their rear legs balancing precariously as their front legs waved in the air. It was amazing how a large animal could balance on such a small container.

The door of the wagon flung open. Michael's reverie was interrupted as Dan appeared in the doorway, a grin stretching from ear to ear.

They looked at each other silently, neither speaking, just staring, reading each other's thoughts. Michael finally sat up, his legs swinging in the air from the bunk. 'You're staying, aren't you?'

'They've offered me the chance of a lifetime. To train for the next six weeks and then be part of the show. And to top it all off, guess who I'll be working with?'

'The blonde girl, Audrey?'

'Yes.'

Michael couldn't help but be excited for Dan. After all, he'd come looking for something different, and Garth's offer certainly was that.

'They would have taken you also, Michael. It's never too late to change your mind. You and me have always been together.'

'Nothing will change my mind. I'm going back. But I'm happy for you.'

Dan lay on the bunk next to Michael, both peering up at the ceiling. 'Maybe there'll be a painting of me and Audrey up there one day, The Great Mr and Mrs McTavish of Wirth's Circus.'

'Maybe there will be,' said Michael.

'The best part of this, apart from working with Audrey, is I'm still with horses. It's just a different game. Instead of the track and the cattle, it'll be a ring, surrounded by hundreds of people who've come to see a show. It's bloody exciting, Michael, and I'm keen to celebrate.'

'Celebrate? Go out somewhere?'

'I ran into Philip on the way back here and he said everyone's going to the pub in town tonight.'

'Too many people for me. You go, though.' Michael sat up and stretched. 'I'm going to soak in the big tub and wash this dirt off.'

* * *

Michael sat in the wagon for a long while after Dan left. He pulled out a worn, leather notebook and crossed another day off the calendar he'd meticulously drawn up. Another day since they'd left the family home. His calendar showed the next six weeks they were committed to be with the circus. Once the last day was ticked off, he'd be happier than a pig in mud and nothing was going to stop him heading back up the track towards Durham Downs.

Once he was back at Durham and had completed the next job for John, then he was going home, home to stay. He could sit at the kitchen table and tell them all about the drove down, how they'd seen the Afghan men and their camels, and ridden through towns where houses lined the streets. There'd be plenty to talk about, and then he'd listen to all their news. A familiar ache filled his chest as waves of homesickness surged through him.

Small photos tucked into the back of the notebook showed the faces of his family peering back at him. His favourite was of his mother. She stood outside the hut, her arm around his shoulder. He was about ten and he snuggled in, looking up at her face as she smiled for the camera. He could almost feel her arm around him now as he looked through the other photos, creased and worn from being taken out and held so often.

There were photos of his brothers and father, his mother standing solidly in the middle of them all. The matriarch, he thought, the one who holds us all together like glue. And a tiny photo of his mother at the piano, his father on the bugle and all of them clustered around, their mouths open as they sang together. He peered at it, wondering if anything had changed since he'd been gone.

A rap at the wagon door stirred him from his reminiscing and he closed the notebook before the door opened. One of the men who worked in the yard stood in the doorway.

'G'day, Donald, what're you up to?' Michael greeted him.

'We thought you'd like to join us for a drink. There're not many of us left and we're just sitting around sharing some whiskey. Only a couple, mind you, before we start cleaning the cages.'

'I don't drink a lot,' Michael said.

'Neither do we.' Donald slurred his words, already well primed from the home-made alcohol.

Michael pulled his boots on and dusted off his hat before following Donald to the wagons parked at the rear of the circus. A few men sat around a fire, and a place was cleared for Michael to join. A large glass of whiskey was passed to him and he rolled his eyes at the smell, the burning liquid causing him to gasp as it ran down his throat.

The men were relaxed, their conversation mainly about the weather and the upcoming weeks of staying put in the one place. The flickering of the fire reminded Michael of nights he'd camped out with his father and the mobs of cattle they'd pushed down from the dry country. The voices of the men were soothing, their manners generous and friendly as they shared the whiskey with him. After the first couple, the liquid went down easier and Michael enjoyed being in the company of workers who, like him, were avoiding the bustle of the town or had night work and shifts to complete.

The men talked about other circuses similar to Wirth's that travelled the breadth and length of Australia, their stories becoming funnier, the conversation louder as they continued to fill up their glasses.

Soon Michael couldn't feel his tongue. The surroundings blurred and moved around him and the chair he sat on swayed. He stood up, refusing what the other men said was the last drink of the night.

'I can't feel my legs now,' he said trying to talk straight. 'Thanks for the drinks, fellas, but I'm off to soak in the tub.'

Raucous laughter and crude jokes followed him as he made his way unsteadily back to the wagon. Before long he reappeared with a bundle of clean clothes, his legs feeling like they were buckling under him. He made a beeline to the bath tent, hoping the water would refresh him, sober him up. No one was waiting their turn and the tub was empty. He had it all to himself.

Michael filled the bath, berating himself for drinking too much as he concentrated hard on pouring hot water into the tub. He used a metal bucket, dipping it into the big drum on top of the wood burner. It was the first time he had ever drunk so much liquor – his arms and legs weren't doing what his mind was telling them to do.

Steam rose from the tub as he plunged underneath, the hot water soaking into his skin. Outside the tent, in the distance, the laughter and muffled conversation of the men who continued to drink drifted across the yard.

Michael breathed slowly, inhaling the steam and scrubbing himself with the scratchy brush provided. In the washroom there was solitude and a chance to stop the spinning in his head.

There was no-one else around to notice anything untoward that may have happened that night. No-one to see the washroom lights turn off. No one to notice a young, scantily dressed lady enter the men's washroom and slip off her robe. Only Michael saw the naked woman standing next to where he lay, her quiet voice asking permission to join him before she slipped into the bathtub, sinking below the water next to him.

CHAPTER 15

t first Michael thought he was dreaming. He shook his head, trying to clear his mind. There was definitely a naked woman in the bathtub with him. He opened his mouth but no sound came out, instead warm lips pressed down on his and a naked body pushed down on him. Her hands moved across him, long hair falling over his face. Her skin was smooth and he held her tight as the water sloshed back and forth.

Everything became a little blurry and he let himself go with the moment, the woman guiding him in his first sexual encounter. The matter did not end in the tub. After drying themselves, the cane reclining lounge at the end of the tent made a much more comfortable support for Michael, who was still drunk and unsteady on his feet. The woman brought towels for both of them and led him across the dark yard to a wagon. She closed the door and took him to her bed.

Being together in a more comfortable bed proved to be as exciting as what had taken place in the washroom, and she praised his ability to perform so well considering they both had drunk so much. By now Michael's mind was clearing a little. Maybe Dan was right, perhaps the circus was a more exciting prospect. Thoughts of home disappeared and he laughed with this woman, who giggled noisily, groaning loudly as Michael pushed his body against hers.

Afterwards they lay together, Michael tingling with the effects of the boisterous lovemaking. He looked at her sleeping, the moon filtering in through a slit in the curtains, throwing light on her body. This was the first time he'd seen a naked woman and he stared hard, running his hand over the curves and folds of her body. He'd like to make love to her again, but she was asleep. Before long the effects of the alcohol and a long day with the horses began to take their toll. He fell asleep, his leg thrown across hers, warm hands resting on her bare breasts and his face settled into the buxom chest of the flying trapeze artist, Layla.

* * *

Layla woke him well into the night, shoving him roughly. Her voice was husky. 'Go back to your own wagon before the others get back from town.' She pushed him out of the bed.

A hangover was already starting to set in and Michael's head was fuzzy, his thoughts confused as he remembered the events of the last few hours. He dressed hurriedly, his legs like jelly, his head pounding as Layla pushed him towards the door.

'The others will be back soon. I've cleaned up the mess in the washhouse. Now here's your clothes, go back to your own bed. If they find out, they'll sack me. Not a word now.'

The yard was dark. Michael licked his lips, the dry sourness leaving a bitter taste in his mouth. He closed his eyes as the details of the night came flooding back.

Concentrating hard on walking back to his wagon, he stopped at a clump of bushes, his retching observed by three elephants, who stood like statues, staring at him. Their huge frames were silhouetted against the inky-dark background; he wondered what they were thinking. They were the only witnesses to what had occurred. He walked quicker, wanting to put his head down on a soft pillow, on a bed that didn't sway.

It was strange; the act of lovemaking had occurred without any warning, and not at all in the context he had imagined. The sweet kisses and whisperings of love and devotion were non-existent, however the rest had swept him away. Layla had left him helpless and wanting.

He lay down on his bed and curled up under the thin sheet. Dan wasn't back yet. Perhaps he was doing the same thing with Audrey. Michael's throbbing head rested on the pillow and he fell asleep before his eyelids even closed.

* * *

The next morning there were a lot of men with sore heads, and not only those who had shared the moonshine out the back. The entire crew had had a big night on the town. Dan looked green, barely able to keep his breakfast down.

'Did you have a good night?' Michael asked him, keen to know if he had made any progress with Audrey.

'I did, yes we did. But I don't like the liquor much. It's good at the time but I have a powerful headache this morning. Just as well you didn't come.'

'I had a few drinks with the men here. They shared a moonshine drink with a mighty kick, so my head's no good either. We make a great pair. I'll be staying away from alcohol in the future. I don't like not being in control.'

'Thank goodness it's Sunday, and not much to be done.' Dan rubbed his temples. 'There was a lot of drinking and then some fighting last night. Some of the townspeople might be a bit sad and sorry this morning. These circus boys are good fighters.'

'How did you go with Audrey?'

'I asked her if she'd like to go to the pictures one night, but she said for me to ask her uncle first.'

'Did you kiss her?'

'She's respectable, Michael. You can't just go around kissing girls. I'm going to take it slow and do it properly. One day I'm going to make her my wife.'

'That's a big statement, coming from you!' Michael's stomach heaved. 'Good luck,' he managed to say.

Last night's intimacy had been Layla's idea, but at no time did he think of saying no or asking her to stop. It had been a night unlike any other in his life, and he wondered when it might happen again. The only trouble was, although Layla was just a bit older than him, she was definitely not respectable. Now Michael understood why many of the others wanted to see the back of her.

* * *

It was a quiet group who sat down to lunch in the dining tent. Some of the men had cuts and bruises from the fighting.

'Maybe we should start a boxing tent,' said Ted, a large man sporting a swollen black eye. 'I reckon I could take on anyone in this bloody town and knock them into next week.'

'Didn't look like that last night,' said Jimmy, a lion-tamer whose arms resembled twisted steel. 'If it wasn't for me hitching you out of the middle of that melee, you'd be a corpse embedded in the main road of Broken Hill.'

'I was starting to turn them, you took me out too bloody early.' Ted turned around, a sneer on his face. 'Well, well, look what the cat dragged in. You look a bit worse for wear, me love. Some lonely drinking all by yourself last night?'

Layla stood with a plate of food in her hand, trying to find a spot to sit down. Most of the men had their backs to her and didn't move over or offer a space.

She flicked her head, moving to another table with spare seats. Michael tried to catch her eye but she either didn't notice him or, if she did, she didn't give him a second glance. His stomach rolled again. He wanted to talk to her, to see her again, but it wasn't respectable. What would happen when it was time for him to go back out on the track? Was she the sort of woman who slept with a man and then moved on?

'She's nothing but trouble.' Jimmy glanced at Dan and Michael. 'Make sure you stay well away from her. If she gets her fangs into you, you've had it!'

Michael looked down at his plate. Sooner or later he'd have to tell Dan. He'd wait until he was about to leave.

* * *

Layla ignored him over the ensuing weeks and, although Michael tried to talk to her, he was unable to see her by herself. Work with the horses kept him busy and, as days turned to weeks and she still paid him no attention, he realised the night was a one-off. She had used him, and Michael admitted to himself, he had used her. Now more than ever he wanted to be back on the track, heading home. It would be a lonely trek back without Dan, but once he was home with his family, he could put what had happened behind him.

CHAPTER 16

The six weeks with Wirth's Circus flew past. Philip wanted everyone ready for the show once it went back on the road and Dan spent the afternoons with Audrey, practising a variety of new acrobatic tricks. These latest tricks, the likes of which Wirth's Circus had never seen before, were performed on the original circus horses as well as the new horses the boys had brought with them to Broken Hill.

Layla continued to avoid Michael so he kept busy, pushing the drunken night of bad decisions behind him and counting down the days until he could leave. At night he lay in bed and looked at the paintings on his ceiling, trying hard to calm the niggling panicky feeling in his gut that wouldn't go away. He reasoned with himself; everything was in order and before long he'd be back with his family.

* * *

On Michael's second last day with the circus, he spotted Layla training with the other acrobats. As usual she was on the outer and it was obvious the other performers were annoyed with her. He stopped what he was doing and watched as she argued with them, gesturing angrily with her hands. Walking quickly away from the argument, she squatted down in the sawdust. Her body curled up and she reached forward to hang onto the railing in front of her, vomiting into a bucket, the sounds of her retching carrying over to where he stood. Michael tied the horses to a nearby rail and walked over to where she was. He held her hair back and supported her as she buckled over, the contents of her stomach ending up in the bucket.

None of the others came to see if she was okay. They resumed their rehearsals, ignoring her plight. Eventually Philip came over. The burly ringmaster spoke angrily, directing his ire at Layla.

'Pack your bags, girlie, because this is your last day here with us. I'll have Matilda make your pay up and get you a ticket on the next train out of here. Your days with Wirth's are finished.'

Michael was horrified. 'She's sick, can't you see that. I don't think it's a reason to sack her.'

'All I can see is a belly getting bigger by the day and a baby that will arrive. We don't put up with ill-reputable women in our team and we don't have room for an illegitimate child. It's time for her to move on.' Philip strode off, his comments ringing in Michael's ears. Michael's head tightened as he squatted next to Layla, clenching his teeth as his stomach churned.

He whispered, a look of horror on his face. 'Is it true? Are you pregnant?'

She wiped her mouth with the back of her hand. 'I guess so, but don't worry, it's not the first time.'

Michael's eyes were wide. 'What do you mean, do you have other kids?'

'No, I got rid of the other ones before they grew. You can get it done in town. It near killed me last time though and I'm not thinking about fixing it that way this time.' She hissed at him, her voice surly. 'This one's yours and I can tell you right now, you're in this as much as I am.'

'How can I be sure it's mine?' Michael's eyes narrowed as he watched her lips curl up in a sickly smile.

She straightened up, her eyes flashing angrily. 'Because you're the only man I've slept with in the last six months. I'd been wary after the other mishaps and I thought I had my dates worked out. It should have been safe, but now I'm late by a week.'

'But it's only been four or five weeks since I . . . since . . .'

Layla wiped her mouth and stood up. 'It only takes that long, you idiot. I get sick straight away. I did with the others.'

Michael was aware some of the others were watching them as they talked. 'How can you know you're pregnant, this early?'

Layla hissed at him again. 'Look at the vomit in the bucket. I've done that every morning this week. Plus, I said, I'm late, and I'm never late.'

The colour drained from Michael's face and he held tight to the nearby rail.

'I'll leave on the train in the morning. If you're any sort of man you'll come with me. It's a hard world out there for a woman and a child by themselves. I'm going to need money.' Layla stood up and wiped her mouth again with the handkerchief Michael offered.

'I can't. I mean I'm going home. No-one knows about what happened. I'm only eighteen. I know nothing about babies.'

'Well, drover boy,' she gave him a sly grin, 'you may be about to learn. I'll be waiting for you on the platform in town at six in the morning.' With that she walked off, throwing her ropes and rings she was working with in the large rubbish bins beside the track.

Dan was observing the pair from the other side of the ring and made his way over to Michael. 'What was that about?'

Michael's skin was clammy; his hands clenched by his side as he stood up watching Layla leave the tent. 'We need to talk.'

* * *

Dan held both sides of his head and rocked back and forth when Michael repeated the events of the night that had taken place nearly six weeks ago.

'How can you be sure it's yours, Mickey? It's not long ago.'

'I can't, but the dates would be right and she says she hasn't been with anyone else. I've kept an eye on her since then and I think she's telling the truth. I watched her because I wanted to talk to her about what happened. She hasn't been into town..'

'I should never have left you by yourself. You know, Michael, she's only just pregnant. They have operations to get rid of babies.'

'I can't be responsible for a baby's death.'

'It's not a baby yet.'

Michael shook his head. 'I'm not sure, but' he paused and breathed deeply, 'she said she's had those operations before and last time it nearly killed her. She refuses to have it done again.'

'Jeez, Michael, what sort of girl is she? She's only a bit older than us but she's already been pregnant. What is she, a prostitute? Does anyone else know about this?'

Michael was shaking, bile rising in his throat. 'No, I can't tell anyone. It's not only her fault. I didn't push her out of the tub and I followed her back to her wagon. I'm as much to blame as she is. I didn't think about her getting pregnant.'

'She's that type. Why don't you let her go, she'll only do it again? Face up to it, she only wants you to support her and the child when it's born.'

'You're right, Dan, but I'm eighteen now and I've only myself to blame. No matter what, I have to do the decent thing. What sort of man leaves a woman in her condition? She'll end up in a care house. She won't be able to work and she's no family or anyone to help her.'

'She should have thought about that before she jumped in with you.'

Michael gulped, a pain pounding in his chest. 'I'll write a letter to Mum and Dad.' He put his head between his hands, closing his eyes. 'It's hard, but I'll be honest.' He stopped talking, the torment of his shame overwhelming.

His gut churned and he felt like he was drowning in the disgrace and disrespect he had brought upon his parents and those in the circus who had placed trust in him. The only thing he could do was to go with Layla and take each day as it came. As he said to Dan, 'There is no decision, the track has been marked.'

CHAPTER 17

December 1934

Michael asked Layla to marry him, so they could raise the baby under respectable conditions. But she refused and her attitude from the first day when they sat next to each other on the train as it slowly chugged out of Broken Hill never wavered. She would have been happy to go by herself, to find a new life amongst the dancers and show people of the city. But bringing Michael with her would ensure an income and someone to look after the brat once it was born. Her choice would have been to get rid of the baby already growing inside her, but the last abortion completed in a small room in the backstreets of Melbourne had gone badly and she was surprised she had fallen pregnant again.

She had been careful not to sleep with any of the men in town or at the circus. Now because of a lonely drinking session and a glimpse of Michael entering the washroom, she found herself in a predicament there was no easy fix for. She slipped a cheap gold band on her finger.

This was the best of a bad situation. Michael was young and would find work in Melbourne. She'd drilled him on what to say and how to act, and to others it looked and sounded like they were husband and wife. No one would question it, but rather assume they were a married couple with a baby on the way. The charade would come in handy when they wanted to rent a room or find work in the city. Once she gave birth, she could return to her vaudeville life; with her contacts, she'd be able to find work. Meanwhile she would let Michael tag along. He was young, good looking and easy to boss around. He'd do perfectly, at least until someone better came along.

CHAPTER 18

Melbourne 1935

ayla was two months pregnant when they arrived in the city; her abrupt instructions leaving no doubt of the rules for their relationship.

'You should have fixed yourself up that night instead of using me.'

'From memory, Layla, it was you who initiated what happened.'

'As usual, the woman gets the blame and it'll be me left with the brat.'

'I'm here with you. It's time you stopped complaining and worked with me to make the best of this situation.'

Layla's eyes narrowed. 'You can live with me through the pregnancy and provide for me when it arrives. The space next to the kitchen is where you sleep and don't ever come near my room, or I shall leave and you won't be able to find me. There are plenty of rich people who'll adopt a little baby and we're not tied by marriage, so you have no real connection to me.'

'It suits me fine not to sleep with you and I'll remind you to keep a civil tongue in your head.'

Once the baby arrived, Michael was kept busy and Layla made sure, even though he was worn out when he finished his labouring work, that he also had work to do at home. Labouring was often wet and dangerous, but the weekly wage allowed them to live where they did. At first Michael thought he could carry on and live separate lives under the same roof. He had a responsibility to Layla and also to his tiny dark-haired daughter, Gracie, whom he had fallen in love with from the moment she was born.

She was a contented baby and hardly cried, happy to lie in his arms and grasp his fingers. Layla had as little to do with her as possible and would be dressed ready to leave for her job once Michael was home in the afternoon.

All his spare time was spent with Gracie, who from a young age was quick to learn and obsessed with the books he brought home for her. She also learned to keep her distance from Layla.

The sight of Gracie walking towards him with her arms outstretched was enough to keep Michael happy. The situation with Layla however, continued to deteriorate and he began to question the way they lived.

Layla often slept the daylight hours away, leaving Gracie to look after herself while Michael was at work. 'Thank God my theatre and burlesque work brings in enough money to keep me clothed and looking as good as I do.'

Michael argued with her. 'This isn't a life for Gracie and don't treat me like your servant. I'd be better taking Gracie and leaving.'

'I bring the most money in, Michael. It's my money that put a roof over our head and food to eat when you couldn't find work. If it wasn't for my acting talents we'd be living in the slums.'

Michael's anger simmered as she continued berating him.

'It's your job to care for that wretched child.' She rolled her eyes. 'You've always been besotted with her anyway and it's pathetic to see how much attention you pay her.'

There were times when he yelled back at her, his deep voice resounding around the tiny rooms. 'She's our child. No matter what, she deserves to be looked after. All you think of is yourself and your drunken theatre friends.'

Layla sneered at him. 'How would you know about my friends. I only ever took you once to meet them and that was only because I needed someone in case I felt sick with that stupid brat still in my stomach.'

'You're a bitch, Layla. Stop and look at yourself.'

Layla's voice would become louder and Gracie would put her hands over her ears. 'You've got no friends here and nowhere to run or hide, let alone have the money to bring up a four-year-old girl alone. Your wage is pittance! I can kick you out anytime and then you'd never see your precious Gracie again.'

At times Michael considered leaving, the fighting and constant barrage of insults wearing him down. But Gracie was the centre of his life and he tried to ease the tension in the house and do everything he could to maintain the peace, keeping her well out of the way of her mother.

Layla became more and more involved with her theatre friends and Michael was sure she was also romantically involved with one of them. He felt no jealousy; all he cared about was his young daughter.

Although he had betrayed the trust his parents had placed in him he had broached the idea of taking Gracie back to his family. Layla had laughed. The child would stay with her and if Michael wanted to leave, that was his choice, but on no terms was he to ever return or ask to see his young daughter.

And so he continued in his trapped existence, handing over his wage to Layla each week and roaming the markets to find the cheapest food. There was no escape and his unhappiness bounced off every crowded street corner of the city he was forced to live in.

CHAPTER 19

As the warmth of spring 1939 imbued the grey streets of Melbourne, life with Layla became more unbearable. Like the tattered strips of paint peeling off the stark walls of their small flat, Michael's life dangled and hung precariously, with nothing but a cold hard surface below.

Once Layla demanded he stay and look after Gracie, now she wavered, suggesting it was time for him to move on.

'I can look after her now, she's four,' Layla said. 'Anyway, many Australian men, the real men, are joining the reserves. They say there's going to be a war.'

Michael's chest ached at the thought of leaving, but the situation couldn't continue and he had already toyed with the idea of joining up. It was time to make some decisions. In the New Year he would join the army. If there was a war he'd do his time and then when he returned he could pick up droving jobs that would bring cattle to the south, and not far from Melbourne.

He pulled the threadbare cover over his body, curled his legs up and rubbed them to try and keep warm.

He could do it.

Once Gracie was old enough, she could travel with him and they could spend time together in a place away from Layla.

As new leaves appeared on the bare branches of the trees lining the streets, Michael became certain about the direction he would take. He'd wait until after Christmas and then see where the war was headed. If they still needed Australian soldiers, he'd be ready.

* * *

Thousands of miles across the oceans in Germany, the days were growing shorter, the cool air of Autumn sending chills through those who sensed the impending disaster. Jewish citizens were barred from working in government jobs or owning their own businesses and any books deemed Jewish or having opposing ideologies to Nazism were ceremoniously burnt. The winds of change moved swifter and those who faced persecution and were able to gain a permit, left Germany as quickly as they could arrange.

In a small office in Germany, Hitler and his generals gathered, peering over a large desk covered with papers and maps. Men pointed to markers on the maps, their fingers tracing the borders of neighbouring countries as they quietly talked. Heads nodded and decisions were made. Long before the trees shed all their leaves, preparing for the bitter winter ahead, German forces gathered, ready to march across the border into Poland and to ultimately succeed in following Hitler's orders - *to send to death mercilessly, men, women and children of Polish derivation and language.*

The relatively young nation of Australia would not escape the tendrils of this war, even with its isolation and distance from Europe. The world was on the brink of another catastrophe that would see the death of millions, incarcerated, tortured and murdered due to their religion, race and nationality.

* * *

Michael listened and gathered any information he could on the events occurring in Europe. On the third of September 1939, he listened in shock to the Australian Prime Minister's speech on the radio. Robert Menzies spoke slowly and clearly, his convictions of Australia's responsibilities in backing Britain and her allies, resonating throughout the room where Michael sat, Gracie snuggled in against his chest.

'My fellow Australians. It is my melancholy duty to inform you, officially, that, in consequence of the persistence by Germany in her invasion of Poland, Great Britain has declared war upon her, and that, as a result, Australia is also at war.

Michael bent his head and rested his chin on his daughter's head. He knew how catastrophic the effects of the Great War had been. The world was once again on the cusp of a conflict that could affect his family and Gracie in the years to come. He kissed the top of her head, his love for her overwhelming and the thought of someone hurting her, unbearable. She snuggled in closer and Michael hugged her tight. Menzies had declared Australia to be at war. The forces would need soldiers, young men to fight for their country, to keep their loved ones safe. He closed his eyes and took a deep breath. He would wait until after Christmas and then he would leave.

CHAPTER 20

By early 1940 Menzies committed twenty thousand Australian men to strengthen the British forces already fighting against the Germans in Europe. Conscription and three months of military training for unmarried men aged twenty-one, re-enforced the home defence forces and freed up volunteers for service abroad. When the first contingent of the Australian 6th Division, consisting of the 16th Brigade, embarked for the Middle East, Michael decided it was time to make a move.

He wrote a long letter to his parents and another one to Dan, letting them know he was going to enlist.

When he had first arrived in Melbourne he had sent a letter to his parents. He told them where he was living and that he had taken on the responsibility of a woman who would be the mother of his child. He only wrote one more time to let them know Gracie had been born. Sometimes he still struggled with the shame of what had happened but over the years his focus was on Gracie and he pushed aside the aching pangs for home and his family.

Michael's thoughts turned to Layla. He had already said his

goodbyes to her. All he wanted was for her to take better care of Gracie; do what mothers were supposed to do.

'Talk to her, read to her and give her some loving care,' he'd told her in no uncertain terms. 'I don't care what else you do while I'm gone, but if nothing else, just care for the child. Be a mother to her, she needs you.'

Layla's whining voice scraped like a knife on a china plate. 'You've spoilt her. I have to use the stick to make her do anything. When she's down in the lane playing with all those dirty brats, she never comes when I call.'

'For God's sake Layla, she's your daughter, have some patience. The way you treat her, it makes her timid. She hardly speaks when you're around.'

'Oh, so now you're the expert on bringing up the kid. What would you know? You've spent all your life living in the middle of nowhere. A drover, nothing but dust and horses. If it weren't for the extra money I make, we'd be living in those slums down the road. A real man would have provided more, not this cold poky flat.'

Michael's thoughts turned to his own mother. Firm, steady and caring, and not a mean bone in her body. 'I think Gracie would respond better if you spoke to her nicely. I could be away for a while. She's going to need you.'

Layla preened herself in the mirror as she answered, her black hair curled in an immaculate bob sat perfectly as she carefully outlined her lips with her newest lipstick. 'I'll be truthful, Michael. There's never been anything between us. This arrangement is over. You can come back to your daughter, but you and I will have nothing to do with each other.'

Anger rose in Michael and his deep voice made Layla jump. 'I will be back and I will see Gracie. I intend taking her on holidays and also back to visit my family.'

'You can come and visit and if you want to take her on a

holiday you can. But she lives here with me and you keep the money coming, unless you want your daughter living in the slums.'

Michael watched Layla apply her makeup. Her demands were definite and as much as he didn't want to leave Gracie even for a short while, at least now he could think ahead to plans for when he returned. He looked around Layla's room, grateful he hadn't shared it with her. He rarely came into her private space. From the start he slept in a tiny room, jutting off from the kitchen. Gracie slept upstairs in a tiny room with enough space for her small bed and a chair, the window with cracked glass allowing a glimpse of the outside world. Much of the building was falling apart and it was hard to keep the cold out, but it was cheap rent and better than most of the other flats nearby.

As much as he disliked where they lived, Michael hated walking through the adjoining suburbs even more. The residents were mostly unemployed and the poorest people he'd ever seen. Children roamed the streets, running after him to see if he'd give them money. Their clothes and hair were dirty, their skinny legs and arms covered in tattered clothes, doing little to shield them from the cold Melbourne winter. The women were bedraggled and he stared straight ahead, walking quicker when they jeered and called out to him.

While he was away he would send money back, so Layla and Gracie could continue to live in the flat. At least it was a decent roof over their heads and it also meant he knew exactly where they'd be when he returned. Everything was in order to leave and all he had to do now was to say goodbye to Gracie.

CHAPTER 21

Fitzroy, Melbourne - January 1940

'But Daddy, who will read to me at night?'

'You're four, Gracie, you can nearly read the words yourself.'

'How old are you, Daddy?

'I'm twenty-four.'

'I'm not as old so I can't remember all the words.'

'Sound them out like I taught you. Remember what the letters say.'

'But sometimes the books are heavy. Who will hold them for me?'

'Lie on your side and you'll be able to read the words.'

'But who will tell me about the pictures?'

'You can make up your own ideas.'

'But what if I have lots of questions about the story?'

'You'll have to save them in your head for me.'

* * *

Gracie snuggled further under the bedcovers, her tiny hands clenching the rolled-over top of the thin, quilted cover. She frowned and her last words came out wobbly as tears pooled in her eyes. Blinking hard to try to stop them, she looked at her father as he tucked the blankets into the side of the bed. His brown eyes never left hers.

'Don't forget to read every night. Read out loud and your words will come to me, wherever I am.'

'How will you hear me?'

'I'll hear you across the sky.' They looked at each other, Michael's tears threatening to push through the cheery barrier he was trying to maintain. He pointed out the window. 'The words will bounce off the stars and if there's a moon, they'll slide down its side.'

A rusty awning protected the window, the ragged edges a silhouette in the moonlight. In the narrow lane below, a rubbish lid, discarded by a cat's departing paws clanged on the cobbled footpath. The aloof feline crossed to an adjacent roof, following an invisible path before stopping near the edge of the red tiles; an upright sentry staring out across the streets of inner Melbourne.

'Why does the cat go up on the roof at night?' Gracie asked.

'Look how high it is. It can see all of Fitzroy from up there. It's probably looking for mice or rats.'

'Why is the cat mean? Why does it kill the mice?'

'To survive, Gracie. Animals eat smaller animals.'

'Do they only kill when they need food?'

'I guess so, or when they need to protect their young.'

'I'm glad people don't kill other people for food.'

It took a long time for her father to answer. 'We're lucky. We can buy our food.'

'Why does Mother say you're going to leave to kill soldiers?'

'Sometimes your mother and I don't agree,' Michael said,

thinking about how Layla yelled and screamed like a crazy woman when he argued with her.

Last week Layla had purposely smashed a photo frame. It was the picture of her and Michael taken at the theatre in the city before Gracie was born. It was the one time she had asked him to come with her and the year was written along the bottom of the print – 1935. Now the coloured frame, usually perched on the thick wooden mantelpiece, lay shattered in hundreds of sharp pieces, the chips of broken porcelain and glass pushed into a corner of the room.

* * *

Gracie had found the photo in the dust under the lounge. She brushed it off and studied it for a long time.

Her mother was upstairs sleeping. She'd come home as the sun was rising. Father was at work so there was no one to notice what she was doing. She took the heavy scissors from the kitchen drawer and cut the picture. Half went in the metal bin outside and she hid the other piece so her mother couldn't find it.

That picture only ever made her mother angry anyway.

Only last week she had waved it around, her face up close to Gracie's. 'Look how good my figure was.' Layla's dark eyes were spiteful and angry. 'See how beautiful I was. I was the amazing Layla De Souza, the main act, right until you came along and spoiled everything. No one would have known I was pregnant. Should have got rid of you then, saved myself all these troubles.'

Gracie waited until her mother left the room. She stood on a wooden chair, so her face was level with the photo. The frame was shiny and smooth and her fingers touched it lightly before making their way onto the photo. If she stood on the tips of her toes she could reach up and trace the lace hanging from Layla's dark wavy hair. Her fingers followed the lace, stroking the outline before sliding down the elegant ballgown stretched tight around Layla's body. The gown spread out along the ground and there were curves and folds of fabric to follow until she reached the bottom of the picture. Her fingers walked slowly across to her father's black shoes, stark against the patterned carpet. She polished them gently, before moving her hand up to his face, tracing his strong cheekbones, trailing across his eyebrows before smoothing down his curly hair.

It took a long while to study the different parts of the photo and she always left Layla's face until last. If her mother had been nastier than usual, she would push her fingers into Layla's stomach, pressing down so hard she needed her other hand to hold the frame upright. Then she would reach up as high as she could and push her lips against her father's face. When his face changed, she kissed it. His lips curled up at the ends and his eyes looked straight at her, crinkly lines stretching from the corners of his mouth as his smile appeared. As soon as she leaned back, the look faded away and unhappiness returned to his face.

Her mother's face always remained the same. Gracie tried hard to change it and once when she was home by herself she had taken a pin from the sewing box and stuck it into her mother's stomach. Nothing changed. Her sickly false smile remained, stuck within the glossy paper. After that Gracie didn't bother with the photo again for a long time. She left it alone and pushed the pin into the back of the couch where no one could find it. Just in case she needed it again.

Now the shelf stood empty, the frame smashed and half the photo tucked away, hidden, where only Gracie could find it. No one cared where the photo was anyway. No one except Gracie.

* * *

'Daddy,' Gracie propped herself up on her elbow, pulling at Michael's sleeve. 'Are you going to kill a soldier?'

'No, your mother shouldn't have said that.' He stared out the window again, the glow from the moon lighting the empty streets and the buildings opposite. Chimneys sat like unsteady blocks on the rooftops, wisps of smoke escaping from their flues, drifting into the clear night sky. The cat was still sitting on the edge of the roof, licking its paws as it watched over the houses, their bricks grey and dirty. 'Listen to me carefully. Your mother doesn't always tell the truth.'

'But you are going away?'

'I am.'

Gracie shut her eyes, tiny tears rolling slowly down her chubby cheeks.

'Don't cry, baby.'

'But I don't want you to go.'

'I don't want to leave you, but hopefully I'll be back soon.'

'What's a war?'

'It's when people from another country want to fight each other.'

'Do they want food, like the cat?'

'Sort of. Anyway, you don't need to worry. I want you to read your books at night and be good for your mother. I'm going to train with the other soldiers in case they need us.'

'Black Beauty wanted to know what the men fought about.' Gracie sat up on the bed, her blue eyes wide and looking straight into Michael's. 'He loved his master, remember Daddy? He fell from his saddle and then he never saw him again.'

Michael sighed; the war horse chapter from the *Black Beauty* story. Their favourite book with frayed edges and a cover worn thin, where his and Gracie's hands had held it many times.

'You won't fall off your horse, will you, Daddy? You're the best rider in the world, so you won't fall off and then you'll come back.'

'I don't think I'll be on a horse.'

'Will the war take long?'

'No, baby, it won't and probably by the time we've trained, the war will be over. I'll come back and we can find new books to read.'

'But I'll want to talk to you when you're with the other soldiers.'

'I know you will.' He pulled the covers back and pulled her over onto his lap. She shivered in the cool night air and he held her close, the two of them squashed into a room, which was more like a cupboard with a window. 'Look at the brightest star. Do you see it?'

They leaned forward, peering through the window. Verandahs hung precariously from the facades of ramshackle buildings on the opposite side of the lane, their windows boarded up, the glass behind, cracked and broken. The cat strode arrogantly along the edge of the roof, its tail vertical as it rubbed its skinny body against a chimney. High above the cat, the evening star flickered brightly.

Gracie whispered, 'I see it, Daddy.'

'Look at the star at night and read the words out loud. They will bounce off the points and I'll be able to hear you, no matter where I am.'

Gracie screwed up her face and Michael could tell she was unsure how the communication would work. She snuggled in closer, revelling in his body warmth. 'But what if it's cloudy or there're no stars out?'

The star is always there somewhere. Sometimes it's hidden behind the clouds.'

'Who will I rub noses with?'

'Nobody, until I come back. Then we will rub noses every day.'

'I know what we can do.' Some excitement returned to Gracie's voice. 'When the moon is big and round like a circle.'

'You mean a full moon.'

'Yes. When it's big and round, I'll rub my nose and look at the moon. And you can rub your nose also.'

'We can do that, Gracie.'

'Are you sure it's going to work, Daddy?

'I'm sure.'

Michael stroked her wavy black hair, twisting the ends around his large fingers, pushing the stray strands back from her face. Her tiny face, so innocent, looked back at him. Trusting blue eyes peering out from behind her long dark eyelashes.

'Do you remember what we call the star?' Michael said.

'It's Elizabeth's star. I remember the story.'

'Elizabeth's Star is a magical star and it will send messages to me.'

'I won't forget, Daddy.' Gracie looked up into the night sky.

Michael's arms wrapped around her. His lips pressed softly down on the top of her head and he inhaled, closing his eyes so he could remember everything about her; the feel of her soft skin against his, the way her fingers clung onto his and the wispy tendrils of hair brushing against his cheek as she pushed her face next to his.

'Will you see the same star?' Gracie asked.

'Yes, Gracie, there is only one Elizabeth's star.'

Gracie was satisfied and Michael breathed a sigh of relief.

'Can we read now?' She snuggled back under the covers, moving nearer the wall so he could lie beside her.

It was their favourite, *Black Beauty*. They nestled together, both holding the book as the words and pictures brought the story to life. Some pages stuck together as if urging them to read faster and finish the book. Michael held the book up straighter and Gracie helped him pry the pages apart, hanging onto the edges so none were missed.

He spoke slowly, adding expression to parts, the sound of his voice soothing Gracie as she lay staring up at him. Her hands dropped, no longer holding onto the book but instead resting on his arm.

Her big eyes looked up, watching his lips as he read. Reaching up, she stroked his face, soft fingers running across the stubble forming on his cheeks. Her index finger traced his eyebrows and he closed his eyes for a moment, cherishing the feeling of her tiny fingers tickling his skin. She touched his hair, her hands patting down the curls she loved to brush.

Her body relaxed and her eyelids drooped. It was very late and they had talked for a long time and Michael knew she would fall asleep before the first chapter ended. As much as he wanted to stretch out his time with his little daughter, he wanted this to be his goodbye. It was better to leave as she slept. The sight of her crying or waving goodbye would be too much to bear and it would make Layla angry.

His voice shook. *'The first place that I can remember was a large pleasant meadow with a pond of clear water in it.'* Gracie's eyes closed and Michael knew she would be imagining she was in the meadow. Her lips moved as he spoke and her words matched his own. *'Some shady trees leaned over it, and rushes and water-lilies grew at the deep end.'*

Tonight, he kept reading, long after her breathing settled into sleep. The story was soothing and there was a surreal calmness as he looked down at his precious daughter next to him.

He stood up, stretching his arms upward, a dull ache in his chest as he contemplated what lay ahead. There wasn't only the sadness at leaving Gracie but also a yearning for the outback; the dusty paddocks stretching endlessly, the mobs of pink galahs breaking the void of silence and the peace found from tracking towards a distant horizon.

But the dusty outback trail would not be the track he would be following and by early morning he would be moving in a different direction.

He bent down and gently kissed the top of Gracie's head, wondering how long it would be before he saw Melbourne city, the outback or his family again.

CHAPTER 22

Woombye Queensland - January 1940

The train trip from Brisbane to Woombye took a few hours and the jolting and clattering of the train dulled Joanie's thoughts and relaxed her body. The ball last night had turned into an early morning party and she closed her eyes, resting comfortably on the wide leather seats.

The New Year's Day dinner at her parents' place was scheduled for six, so there would be plenty of time to get ready and help her mother prepare the food once she arrived. Closing her eyes, she dreamed of a long cool bath in her parents' bathtub, the water refreshing her body after the hot trip in the train.

When she was little, she'd needed a small wooden step to help her get in and out of the tub, without coming to grief on the terrazzo floor. Back then she loved to slide up and down on the slippery surface of the tub, enjoying the water sloshing over her body like the waves of the ocean.

She stared out the train's window, her image reflected in the glass. Bright green eyes, framed by long lashes looked back and she smiled, pleased the natural thickness of her lashes did not require the added makeup of mascara. She barely used makeup, much to the chagrin of her girlfriends who spent long hours getting ready before any outing. Even her hair was better left as it was, with only a brush passed quickly over it before going anywhere. She pinched her cheeks and pushed her hair back behind her ears, tilting her head from side to side.

She had changed in many different ways since leaving the security and familiarity of the small town she'd grown up in. Not only did she look older but she had changed emotionally and socially. In the larger city she mixed with others who came from different parts of Australia, socialising with young men and women who similarly enjoyed the dance halls and eateries in and around Brisbane.

Woombye still held a special place in her heart. It was where she had been born and lived for most of her life. Her school friends, her family and everything she held dear was in and around the tiny country town. Her father's trading store in Blackall Street had been her workplace since the day she left school at the age of fourteen. The job had kept her busy and given her valuable trading and bookkeeping skills. However, by the time she turned nineteen she knew she wanted more.

It was her parents who insisted she spread her wings. They were the driving force in encouraging her to make a change and experience life in a bigger town, somewhere offering more exciting and varied experiences.

Now she couldn't imagine living anywhere else. The bustling city of Brisbane became her home and she found her working niche in an office of one of the busiest trading shops in Queen Street; McDonnell & East. The manager, who had known her father for years, readily took her on and had been rewarded with a worker with a natural ability for trade and bookwork. A strong work ethic and bright mathematical mind allowed her to move into some of the more rewarding roles. It didn't take long before she was working directly with the managers and more senior assistants, who noted, "the young country girl", was very quick to pick up and remember what she was taught. The male staff were also quick to notice she was single.

It hadn't taken long for the invitations and requests to flood in and Joanie was kept busy accompanying a variety of young men to picnics and dances. She'd also become friends with some of the other girls at work and there was no shortage of company when she needed to buy a new dress, to go for a cup of tea at the new café in the store or to roam the shops looking for shoes for one of the upcoming social events.

The wide streets of Brisbane with the steel tramlines running down the middle became as familiar to her as the country lanes and tracks she'd grown up with. A tiny, shared flat overlooking the main street of the city was a cosy retreat at the end of her busy working days, and Vera, the girl she rented with, became her new family.

Vera was a nurse from Sydney, and accustomed to cities and finding the best places to dine and dance. She took the naïve Joanie under her wing and when they weren't working, they could be found together, arms locked, strolling through the city streets, trying to find the best deal on silk stockings or looking with envy at the elegant dresses in the fancy shops.

After living in Brisbane for a year she couldn't imagine being anywhere else. Once work was over for the day, the focus was on, where to meet and what to wear. The lounge became their change room and dresses and shoes scattered over the chairs, revealed the difficult decisions about how to look the best.

'Time to get those curlers out of your hair, Vera,' Joanie said, as they got ready for the most important event of the year.

'Not everyone's as blessed as you are with your wavy blonde hair and lovely green eyes,' Vera complained, teasing her blonde hair so the curls she had created would hold.

'My hair does what it wants.'

'Oh, please.' Vera pulled a comical face. 'Go with it my love, the men go crazy over you.'

'They go crazy over us all. What is it with men? I don't understand why they want to get serious. I want to go out and have fun, to dance and be friends with them. I'm not ready to settle down.'

'Me either.' Vera flopped down on a wicker chair, positioned to take in the events of the street below. 'There's no way I'm going to end up like my mother, cooking and cleaning all her life and taking orders from my father.'

'Not all men are like your father.' Joanie watched a tram making its way up the street. 'My father has always encouraged me to be independent and follow my dreams. Hence,' she positioned a hairclip into the front of her hair, 'I live here in this magnificent city apartment with gold taps and crystal chandeliers and do exactly what I like.'

They both laughed, casting their eyes around the dimly lit tiny space they called home, the remnants of last night's dishes and glasses still stacked along the kitchen bench. Joanie stood on her tiptoes and spun around. 'We are two independent young women and we are on the brink of a new year.'

Vera added, 'To love and friendship, freedom and new experiences, perhaps even adventures.'

'Always the wordsmith,' Joanie said as she straightened her dress. 'It's going to be a fantastic new year. I can feel it. And you're right, there are adventures ahead.'

'1940,' Vera said the numbers slowly. 'It sounds weird, almost ominous. I'm not so sure what's ahead, but there's something in the air.' Passing a silky pair of gloves to Joanie, she paused and gave her a tiny kiss on her cheek. 'Let 1940 be a fabulous year for both of us.'

Joanie's face glowed, her eyes wide and excited. 'Wonderful things are going to happen in the New Year. I just know it. Now let's get going. Cloudland's ball awaits.'

CHAPTER 23

New Year's Day 1940

The New Year's Eve Ball continued long after the bells at midnight and the sky was lightening as Joanie and Vera tip-toed up the narrow stairs to their flat, holding their high-heeled shoes.

'My feet are aching,' Joanie giggled, 'I love dancing but some of the boys need to learn how to dance properly and not stand on a girl's toes.'

'You danced with so many. Did you keep count?' Vera whispered.

'There weren't that many. I tell you what though, you have to remind a few where it's acceptable to place their hands when they waltz.'

Vera rolled her eyes. 'It's amazing how they seem to forget where your waist is and think it's okay to slide their hand lower down your back. I saw you dancing with the boss's son. He's the best-looking boy I've ever seen.'

Joanie grimaced. 'I had to stop dancing several times with him. He's got the loosest hands and,' she sighed, 'he's asked me out many times, but to tell you the truth, he's about as boring as they come. All those gorgeous looking boys and not one either of us is interested in,' Joanie added.

'Perhaps we'll end up single forever. I'm glad we're not chasing after a husband, because so far I've found no-one who I'd let park their shoes under my bed,' Vera replied.

They both giggled as Vera struggled to put the key in the lock and open the door. 'Home sweet home, now off to bed, young Joanie. You only have an hour or so until you have to be at the train station and your father will be waiting for your answer to his question.'

Joanie gave Vera a kiss on the cheek. 'Fancy father ringing me at work. It's completely out of the blue and he's thrown a spanner in the works, as he would say. I do like the sound of it though. Goodnight, my friend. Today is the first day of the rest of our lives. 1940. I'm telling you, wonderful things are going to happen this year.'

* * *

A cool bath and clean clothes freshened Joanie up after her late night and the train trip back to Woombye. She rested on the bed in her old bedroom, staring up at the ornate ceiling rose, a light bulb attached to a long cord hanging from the middle. Tall French doors opening up onto the verandah were flung open, attempting to catch any breeze that might filter through. The summer humidity was stifling, and she wiped her face with a damp towel, running it over her legs and arms before using it to chase a couple of flies away.

She stretched her body, staring at the pink and yellow glass panes of the windows on the other wall of the bedroom. When she was little she had loved the rays of coloured light, reflecting across her bedroom when the sun hit the glass at the right spot.

The house held fond memories. It was still home. Even though she wouldn't want to come back and live here, it pulled at her heartstrings. It was in this yard that her father had helped her climb the jacaranda tree, where she had watched chickens hatch and played with her toys on the same wooden floor she looked at now. It was strange to be lying back on her old bed, in a room where she had spent much of her life. From where she lay, she could see the letter box and low picket fence, the road not far in front. A path led from the front gate to three stairs, a wide verandah running along the front of the house. Short thick stumps held the house off the ground, the air circulating underneath, cooling the rooms above it during the heat. Woombye's weather was what Joanie's father described as the perfect temperature. Although it could be one hundred degrees in summer and thirty-five in winter, the extremes were short-lived. Overall, the days and nights were comfortable, the green hills and prosperous farms in the area, testament to good soil and weather conditions.

Her mother's cocker spaniel, Raj, scratched and whimpered at her bedroom door, reminding her it was time to get up and get ready. She stretched again, revitalised and looking forward to the dinner and catching up with not only her mother and father, but also childhood friends, Peter and Andrew.

* * *

The two boys were already seated by the time Joanie came to the family table. They were brothers with only two years between them and had gone to the same school as Joanie. The younger of the two, Andrew, was twenty-two, the same age as Joanie, while Peter was two years older. Similar to Joanie, they had also left

Woombye a few years ago, finding work further afield. They stood as she took her seat, her father, Reg, pulling out the chair for her.

There was plenty of chatter and laughter, the discussion covering where they'd been and what they'd done since the last time they caught up. Peter and Andrew both suffered from itchy feet and to be part of the movement. 'The movement', Andrew stated, 'was the need to be off and help fight the dirty Germans, sending them back to where they came from. That's what the posters say anyway.' He sighed and Joanie could tell he wasn't convinced.

Peter appeared to be more eager, declaring they were joining up and leaving on the train next Monday, otherwise the Germans would be on their doorsteps before they knew it.

Andrew winked at Joanie. 'I reckon they'd have trouble finding their way here.'

'Hitler found his way into Poland easy enough,' Reg said. 'He went in from all directions, north, south and west.'

'Thank goodness Britain and France were quick to declare war. Those countries are all close together over there,' Joanie added, 'and Menzies has backed them. I didn't think you two would be so quick to join up though. It's a million miles away.'

Andrew raised his eyebrows. 'It's Peter's idea. I'd be happy to wait and see but he's keen to get out there and do his part.'

Peter sat tall, his voice deep and stern. 'Hitler has given orders to kill without mercy all men, women and children of Polish descent. He insists that Germany gain the living space it needs.' He leaned forward, across the table. 'They are the words of a madman and I fear if we don't do our part, it could be the motherland or us here who will suffer the consequences.'

Joanie frowned. She hated all the talk about war. It was the same at work. The men did nothing else except scour the newspapers and listen to the radio in their breaks. 'Oh, Peter, it's so far away. Look at how many lives were lost last time.'

Peter shook his head, as if she was naïve. 'Men died on the

shores of Gallipoli and in the fields of France to protect us. Now, less than twenty years later the Germans are threatening us again. I'm telling you Hitler is a crazy man and if we don't stop him, he'll take over the entire world.'

Joanie's mother, Edna, pushed a strand of hair behind her ear, her modern bob, stylish, the floral dress she had sewn last week, fitted, and pulled in at the waist accentuating her slender figure. She had recently celebrated her forty-eighth birthday, but her skin was smooth and unblemished, only a few wrinkles gathering at the corners of her eyes. Her childhood had been spent in England, her hands and arms clear of the spots and blemishes of others her age. She passed the dishes around, the boys needing no encouraging to stack their plates high.

Edna had cooked up a feast and the silky-oak table was brimming with plates of food. The dining room they sat in was reserved for special occasions, the long sideboard with its oval mirror, decorated with large vases of roses and carnations, picked from the garden in the front yard. Taj nestled on his special rug nearby, a swirly patterned carpet underneath, the polished timber furniture and flickering candles, imbuing an inviting warmth to the room.

The delicious aroma of the food wafted across the table. It had been a while since Joanie had been treated to a family dinner and the food was in stark contrast to what she and Vera usually survived on. Wisps of steam floated up from plates loaded with succulent roast chicken and potatoes, fat long green beans and clumps of broccoli joining the other vegetables on the plate. An elegant gravy plate was passed from person to person, the aroma of the hot juice wafting across the table.

Joanie's eyes met Peter's across the table, and she smiled, the sternness fading from his face as he poured a small amount of wine into Joanie's glass. The two had spent most of their younger years trying to outdo each other in every sporting or academic event held in the small town. Peter was taller than Andrew by a head, although their muscular builds, short blonde hair and green eyes, were similar. It was hard to decide who was the most handsome; the kind eyes and concerned face of Peter or the cheeky grin and energy of Andrew.

Andrew was also one of her closest friends. He was the rogue out of his large family, which consisted of ten children. Joanie spent much of her childhood either looking for him because no-one could find him, or hiding him from the local constabulary or more frightening, his mother. It had been Andrew who swam with her across the wide river she wasn't allowed to swim in without her father, Andrew, who made her climb the tallest spikiest Bunya Pines in the mountains behind where they lived and Andrew who doubled her day after day, year after year on the back of his fat pony named Spot.

Often, she would help the two brothers when they came into her parents' store, the tribe of their younger brothers and sisters tagging along behind. Their mother, Ethel, often sent them with a list of items needed to run her household in the desired manner. It was rare for Ethel to visit the shop herself, however on occasion when she couldn't locate one of the older children she would march down to the store. Joanie always made sure to speak in her best manner and try and find the tiniest items the boys' fearsome mother demanded when her grand presence graced their shop.

Usually it was a tiny object, a silver thimble or a new gramophone needle she needed, that would send her down to the main street. 'I've got too much to do at home. I don't need to waste my time, waiting here for you to find something in those backrooms. You think your father would have it all in order by now; he's been doing it for long enough'.

She would huff and puff, her short stout legs pacing up and down on the wooden floorboards, her round face reddening, as she waited for Joanie to find the desired object. Joanie would sigh with relief when she was able to put her hand on the item needed.

'I swear I only keep half that stock out the back for Ethel

O'Rourke,' Reg often told Joanie. 'She's one fearsome woman. No wonder he does what he's told.'

The, 'he', her father was referring to was Ethel's husband, father of Peter, Andrew and the other eight siblings. The long-suffering husband of Ethel, Percy, was a skinny bow-legged man, who had the most missing teeth out of anyone Joanie had ever met. He was a lot friendlier than Ethel and often chatted to Joanie when she went to the Post Office where he worked. When he finished work in the afternoons, he hurried straight home to help in the house and take care of the kids.

'You won't see my husband going to the pub in the afternoon,' Ethel loved to say. 'He comes straight home and does his chores. Of course, he has a proper job, not just running a shop or working in a store. He's a Postmaster.'

Edna once passed comment to Joanie and Reg on that subject. 'Perhaps it would do Percy good to go to the pub. It would be wonderful to see him relaxed and smiling. Not, always looking like a frightened rabbit.'

'Why does Ethel O'Rourke look down her nose at us?' Joanie asked her father. 'It's like she thinks she's better than us.'

Edna happened to walk in on the conversation. 'Sometimes Ethel O'Rourke can walk straight past me in town and not acknowledge me or say hello. She sticks her nose up in the air and pretends like I don't even exist.'

'Why does she do that? Peter and Andrew spend more time here with us than they do with their own family,' Joanie asked, aghast someone would be mean to her mother.

Edna sighed and began sorting out some deliveries. 'It's all to do with religion, Joanie. You'll find her friends are all in the same church.'

'You mean, they think their shit don't stink!' Reg said, his rare swearing causing Joanie to laugh out loud and Edna to frown.

'I'm sorry, Edna, but it gets right up my nose that sort of attitude.'

Edna quipped. 'It's quite amusing actually; because Mrs O'Rourke struts around like she's the Mother Mary herself yet treats others in a very unchristian like manner. If only she knew what those daughters of hers got up to behind her back.'

Reg chuckled as he started getting stock ready for the day. 'What do they do? I mean I've heard the stories about the girls, but do you really think they're true?'

'Where there's smoke there's fire. I can hear the gossip when the women talk in the shop. I might be out the back, but I can still hear what they're saying. Mrs O'Rourke would have kittens if she knew what really went on.'

'At least the boys are polite,' Joanie said. 'Andrew can be wild at times but he's always respectful. Peter's the same and I think of them as brothers.'

'They're great lads,' Reg added, 'and we're lucky to have them.'

CHAPTER 24

*D*uring their school years, Joanie thought the three of them being together would last forever; that they'd be friends for evermore. The two boys however, were ready to go out in the real world to earn some money and both left school at the same time.

Andrew was restless and had long ago realised there was more to life than what his mother wanted for him; a job in Woombye or nearby, marriage and a mob of kids. He had 'gone off the tracks' a little as Edna liked to say and always seemed to have a different girl on his arm.

None of the relationships lasted and he drifted from one job to the next, never settling or finding whatever it was he was looking for. He had confided in Joanie that he was going to leave. He'd head north and then over to Western Australia. He'd been told the ground was red and the ocean a vivid aqua. At night the sky stretched from the eastern horizon to the western horizon and was covered in so many stars there weren't any gaps in between.

Joanie thought it was a grand idea. She'd heard that in Broome there were pearls in every oyster shell. The shops in the town could string them together and make them into necklaces worth hundreds of dollars.

Andrew's eyes had lit up. 'Maybe I could become a pearl diver and bring you back a shiny string of beads.'

Joanie had laughed, reminding Andrew he hated the ocean. When they had visited the beach he wouldn't go past his ankles. He'd swim in the river but not in the sea.

'Jeez Joanie, you never forget a thing. I'm a great swimmer. I can easily swim across the river but I don't like the ocean.' He flexed his muscles, his young body fit and robust.

'I know you can swim and for goodness sake, put those muscles away.' She'd nudge him playfully. 'You're scared of sharks, aren't you? Big strong Andrew, scared of the sharks eating him.'

'Watch out.' He playfully boxed, his hands curled up and jabbing in the air, pretending to square up with her. 'I'm going to be a champion boxer next year. Kevvy down at the boxing shed reckons I'm perfect.'

'Don't try and change the subject. What about this dreadful fear you have of sharks? You didn't even want to come out where the little kids were,' she said, trying to avoid his teasing punches.

Just as Andrew was starting to jump all around her and act like he was in a boxing ring, Peter's voice bellowed from behind them. 'Andrew, Mum is going crazy at home. You were supposed to be there to bring in the wood and dig a new garden.'

'Jesus, Mother Mary, God of saints and hail all the holy fathers,' said Andrew, his fists held in mid-air as he stopped his boxing antics, gave Joanie a hasty wave goodbye and started sprinting down the street towards his house.

Peter appeared and Joanie fixed her hair, straightening her dress to make sure she looked good.

He changed his tone as he neared her. 'Sorry to interrupt the boxing but Mum will kill him if he doesn't get home.'

'Where are you off to, Peter?' She knew her voice had changed from a moment ago. She tried to sound more mature than when she had been playing around with Andrew. She pulled her shoulders back and smiled sweetly.

'I've got to go and round up a couple of the kids from the churchyard. They've been helping Father Scott, stacking his whiskey and wine bottles. It keeps them busy for ages, especially if there's been visiting clergy.'

'I'll walk with you,' she said, excited to have some quiet time with Peter, without the antics of Andrew to distract them all.

They walked together, Joanie aware that sometimes his arm brushed against hers and at times when he looked straight at her, she blushed and felt strange. It was a feeling she hadn't experienced before, and it confused her.

* * *

Now, years later and on the first day of the New Year, Joanie sat opposite the two brothers. Their blonde hair was neatly combed back and they had dressed for the occasion, their white shirts pressed, tailored trousers and shiny shoes completing the outfits. Although Peter's tie was knotted tight and sat just as it should, Andrew had relaxed and had undone his tie which now hung on the back of his chair. He gave Joanie a cheeky grin as he rolled the sleeves of his shirt up, revealing tanned muscled arms. The fact none of them were married at this age was unusual and Joanie wondered how different life might have been if the events so many years ago had been different.

Even now, that day she had walked with Peter to the church to gather up his younger siblings was still vivid in her mind. She had been sixteen and he would have been eighteen. It was the first time when she realised she felt differently about Peter than how she felt towards Andrew. It was also the first time she'd felt a fluttering in her stomach, a tightness in her throat and an overwhelming desire to kiss him.

People she knew passed and said hello, but her attention was firmly focussed on Peter. Her heart thumped when he finally plucked up courage, gazed into her eyes and asked her to come with him to the next dance in town.

It was a strange invitation and not offered in the way she'd dreamed he might ask her out. Instead, he waited until they were nearly at the church and there was no one else around. He mentioned he was going to the dance on Saturday night and asked if she would meet him there. He also suggested that perhaps it was better that she didn't mention it to anyone.

At the time she thought his idea strange but dismissed her worries. Perhaps he didn't want Andrew to know; after all she was only sixteen.

* * *

The night of the dance she had waltzed with Peter several times, aware he had also danced with other girls. She tried to mask her annoyance as he offered his arm to others, her frustration easing when he finally whispered in her ear to meet him out the back of the hall and to make sure no-one saw her leave.

Joanie had nervously left the hall in secret, making her way through the shadows towards the silhouette of a huge fig tree. Peter was leaning back against the broad trunk, only his face visible in the moonlight. Her heart beat faster as she came to where he stood and he took her hand, leading her across the moonlit paddock to look out across the hills.

His fingers squeezed gently around her hand as they walked and when they stopped, far away from the glare of the dance hall lights, he turned and bent his head down to kiss her. It was her first kiss and his lips were warm and moist on hers. His hands caressed her arms and back and she leaned against him, enjoying the strange squirming feeling in her stomach as his body pressed against her breasts. She kissed him back, her lips tingling, her eyes closed as she disappeared into the moment. They kissed for a long time, neither speaking afterwards as they joined hands again before walking back to the dance.

CHAPTER 25

There were many times after that first kiss when they found opportunities to escape from everyone. Their favourite spot was under the grove of trees down the far end of a paddock. Sometimes they stole away to an old barn, further from town.

She thought of that day now as she passed Peter a bowl of gravy, her cheeks burning as she remembered his hands on her body. She had been sixteen back then and the sun had been high in the sky when he picked her up in his father's Chevy pickup truck. It was spring and the hills were lush , the paddocks full of fat grazing cows, their calves cavorting with each other or sleeping in small groups in the sun. Joanie sat up high in the truck, feeling very grown-up in a polka dot dress her mother had recently made for her. The middle section was pulled in tightly with a wide stripy belt and she pushed her chest out, hoping Peter would notice. When she glanced at him, he was looking at her, his eyes roaming from her face to her body as he held tight to the steering wheel, remembering to look back at the road when she reminded him.

They talked about the usual topics while the car bumped along the narrow road, Joanie hanging off every word he said, fidgeting with her hair and her dress as she held back the questions of where they were going. She longed for his kisses and to feel his body pressed up against hers and she took a deep breath when he parked his car outside an old barn. When he opened the car door for her and held out his hand, she took it, butterflies in her stomach as his hand grasped hers. She followed him through the squeaky timber doors, a possum's red eyes looking down at them from a corner of the barn.

'There's only a possum here,' Peter whispered to her, his lips moving up and down her neck. 'Nobody else but you and me.'

She would always remember that afternoon. Even later in life when she reminisced, she would twitch her nose, as if she could still smell the dusty hay floating on the rays of sunshine filtering in. He had been so handsome, so strong and loving, and her stomach had ached as he pulled her in towards him.

Hay stacked high closeted them from the outside world and they clung to each other, their kisses long and passionate.

Although Peter's kisses and caresses sent goose bumps running over her body, Joanie needed to ask a question she had been pondering for many months. She pulled away from him, pushing her hair back from her face. 'Can we stop for a moment? I need to ask you something.'

Peter stopped kissing her, his hands stroking her arms. 'You can ask me anything.'

'Why do we have to meet in secret? You've told me you like me, so why do we meet where no one can see us?'

Peter tried to kiss her again, but she pulled away, the silence deafening as they sat and stared hard at each other.

Finally, he spoke. 'I don't want to ruin everything. I like being with you, touching you, kissing you.'

'I like that also. But I want more.'

His fingers traced the top of her bodice, gliding softly underneath. Her skin felt like it was on fire where he touched, where his fingers rested. She tried to breathe evenly and keep her senses, but now his other hand was moving up and down her leg, stroking slowly under her dress. 'You mean you really want more,' he whispered, his hand moving higher up the inside of her leg.

Overcoming the desire to continue, Joanie sat up, pulling her dress back down over her knees. Peter pulled his hand away. 'What's the matter, am I going too fast? You said you wanted more.' He leaned over and tried to kiss her again. 'We can just kiss if you like.'

Joanie adjusted her clothing. 'I didn't mean I want you to go further. I meant I want more than meeting in secret all the time. Why do our feelings for each other have to be hidden? You never hold my hand or let it be known we're together. I want you to come and ask my father if you can take me out.'

Peter grabbed both her hands, his eyes pleading. 'I know it would be the right thing to do, but I can't. Not at the moment.'

Joanie frowned. 'I'm good enough to kiss behind the shed or here in the barn, and if I let you, I'm sure you'd go further. I'm good enough for that, but not to be together in public?'

Her voice was angry, and she stood up, pulling her hands away from his.

Peter pleaded, 'I need to talk to my mother. I'm sure she'll come around.'

'She's known me since I was born. I've grown up with you and my mother and father treat you and Andrew as family. Are you telling me she doesn't like me? Is that why we can't be together?'

'It's not that she doesn't like you.'

'What is it then? You tell me, because now I'm confused. I thought we had feelings for each other. But it's clear, you don't feel the same.'

Peter stood up again. Already at nineteen he was six-foot-tall and towered over Joanie. He appeared to be struggling with the way the conversation was going and used his most consoling voice.

'I do, Joanie. I want you to be my girlfriend, I always have. Ever since we were at high school, I knew you were the only girl I was ever going to want.' Peter tried to stroke her arms but she pulled away, her body tense. 'It's your religion.'

'What?'

'It's because of your religion.'

'That's strange because I don't have a religion.'

He looked down at the ground. 'The fact is you and your family aren't Catholic.'

'Don't we all believe in the same God?'

'You know how it is. Mum's practically married to the church and lives by its teachings. If you're not Catholic, you're a heathen in her eyes.'

'Your mother says that? I thought she was a good Christian?'

'She is, but she constantly reminds us about the sins of people who aren't Catholics and gets Dad to lecture us also. Mind you, I think he says it to keep the peace.'

'And is that what you're going to do? Agree with your mother to keep the peace. Are you nineteen, or ten?'

'It's hard, Joanie, she's my mother and she's already asked if I have feelings for you. I've tried to keep them hidden but somehow, she knows or she's guessing. She keeps telling me I have to marry someone from the church. If I take up with someone who's not from the church, I'll be disowned and no longer welcome in the family.'

Joanie was starting to lose patience. 'How dare you! You actually let your mother and father talk about me in a disparaging way. What sort of person are you?'

'There's no use getting angry. Our families have different beliefs.'

Joanie's face burned, her words loud. 'Your family and my family have known each other for years. You've spent more time at my place than your own.'

Peter sighed. 'I'm fond of your parents and I want us to be together. But at the moment it's not a good idea to come out in the open. They've told Andrew the same thing. He's not to get any ideas about you or any other girls who aren't from the church.'

Joanie shook her head. 'Have they seen the girls Andrew takes out? At least Andrew has a mind of his own and is taking out whoever he wants. I don't see him slinking behind trees or sneaking away to barns to meet with his girlfriends. He's out in the open about it. I guess even though he's younger than you, he's a lot more mature.'

'I can't change their minds, it's the same for all the kids in my family. We've all been told and that's the rules. What am I supposed to do? They're my parents and they make the rules. And that's why I want to meet you in secret, until I can work it out.'

Joanie's chest was tight and tears of anger stung her eyes. There was no-one in the world who was more giving then her parents. They had brought her up not to judge people and it made her feel sick to think Peter's parents thought so little of them. How dare they criticise her or her parents!

She seethed with anger, her voice loud and trembling as she faced Peter and looked him straight in the eye. 'I'm telling you, Peter O'Rourke, if you can't make your own mind up about me, then we should forget about it. I'm not going to tell lies and sneak around for anyone.'

'But no one would need to know. There're plenty of places we can meet. I won't do more than kiss you. I need time to sort everything out.'

Joanie felt confused. She loved Peter and sometimes she dreamed about the future. Maybe one day they'd get married and live in a little wooden house with lots of kids running around. She never even considered religion would have an impact on their relationship.

Peter tried to put his arm around her. 'I'm sorry, Joanie, but it's how it is. I don't want to be kicked out of home. What am I supposed to do?'

'You know what, Peter, how about you stick with your family. You get up and go to church with them on Sunday and play with those stupid beads and drink that horrible wine. If they don't think I'm good enough for you, then I don't want to be part of your family anyway. Ever! Maybe it's a good thing this is happening before anything even really started.'

'There's no need to yell at me. I've always known I have to marry someone from the church.'

'I thought you liked me.' Joanie was upset, her voice shaky.

'I do. I'm sorry.'

Joanie was silent, her mind reeling. It was clear why Peter kept them a secret. It had been drummed into him since he was little. He would go to the Catholic Church, high up on the hill every Sunday and sit in the front row with the rest of his family. There was no question about it. He would marry a Catholic girl. There was no surer thing in the eyes of Ethel O'Rourke.

Joanie straightened her dress and glared at him. 'Right then, drive me back home.'

'Please Joanie, let's be together for a bit longer. I'm sorry.' He tried again, stroking her arm.

But her voice was loud and angry, the words resonating throughout the barn, causing a large owl perched undetected in the rafters, to flap its wings noisily and peer down at the commotion below. 'Oh, don't be. I couldn't care less. It's your choice and you've made it.'

She muttered loudly as she stomped off, roughly brushing stray bits of hay from her hair and clothes. Peter followed; his reply lost in the wind swirling around the yard. The owl and the possum both perched high on the beams looked down, the only sign of movement remaining, the dust and hay floating through the air. All traces of romance had disappeared, sucked out with the last gust of wind as the heavy doors banged shut. Dimness and quiet returned to the barn. The owl ruffled its feathers and closed its eyes while the possum took one last look before retreating back into the corner of the barn.

CHAPTER 26

Blinding sunshine greeted Joanie as she strode defiantly from the barn. She clenched her fists in tight balls, wanting badly to hit the side of the car as she pushed past Peter when he went to open the door for her.

'I'm capable of opening a door myself,' she said, sliding onto the seat and forcefully closing the door behind her.

Neither of them spoke until they pulled up outside her house.

'I'm sorry. Just give me time.' Peter turned towards her.

'No, forget it. If your family is going to judge someone by their religion, then I don't want to be part of that. Goodnight, Peter, and don't bother calling.' She slammed the car door as hard as she could. 'What's so good about being a bloody Catholic anyway?'

* * *

That night she had lain in bed, her tears saturating the pillow, her face hot and flushed as she went over the events of the day. If he loved her that much, he would do anything to be near her. It was time for her to make some decisions. Perhaps a move away from the small town and the same people she had grown up with would be a good thing for her.

If she worked at her father's store, she'd gain experience and then be able to get a job in one of the bigger cities. She took deep breaths. She hadn't wanted to leave Peter or Andrew before as they'd always been her constant companions. She'd thought she was in love with Peter but now, now she wasn't so sure.

How dare his parents think she wasn't right for him because of her religion and who'd made the rule you had to marry someone from the same church. How ridiculous and medieval their attitudes were! She sobbed loudly, squeezing and shaking her pillow roughly. Her stomach churned with fury as she pressed her face into the pillow, her eyes sore from crying. She closed them, waiting for sleep to come and for the day to be over.

* * *

That night had happened over six years ago, but she still wondered what might have been. What different direction would their lives have taken?

Even now Joanie wasn't sure if she'd forgiven him for not standing up to his parents. Although there'd been a string of admiring suitors over the years, she remained single. Peter also remained single. He had come close to, "tying the knot", as her mother would say and Joanie had listened with interest a few years ago to some gossip via her friend, Norah.

Peter had been engaged to one of the local girls but broke off the engagement only weeks before the wedding. Norah delighted in repeating the story to Joanie when she visited Brisbane. 'Boring little Theresa Murphy. I couldn't believe it when they got engaged. She should have been a nun she was so pious, and prim and proper. Always winning the baking award at the annual town fair. What a perfect little Catholic wife. I bet his mother chose her for him.'

'Do you know why he broke it off?' Joanie was curious, but not surprised Peter had become engaged. Theresa Murphy would have been a perfect choice in his parent's eyes.

'No, he just said he couldn't go through with it. The venue was booked and the invitations about to go out. Her family was devastated. It was the talk of the town for months.'

* * *

Gazing around the table tonight, on the first night of the New Year, Joanie pushed the resentment towards Peter and his parents aside. She felt a warmth and closeness to the people who sat around the table, sharing food, laughter and love, all with different roads travelled and with plenty more to come.

CHAPTER 27

January 1, 1940

Reg sat quietly at the end of the table, listening to the chatter as he watched his daughter and the two young men who over the years had become like his own sons. He was turning forty-nine this year and his body was no longer that of a young man's. His shoulders had stooped a little and his once thick brown hair, had greyed and thinned. Stray wiry greys pushed out from his eyebrows, his skin weathered and wrinkled, lines running across his forehead and gathering in the corners of his eyes. Edna still told him he was the most handsome man in the world and his eyes the greenest she had ever seen.

Owning the store had been easier on his body than many of the other occupations that men did. He was blessed, not only with his home and family but also the cards that life had dealt him. He intended to live a long healthy life and he made sure he walked and gardened to keep his mind and body fit. In spirit, he still felt the same as he had thirty years ago, those years when he had first fallen in love with his beautiful bride. But his body didn't move as quickly as it once had.

He looked at Peter and Andrew. They were young and fit, the best years of their lives ahead of them. Andrew wore a cheeky grin, his eyes sparkling and face animated as he told a funny story. Peter looked content, his eyes focussed on Joanie, who seemed unaware of the way he looked at her. Reg could see it. He had always seen it. It was there when they were teenagers and tonight, the same look was in Peter's eyes.

It would have pleased Edna and himself if Joanie ended up with Peter. He was a sensible and caring young man and would have taken good care of her. Reg always doubted it would happen though, knowing full well the wrath and determination of Ethel O'Rourke. They had lived in this small town long enough to know exactly how some viewed others and who they wanted their children to wed. Perhaps it was for the best. Fate, as Edna said.

Tonight, Peter also thought about the night so many years ago with Joanie. Thank goodness he was no longer the docile, compliant son his mother wished for. He had left the tiny town of Woombye straight after he broke off his engagement to Theresa, the distance allowing him time to clear his mind. The last couple of years he'd worked with sheep down in the cooler pastures of Victoria.

Over the years he often thought about Joanie. His feelings for her had been an added factor in his decision to call off the wedding. The attraction to Theresa had been purely physical and although they never slept together, Theresa could do amazing things with her mouth and hands that Peter now hoped like hell she wasn't confessing to Father Scott on Sundays. It had all gone terribly, a big mess, or as Andrew liked to declare, 'down the gurgler in the blink of an eye.'

Peter wanted to tell his mother what sort of girl Theresa Murphy really was. He wanted her to know that many of the girls who had the look of purity as they took the bread and wine on Sundays, were not virginal angels. What you saw, was not what you got.

Now as he stood, ready to make the toast for the New Year, he gazed fondly at Joanie, so different to any other girls he had met. She was the picture of beauty, her hair bouncing in wavy blonde curls on her shoulders, her face alive and full of fun and laughter. His chest heaved when he thought about how he had lost his opportunity with her. He should have asked her to marry him. They had only been young, but they could have run away, or just had her parents' blessing for the marriage.

Tonight, he was going to make sure he didn't mess up. All he needed was a chance to talk to Joanie alone, so he could tell her that she was the only girl he had ever loved. He'd made a mistake and now, with a wiser head on his shoulders and his thoughts in perspective he was never more certain that she was the one for him. Even though he was going to join up and be overseas for a while, he wanted them to be married before the year was out. They could be wed before he left, with or without his family's blessing.

CHAPTER 28

*E*dna smiled as she gazed around the table, filled with content that the people dearest to her were together. She watched Peter and Andrew, curious at the interactions between them and Joanie.

When they were younger, the boys' friendship had filled the gap of her being an only child. During the teenage years they had remained close and Edna had breathed a sigh of relief when a lingering romance between Peter and Joanie had ended.

A relationship between them would never have worked. Not because they didn't have strong feelings for each another or weren't suited. The fact was, Ethel O'Rourke would never be swayed on who her sons could and would marry.

Andrew was also very attentive to Joanie. The younger and livelier of the two boys had always been there, waiting patiently. Was it just a close friendship, or was there something more to the hours he'd spent with Joanie in Brisbane?

In the past there had been whispers of romance when the two had been sighted together in the city. Joanie however, maintained they were just friends and there was nothing between them. Edna was not so sure. Her daughter's face was alight with excitement, her wavy hair pinned back with a hairpin—she had told Edna—Andrew had bought for her. Her hand rested on her father's, and she entertained them with comical stories of living in Brisbane. The descriptions of Vera and Joanie's attempts at cooking and chores, made them all laugh so much that tears ran down Reg's face.

A lump came to Edna's throat. The years had flown past. The three young people at the table were on the cusp of new beginnings, once again heading away from the town they had grown up in. The boys had announced they were joining up in the next couple of months; Joanie had long ago spread her wings and now another exciting opportunity presented itself. Reg straightened his shoulders and took his daughter's hand in his. With the other hand, he clinked a silver teaspoon on his glass, to get the other's attention.

'I'd like to make a toast tonight, a tribute to the three of you, all bound for different parts of the world. To Peter and Andrew, to wherever the wind may blow you and to...'

'Wait, Dad, wait.' Joanie interrupted, giggling loudly as she held out her champagne glass to be refilled.

Andrew tilted the green bottle, the bubbling liquid flowing into the glass. 'Only the best for tonight.' He winked cheekily at Joanie who laughed with him, raising her glass, now ready for her father to continue.

'May you all travel in safety,' Reg said.

Andrew spoke first. 'Now you have to tell us your plans. What is this adventure you keep hinting at?'

Edna's eyes rested on Reg as he leaned back in his chair and winked at her. They had been married and in love for many years, the special connection between them giving an insight into each other's thoughts. This latest proposal would involve them being apart, perhaps for one or two years. But there would be opportunities for her to visit Reg once he was settled in. She could stay for a month or two and then return. It would be difficult to be separated, but there were many more years ahead and this opportunity held the promise of a great adventure. She wanted Reg and Joanie to experience it together, as father and daughter.

'We have been presented with a proposal and our family has had lengthy discussions,' Reg said. 'The end result being, we are going to take advantage of an opportunity for adventure, more so for Joanie and myself.'

The two boys leaned forward, their eyes intent with the mention of adventure. 'Edna, Joanie and I have come to an arrangement. Edna will for the time being and with the help of Stanley our trusted worker, run the shop. We have scouted around and found another worker who will also assist in the shop in return for the rent of our cottage next door. This is of course a temporary arrangement that will allow Joanie and I to avail ourselves of this new opportunity.'

Peter put his glass down. 'You haven't said what the opportunity is.'

'C'mon, you two, spill the beans. What are you up to?' Andrew sat tall, his dark eyes looking straight at Reg.

'Maybe we should have another drink first.' Joanie laughed as both boys howled her down. Their indignant responses were so loud and raucous that Raj lifted his head and barked.

'Goodness me,' Reg said, 'you two have upset poor Raj. Maybe Joanie should go and quieten him.'

'She's not going anywhere until she tells us your plan,' Peter quipped. 'What are you up to?'

Joanie's eyes darted from Peter to Andrew. 'Dad has been asked to do a two-year stint looking after one of the stores of Burns Philp and Co. It would be a managerial position and he would need to relocate. The company has also asked, considering I have experience in bookkeeping and finance, if I could join him.'

Andrew's face lit up. 'I love the way you march to the beat of your own drum, Joanie. Now tell us, where exactly are you going?'

CHAPTER 29

*P*eter's face was expressionless, and Edna found it hard to read what his initial reaction to the proposal was.

'I had a similar opportunity when I was Joanie's age.' Edna smoothed the tablecloth in front of her. 'I travelled from England to India with my father. It was a wonderful experience and one I have always remembered; a special time for a father and daughter.'

Peter's words were terse and he leaned across the table, looking straight at Joanie. 'Where are you going? Surely not India.'

Joanie took a long sip from her glass, before looking up and meeting Peter's eyes. 'Dad and I are booked to leave on the fourth of March, aboard the *MS Malaita*. It's a Burns Philp ship and we sail from Brisbane to Rabaul.'

Peter and Andrew spoke together. 'Where?'

Reg swirled the wine in his glass before downing it in one gulp, his voice steady. 'Rabaul, it's on the Gazelle Peninsula in New Guinea.

'Until a couple of years ago it was the capital of New Guinea,' Joanie said.

Peter did not even try to hide his discontent. 'Why isn't it still the capital?'

Reg gave a little cough, placing his empty glass on the table. 'A volcano erupted. The town is surrounded by a ring of them. Mountains on one side and a magnificent harbour, perfect for the trade ships on the other. It's a major trading town with most of the same facilities we have here. It's not the ideal location for an administrative capital so they're moving some of the government departments to another town.'

Peter blinked rapidly, a look of disbelief on his face.

'My God, I'm jealous.' Andrew stood, pushing his shirt sleeves up higher, his words animated. He lifted his glass high to clink with Joanie's. 'What an adventure and imagine what you'll see in such a remote outpost. Tell us more about this faraway place.'

Joanie's eyes were alight, her cheeks glowing, perhaps from the glasses of champagne she had drunk in her excitement of breaking the news. 'They say the town is starting to look a bit like it used to, that is, before the eruption. There're a few shops, restaurants, a radio station and even a picture theatre.'

'Quite civilised really,' Edna said, 'and plenty of other Australian families for Joanie and Reg to mix with. It will be an experience for them both and one they might not get the chance to have again.'

'You're quiet Peter, what do you think?' Edna had been watching Peter as he listened to Reg.

'I suppose it's a fabulous opportunity to see the New Guinea wilderness. But is it safe? Aren't they all head-hunters and cannibals who don't wear clothes and carry spears and axes? They say there are also some Germans living in New Guinea, leftovers from before the Great War.'

Joanie put her glass down and sat upright, her eyebrows raised. 'There are people from many different parts of the world living in New Guinea: Chinese, Europeans and Melanesians, and the local population. From all accounts it's quite civilised.'

Reg turned towards Andrew. 'The current manager of Burns Philp is an old friend of mine, Bill White. Along with his wife, Leila, and their two daughters, they have lived in Rabaul and run the business for a good number of years. Joanie and I met with him on his last visit to Brisbane. They don't really want to come back to Australia, they love Rabaul but they need to return to the city so one of their daughters can have treatment for an illness.'

Joanie tucked her hair behind the clip she wore. 'Dad and I will run the store and Mother can sail up on one of the ships if she gets lonely or wants to see the place.'

'One hell of an adventure, I'd say.' Andrew filled their glasses. 'I propose another toast. To new sights and exotic places where none of us have been before.'

Peter waited until Andrew stopped talking, his question to Reg coming out loud and abrupt. 'What about the war? Isn't it a strange time to be travelling when there's a war happening?'

Reg sipped his drink, smiling at Edna as she cleared the table. 'The war is a long way from here and Rabaul is no different. We're isolated in Australia, protected by our distance and the might of the mother country.'

Joanie laughed. 'The Germans won't bother with a little town in New Guinea. It won't even be on their maps.'

'The allies will have the war in Europe under control and finished before the end of the year. Mark my words,' Reg said. 'I know you're keen to sign up, but let them fight it out over there.'

'What about Japan?' Peter asked.

'They're only disagreements about iron ore and trade agreements. Australia will avoid confrontation with them at all costs,' Reg said.

'The war in Europe might finish quickly but I want to defend the mother country. It's our duty.' Peter looked back to Joanie. 'I'll be signing up as soon as I can.'

Joanie's voice lost some of its merriment. 'And what about you, Andrew? Are you keen to sign up or is it because Peter is going?'

Edna recognised the anger simmering behind Joanie's question and held her breath, waiting for Andrew to answer.

Andrew shook his head. 'You know me too well, Joanie. Peter knew Mother would take it better if I were there to look after him. You know he was always the golden-haired boy.' The younger brother raised his eyebrows. 'Peter could never do anything wrong.'

'Hmmph,' Peter replied. 'You were always in trouble as a kid. I don't know how you got away with what you did.'

'Nothing wrong with stealing the priest's wine. Give to the needy, isn't that the rule?' Andrew laughed, throwing Joanie a cheeky wink that brought a blush to her cheeks.

Edna passed a bowl of fruit to Andrew, her stomach churning at the thought of the boys being sent into a conflict. 'What does your mother think about you both signing up?'

Peter rolled his eyes. 'She's not opposed to the idea. The priest gave a lengthy sermon last Sunday about the responsibilities of serving God against the heathens and the evil Germans.'

Joanie's reply was sarcastic. 'The church always came first with your mum, didn't it. It must be wonderful to have continual devotion.'

'Bloody hypocrites, the lot of them.' Andrew spat the words out.

'Now, Andrew, I'm sure the others don't want to know about our family or church business. Tell us some more about this new managerial job, Reg. What does a store like Burns Philp sell in a remote place like Rabaul?'

CHAPTER 30

*J*oanie had mixed emotions about the boys joining up. Surely they could wait a bit longer and not rush into entering into a war that could end soon. The move to Rabaul was an important event for her family but Peter and Andrew joining the war effort was an even bigger change. Tonight might be the last time they were all together for some time.

'We thought of going to Melbourne,' Peter said. 'If you join down there you've got a better chance of getting to the Middle East, quicker than if you signed in Brisbane.'

Andrew stood up and stretched, squashing his tie into his pocket, before bending down and planting a kiss on Joanie's cheek. 'It doesn't matter where we go, it'll all be the same. But,' he reached over and ruffled Peter's hair, adding a playful punch, 'wherever he goes, I go.'

Joanie frowned. She'd grown even closer to Andrew since she'd moved to Brisbane and when he'd visited her last time he'd told her she was beautiful and his favourite girl in the entire world. He'd said she was the ultimate woman, independent, free-thinking, and similar to him, not wanting to settle down to the domestic routine of married life.

Now he wrapped his arms around her, squeezing her until she squealed. 'Look after yourself, little Joanie. I'll come and visit before we all go our separate ways.'

Joanie walked out with Andrew, closing the front door behind them. The night air had cooled the heat of the day and cicadas sounded in the bushes next to the house. They stood side by side on the front verandah, the lights of the main street flickering in the distance, the town peaceful, and a long way from any war. She'd hoped Andrew wouldn't enlist, that he'd resist the lure of fighting and find a job that contributed to the war effort, but safely in Australia. She linked her arm through his. 'I'll miss you terribly. I'd much rather you stayed.'

Andrew kissed her cheek softly, his eyes adoring as he looked into hers. Thank goodness, they had spent time together in Brisbane, away from everyone, away from the restraints of the small town and its gossip and innuendo and particularly away from the influence of Peter.

There had been an especially romantic night in Brisbane only last month and Andrew had surprised her with flowers and a small china teapot he had bought in an expensive Sydney store. 'This teapot reminds me of you,' he said, 'Bright and bubbly.'

Vera had been on night shift and Joanie and Andrew had sat together on the lounge, the colourful lights of the city visible through the window.

'And what may I ask, or who were you visiting in Sydney? I'm sure you didn't go all that way just to buy me a teapot.' Joanie was not overcome by Andrew's romantic gestures and knew he had a number of girls, who he declared were all his sweethearts.

He'd wrapped his arms around her, kissing her on the lips. 'You know you're special to me, Joanie.'

'You have a special place in my heart also, Andrew.' She stroked his arms, returning his warm kisses. He hugged her firmly, no doubt feeling secure that there were no gossiping acquaintances around. How they would love it, she thought, a scandal, Joanie Black, kissed by one of the most eligible bachelors in Woombye. She laughed and looked up into his eyes. 'I wasn't born yesterday and I'm well aware your good looks and winning ways, have quite a few women besotted across the length and breadth of the country.'

'That is an exaggeration.' He twirled her hair with his fingers, bringing it up to his lips.

Andrew changed the subject. 'You know Peter will want to see you when you come back home.'

'I know. I'm going to have to be honest with him.' Joanie sighed.

'He's got his heart set on you and heaven forbid if he ever found out I'd visited you here.'

'You and I have always been kindred spirits, Andrew. Peter is the same. Maybe once I was in love with him, but it was a schoolgirl crush and time has marched on. Now I want more. More than what your sisters have, with their huge church weddings and hordes of children.' They both stood up, Joanie straightening her hair and dress.

Andrew stood next to her and took both her arms, wrapping them around his body. They pressed up against each other and he bent down and kissed her.

They stood for a long while looking at each other, Andrew gently stroking her face, his fingers warm on her skin. 'You will reach your dreams Joanie. God knows what they are at this point in time, but one day both of us will get what we want. Now let's drink this wine and get our dancing shoes on. The night is young and so are we.'

Joanie giggled, wiping his lips and laughing as he playfully took one of her fingers gently between his teeth. 'One day someone will catch you,' she said, pulling her finger away.

'The world is our oyster,' Andrew replied, as they made their way out into the city, their arms wrapped around one another, both of them without a care in the world.

* * *

That was three months ago and there had been a few more catch-ups in Brisbane where they could enjoy the freedom of being away from prying eyes. Tonight in Woombye, Joanie wasn't surprised that Andrew was leaving the dinner party before Peter, because there was no way they would be able to talk and hold each other, like they had in Brisbane.

* * *

Reg and Edna had retired to bed not long after Andrew left, leaving Joanie and Peter sitting together on the verandah.

A full moon hung in the western sky, the beam of light filtering down to the empty streets of the small town and beyond that the undulating hills surrounding Woombye. Cows in the paddocks shuffled against each other, a calf calling out, breaking the silence of the humid summer night.

'I wonder what the hills are like in Rabaul?' Peter said. 'It will be very different from here.'

Joanie swivelled on her chair so she faced him. 'You don't think it's a good idea for me to go, do you?'

'I'm surprised your family is encouraging it. I mean, a young single woman in a remote place, surrounded by cannibals and volcanoes!'

'The volcano erupted a couple of years ago. Mr White says the worst is over and there're only minor eruptions every now and then. And as for the natives, I won't be mixing with them socially, they'll be working for us.'

'It'll be hot.'

'Apparently it's stinking hot.'

He shook his head. 'There's a war happening. Right at this moment across the ocean, men are marching across Europe to defend their countries.'

'There are Burns Philp ships sailing between Brisbane and New Guinea every week. If there's any trouble, we'll just catch one back.'

Joanie opened a small silver case, took out a cigarette and placed it between her lips. Peter held her gaze as he took the matches from her to light it. She inhaled and then blew tiny rings of smoke that rose into the night air in perfect formation. They watched as the smoky circles spiralled upwards, melting into the darkness above.

The end of the cigarette burned brightly as she inhaled again. Peter took the cigarette from her, blowing thicker rings that stayed longer in the air. They laughed. When they were younger they had competed to see who could create the best smoke rings. Peter had always won; his smoke rings lingering a long time before disintegrating into the air.

He passed the cigarette back, and Joanie took a few more puffs before stubbing it out on the silver ashtray perched on the windowsill. They sat in silence, Joanie lost in her thoughts, the smell of the cigarette bringing back memories of teenage years and lost moments.

Eventually she broke the silence. 'And where will you be, Peter? Where will the war take you?'

Peter looked down at the ground. 'Who knows, but,' he turned towards her, 'I was hoping when I come back, we might be able to try and work things out. Maybe there's a hope we could be together.'

Joanie said nothing, her eyes cast down as she struggled with a reply.

'I have very strong feelings for you, Joanie. I should have done the right thing years ago.'

Her voice was steady and clear when she replied. 'If we'd

become a couple I would never have left Woombye and worked in Brisbane. I would have stayed here in this little town and we'd probably have six kids by now.'

'And would that have been so bad?' His voice was wistful.

She raised her eyebrows. 'Your family were never going to allow it.'

'I came home to say goodbye and,' he took her hand in his, his eyes looking straight into hers, 'because I knew you were going to be here.'

'We're both going away soon. I'm not sure when we'll meet again.'

Peter's eyes never left hers as he spoke. 'I love you, Joanie. I always have. I should never have let you go.'

She took a deep breath, unsure how to respond. The annoyance at his weakness and how he had sided with his parents still rankled her, even after all these years.

'Thank you, Peter.' She tried to keep her voice calm. 'You've always been someone I've cared for. I'm going away though and I, well… both of us have no idea where, when or for how long we'll be gone.' She avoided declaring her love for him. He was often in her thoughts over the previous years, but so was Andrew.

Peter would not know Andrew had visited her in Brisbane, the two of them dancing until the early hours of the morning. No one except Vera knew that she was as fond of Andrew as she was of Peter, who now sat next to her, for the second time in their lives, declaring his love for her.

They sat in silence looking across the front yard. The stars in the distance were scattered across the sky and the pointers dangling beneath the Southern Cross twinkled brightly, pointing to an invisible destination far on the southern horizon.

Peter was persistent, his voice husky and full of frustration. 'I hate that we have to wait. The war may seem a long way away for you, but it's not just the Germans we need to worry about.' He cleared his throat. 'To the north of here the Japanese army is moving across China, murdering anyone who stands in their path.' He reached across and took her hand. 'We're still young and I don't want to waste any more time apart.'

Peter seemed to be collecting his thoughts and she waited for him to take a breath before speaking again. 'I'm asking you to wait for me. When I return we can be married.'

Joanie cut him off, not wanting to listen to anymore. 'I'm not Catholic.'

'I'm not one myself anymore. I haven't been to church or followed the faith for the last couple of years.' Peter sat up straight, looking across the paddocks, the low calling of the cattle sounding out across the emptiness. He turned and looked directly at her. 'Will you write to me from Rabaul and give my proposal some thought?'

'Peter, I need to be honest with you. Once I did have those feelings for you, but now, I must be honest. I love you like a brother; nothing more. I'm sorry.'

He was quiet for a long while, his hand still holding hers. 'I hope when we both return, your feelings may change.'

'Perhaps,' Joanie replied, weakened by the intimacy of his body next to hers and the way he looked at her. 'Perhaps.'

'Whatever happens I will come back here and ask you again Joanie. I won't give up.'

She kissed his cheek, relieved she had time up her sleeve to work out exactly what she wanted. Simple, she thought, with a sense of relief as she gave Peter one final hug before turning back inside.

CHAPTER 31

Brisbane to Rabaul - March 1940

Joanie and Reg set sail from Brisbane on the *Malaita II*, on the fourth of March 1940. Edna was tearful when saying goodbye but firm in her resolution that it would be an exciting adventure for both of them. Their time away would go fast and ships regularly travelled back and forth, so if Reg and Joanie needed to return, or if she wanted to visit them, there would be plenty of opportunities. She hugged Joanie tight, advising her to look after her father and see as much as she could.

Going to Rabaul was going to be the experience of a lifetime and very few single females ever got to do something so exciting. Joanie had felt the envy of some of her girlfriends when they'd gathered for a going away party the previous week.

* * *

Most of Joanie's friends were married, some with babies and toddlers in tow. When the farewell party ended, she walked arm-in-arm with her best friend, Loreen. They'd gone to school together and Loreen had married the boy next door and settled in Woombye. Although her life had taken a different direction to Joanie's, she'd always understood her friend's decisions to do things differently.

'How did the boys take it?' Loreen asked, as they headed away from the small café where the party had been.

'Oh, you know, typical responses. Andrew, of course seeing it as I do, as a great adventure.

'And what about the handsome Peter?'

'Just as I expected. Worried about the dangers, the war, which is a million miles away, a volcano that has already erupted and the fact the natives might eat me!'

The girls stopped in front of an alleyway. The show was coming to town and some of the vendors had arrived a few days earlier, their tables set up with trinkets and jewellery for sale. Joanie picked up a pink rose brooch, its petals delicate and shiny.

Loreen took it from her hand and turned it around, checking the clasp on the back. She gave it to a man behind the table, who held his hand out as she passed him some coins. 'Let me buy this for you. I want you to wear it and remember me back here in this tiny little town you always wanted to escape from.'

Loreen pinned the brooch to Joanie's shirt, the street lamp above throwing enough light so they could see what they were doing. It had been a fun evening and they giggled and jumped, squealing like children as small beetles attracted by the light, fell on them. Joanie flicked the bugs away and the colourful beetles flew off, back into the glare of the lamp. 'I need to get used to them because there will be bigger ones where I'm going.'

The man who sold them the brooch watched as they spun around, checking each other to ensure there were no large beetles clinging to their backs. He called out, waving them back towards his stall. 'It isn't busy tonight. My wife will read your palms as a gesture of goodwill for your purchase.'

* * *

A small dark-haired woman sat behind a table towards the back of a tent, the lamp on the table sending prisms of colourful light across her face. Loreen and Joanie grinned at each other, both of them ready for some entertainment to finish off the night.

Loreen grabbed Joanie's hand and they made their way to the back of the tent.

The lady's dark eyes glanced from one to the other as she beckoned them to sit on the tin chairs in front of her table. The girls giggled, sceptical about the practices of the gypsy lady. She rolled her eyes as she took Loreen's hand and turned it over. Her lips pursed and the girls stared at her face, her lipstick glossy, an immaculate shading on thick lips. Dark eyelashes, heavy with mascara fluttered, as she peered at Loreen's hand.

'You will have three boys. The first one is within you now.' Both girls stopped laughing and looked at each other. 'They will be fine boys and good men like your husband. Your husband will not go to the war. His eyes will not allow it.' Loreen wore a gold wedding band so it was an easy guess she was married. The part about her husband was a bit eerie though. Loreen's husband had been born with limited vision and although he worked on his father's farm, many things were difficult for him to do due to his poor eyesight.

The lady continued. 'This first boy will like music. It will be him who puts the jigsaw together.'

'What jigsaw?' Loreen rolled her eyes, wondering what was going to come out of the soothsayer's mouth next.

The second boy will go to war, but will return.

'He might be too young. He hasn't even been born yet.'

The women looked up, her voice changing and a look of annoyance on her face causing Loreen to be quiet. 'I did not say which war. You are young now, but one day you will show the wisdom needed to look after such fine sons. The last boy,' She closed her eyes as if in a meditative state. 'His birth will signal a great change for the world,' She closed her eyes tighter as if she was trying to see something. When she opened them her voice was steady and confident, 'It will be the end of the war.'

'What year is that?' Joanie asked. 'It can't be too far off. Maybe this baby is coming next year.' She giggled, doubtful about the information and amused by the dramatic tone of the lady's voice.

'It is not close. The birth is the third boy. That is all I can tell.'

Joanie tried to work out the years. The lady was not producing accurate information. The war would be over by Christmas next year. There was no way Loreen was going to be able to produce three boys in that time.'

'Are there triplets or twins?' Loreen asked.

'No.'

'Can you tell me more about the last son born?'

'No, I cannot. The smoke is great and conceals the rest of his story.' She pushed her fingers along the lines in Loreen's hand. 'It is a good story. It will be a very good story for him and the others.'

She placed Loreen's hand down and smiled. 'They are all good sons. You will be blessed. Remember, the boy with the music will be the one to solve the puzzle.'

Loreen leaned back in her chair. 'Thank you. Who knows what the future will bring, but if you are right and I have three sons, I would be happy indeed.' The girls laughed again and Joanie leaned over the table, the gypsy lady holding out her own hand to take Joanie's.

Outside the street was quiet, apart from the low voices of a few people walking past.

Using her finger the gypsy tracked along the lines in Joanie's hand. She placed it down on the table, her eyes downcast as she spoke. 'You also will have a good life and a husband and two children.'

Joanie sat upright. The tone of the fortune-teller had changed. 'You see something, don't you? You can see something there, but you aren't going to tell me,' Joanie said.

'There are some things better left unsaid.'

'What is that supposed to mean. You can't not tell me what you read in my palm.'

'It is true what I said, you will have a good life but there is a message you must abide by.'

'What is it?'

'When they say to leave, you must go. Apart from that I cannot read anything in your lines. I'm sorry, but that is all. There are many times when I cannot read a palm. Perhaps I am tired after all the questions of your friend. I won't make up information.'

Joanie laughed. 'Oh, is that all. That makes it all clear because I'm about to go somewhere and there are some who say I shouldn't go. You had me worried there for a moment, but now the message is easy for me to understand.'

The lady started packing up. 'You girls should be heading home. It's getting late and I hope you don't have far to walk.'

'We're just down the road. Thank you so much. The readings were fun and if Loreen has three boys, we'll remember you told us so. It's also confirmation I'm doing the right thing going.'

* * *

The gypsy lady stood and watched the girls, their arms linked as they walked down the street. She observed them until they were no longer visible. For a long while she stared into the space where they had walked, her eyes closed, her body swaying. She opened her eyes when her husband touched her on the arm. 'You have finished for the night, let us pack up.' He looked at her, his eyes narrowing at the sorrow in her face.

'Sometimes I wish I never had the gift of foretelling the future,' she said.

CHAPTER 32

On route to Rabaul – March 1940

Joanie shared a cabin with Jean, a high-spirited young nurse who had recently finished her training and was about to start a job at the government hospital in Rabaul. Jean had dark brown hair with brown eyes to match, her tanned skin, a result of many days spent sunbaking on the wide beaches near to where she lived. Her sister, Isabel—who was the image of Jean—was also on board. Isabel and her husband, Bert, lived further up the mountain ranges and were managers at a large plantation that they hoped Joanie and Reg would have time to visit.

The first three days had seen gusty winds and rough seas and Joanie and Jean had spent much of their time on their bunks or walking around the decks, trying hard to ignore their persistent nausea. Their cabin was small yet comfortable; two narrow beds separated by a timber dressing table, thankfully with a sink, mirror and a small amount of space for the girls' collection of creams, hairbrushes and make-up. Neither had been on a ship before and with no port-hole to look out of, it was a relief when the wind died down and the white caps of the ocean dissipated, leaving behind a tranquil, glassy surface.

By the time the *Malaita* sailed past the scattered islands of the North Queensland coast, the two of them had regained their energy and also become best friends, promising to visit each other once they were settled in. They spent their days together, leaning over the polished rails of the ship, watching large pods of dolphins swim alongside, their sleek grey bodies diving in and out of the waves. When no-one else was around they challenged each other on the deck with cartwheels and handstands, dissolving into fits of giggles when one of the other passengers appeared, frowning at their unladylike antics.

Reg had also made some friends and spent his time playing cards with some of the other men or writing letters to Edna. He had been sea-sick too for the first few days and still couldn't get used to walking through the narrow corridors, the floor constantly moving upwards and downwards, the rattling of the walls setting his nerves on edge. His legs were shaky, his feet pressing hard onto the floor as he grasped for the handrails with every lurch. He was relieved when after five days of sailing, the *Malaita* reached Cairns, the north Queensland town offering a break from the confines of the ship with solid ground and an assortment of food outlets and small shops to visit.

* * *

In front of them lay the final part of their journey and within days they would be crossing the strait towards the southern tip of New Guinea, before heading for New Britain and Rabaul, 372 miles, east of the mainland of New Guinea.

* * *

Cairns had been a welcome relief, but the final leg of the journey beckoned. As the coastline of Australia sank into the horizon, the ship pushed through white-capped waters. Sea gusts barrelled across the decks as the bow plunged through the waves of the Coral Sea. Over a thousand miles lay behind them, with Rabaul only a thousand or so more to the north. New Guinea was closer to Australia than Joanie had realised, with Port Moresby only 500 miles north of Cairns, three times closer than Canberra was.

The blustering winds and choppy waters that had plagued them after leaving Cairns, eventually rolled into calm seas, the weather settling and the skies clearing. Joanie settled into the rhythm of life on board, her days spent on the deck with Jean as they took turns spotting the small islands dotting the ocean. The next eight days flew past, the glassy water an easy surface for the ship to glide across. The main island of New Britain was soon visible, its steep coastal mountains rising dramatically from the water, their tops covered in threatening dark clouds. In contrast to the brooding skies, the water was the bluest colour imaginable and seabirds following the ship dove in and out, often with a small fish in their beak as they surfaced.

Reg joined them on deck as the ship steamed through Blanche Bay, a small town called Kokopo appearing on their port side. Wharves and sheds lined the shoreline, the docks they were passing, all important centres for the Burns Philp ships that regularly called in there. The land they sailed next to was part of the Gazelle Peninsula, and not too far to the north, their final destination; Rabaul.

* * *

As the ship rounded the headland of Matupi Point, Joanie stood with her father, their arms resting on the rails of the ship. They leaned out to get their first glimpse of the place they would call home for the next two years, grinning at each other as the steamer sounded its horn. The lingering boom bounced off the ranges, reverberating across the waters around them.

Joanie hung tight to her hat, the tropical heat searing the decks and humidity hanging heavy in the air. Whitewash swept either side of the boat as the ship pushed forward, rounding the peninsula, the port now clearly visible.

'Listen to that.' Joanie squeezed her father's arm, her voice full of excitement.

'That's the sound of the conch shells.' Isabel came up behind them. 'The natives blow into the shells and the noise travels over the countryside. It lets everyone know the ship has arrived.'

'It's haunting,' Joanie said. 'The sound bounces back from the mountains.'

'You're going to come across a million things that are different here. That's why we love it so much.'

As the ship entered the harbour, the colour of the water darkened, the waters so deep even the largest ships were able to pull in right next to the dock.

Isabel pointed across the glistening ocean, a fast approaching convoy of canoes slicing through the calm waters towards them. The women rowing made it look easy, their produce balancing precariously in the narrow hulls. Larger boats followed, a variety of food and goods stacked high in their holds, the excitement contagious, as everyone competed for the first sales. The arrival of a ship was a big day for the locals to trade, to gain a penny or two, or barter for tobacco they could then trade on again when they went inland to their villages.

The welcoming flotilla continued to fill the harbour, the water dotted with convoys of canoes and small boats, those on them waving and calling out to those on the ship. Behind the boats the shoreline bustled as people scurried back and forth, waiting for not just the passengers but also the trading cargo and mail the ship brought with it.

Standing on her tiptoes, Joanie gazed along the shoreline. Women walked back and forth, huge baskets on their heads laden with bananas, pineapples and other fruit. 'It's amazing. So many different people, and ...' she took a deep breath, inhaling the variety of aromas filling the air, 'the colours, the smells. I didn't envisage anything quite like this.'

Jean joined them, squealing with delight as she looked towards the dock. 'How could you explain this to anyone! There are people and colours everywhere.' She gripped Joanie's arm, jumping up and down. 'This is it, Joanie. The start of our adventure.'

'You girls have new places to explore and people to meet,' Isabel said. 'Wait until you go to the markets and taste the exotic fruits. The trade will be busy and the area packed, but then it's all over by noon and everyone will pack up and go home.' She smiled at the two girls. 'Now gather your belongings and get ready for the welcoming party. Rabaul is a beautiful town and the people the friendliest in the world. Apart from the eruptions and the smell from the volcano I'm sure you're going to love it.'

Jean held her hat in the air, waving it high in welcoming sweeps. She linked arms with Joanie. 'I'm ready for those tropical discomforts and I can't wait to start my work at the hospital. We two are the luckiest girls alive!'

'Bill told us about the previous eruptions,' Reg said, shading his eyes as he surveyed the terrain. 'He warned us about the instability and,' he sniffed the air, 'the smell we could expect.'

'That's right,' Isabel said. 'The last big one occurred three years ago. Unfortunately, hundreds of the locals and some Europeans didn't escape.'

'Were they killed?' Jean asked.

'It was a disaster; a tragedy for the entire town. But not to worry,' she reassured, 'the eruptions only occur every forty years or so and you'll get used to the shaking earth and spits of smoke.

It's a good sign when there are a few little eruptions. It means they're letting off steam slowly and it also means there won't be any bigger ones. Rest assured you're safe. The township has been rebuilt and the gardens are back to what they were before.'

It was hard to imagine billowing smoke or fire and lava running down the slopes of the countryside. The idea of eruptions seemed as foreign as the dark thick jungle clinging to their slopes.

The ship changed course a little, pulling into the dock. The harbour was a circle; an ancient caldera. If you looked hard enough you could visualise what it once was; a huge crater, with steep sides, its middle now filled with water. Previously land-locked for hundreds of years the wind and waves had caused the western side to weaken, the continual pounding finally wearing down the crusty wall, sending it crumbling into the ocean.

Reg looked around. 'It's like we're sailing across the mouth of a volcano. My goodness that smell is strong.'

'It's the sulphur,' Isabel said. 'You'll get used to it. It never really goes away.'

'What are the names of the mountains?' Joanie asked.

'That one is called, *Mount Tovanumbatir* or *North Daughter,* and the other, *Mount Kabiu* or *The Mother.*' Isabel pointed to the south, 'You can see the tip of the one known as the *South Daughter,* or *Mount Turagunan.*'

Joanie followed the deep lines in the valleys down to the flat strip of land at their base. In the narrow area between the ranges and the sea, clusters of buildings and rooftops were visible, their colours half hidden beneath the green foliage lining the streets between.

'There's the township,' Isabel said.

'The colours of the land and the ocean are stunning. It takes your breath away.'

'Aye, Joanie, it's something we'll never get to do again.' Reg picked up their luggage. 'Now let's get our bags. By the sound of the people on the wharf, we're about to disembark.'

CHAPTER 33

Rabaul's rows of neat houses perched along tidy streets, their white-painted timber walls and picket fences giving a pristine, suburban look to the town. The backdrop however, left no doubt that this town was not like Brisbane or Woombye; New Britain was an entirely different landscape.

Clouds sagged with the constant threat of rain, their brooding shapes hovering above the lower slopes behind the township. On the sides of the mountains, certain areas were a dark purple, and Isabel told them that below, hidden by the impenetrable foliage, were deep craters gouged out by earlier eruptions. Joanie took a deep breath and tied her hair up, beads of sweat trickling down her back and neck. On the shore, men called out to those on board, heavy ropes and gangplanks, tied and placed in position.

Reg fanned himself with his hat, the humidity overpowering as they followed Isabel and Jean, ready to make their way onto the shore.

* * *

Joanie closed her eyes, standing firm as her feet touched the timbers of the dock. The ground swayed beneath her, the heat stifling as she pushed her hat down on her head, trying to shield her face from the glare. She hesitated, breathing in unfamiliar smells and hoping the spinning in her head would stop.

Isabel took her arm. 'It's a mixture of the senses. There are many different smells and don't worry, you'll get a rocking motion for a while. Take my arm and follow your father. The boys will take your baggage.'

Joanie stared in amazement. She had never seen a New Guinean native before and the sounds of their language were a sing-song chatter, a musical background noise. She smiled back at them, their friendliness making her feel welcome.

A boy picked up her bag, positioning it neatly on top of other baggage on his head. Her father looked back at her, a grin stretching across his face as a line of boys passed them, all with baggage stacked high on their heads. Thank goodness for Isabel's supporting arm as she guided them away from the ship and through the throngs of people who had gathered for the welcoming.

A group of local women walked in front of them, their hips swaying from side to side, their heads covered in dark fuzzy hair. They wore colourful blouses and Isabel said that the wraparound material they wore like a skirt, was called a *laplap*. Woven bags, called *bilums*, hung from their foreheads, the rounded bulk hanging down their shoulders onto their backs. The women transported fruit, vegetables and a variety of other wares in them, supporting the weight of what they carried, from their foreheads and shoulders.

They laughed and jostled through the crowds, their dark skin contrasting sharply against the bright colours of their clothes. Strange markings ran like ink drawings on their faces, arms and legs and a multitude of colourful adornments dangled around their necks.

Isabel guided them through the markets, explaining what the different varieties of food were for sale and how the markets were run. Vegetables and fruit of every shape and colour spilled over on tables lined with banana leaves: mangoes, bananas, limes and pawpaws sat alongside sweet potatoes, taro, melons, sugar cane and coconuts. The markets were known as, *The Bung* and were the central location for vegetables and garden food to be sold or bartered. The government hadn't liked the way the original markets had displayed the foodstuff on the ground, so they built a market hall and put in long bamboo tables, which was also drier in the wet weather.

The earthy hues of hundreds of baskets occupied every available surface while tropical fish and poultry, filled woven containers hanging from the rafters. A mixture of smells wafted across the area; body odour, raw fish, rotting vegetables and tobacco, as well as a sweet coconut aroma coming from a large pot of bubbling liquid. Hundreds of locals who filled the area chatted excitedly in their native languages, using pidgin English when they talked to the Europeans and Chinese traders. Joanie took deep breaths as she gazed at the crowds, the mixture of exotic sounds and smells, tantalising her senses. Excitement rippled through her body. They had arrived in Rabaul.

CHAPTER 34

*J*ean and Isabel bid Joanie and Reg farewell as a store man from Burns Philp arrived to drive them to their new home, situated a short distance from the town. Bill and his family had lived on the property for a number of years and although the building and gardens had been mostly destroyed in the 1937 eruption, the efforts of the working boys who now gathered to meet their new employers, had restored the property to its former grandeur.

The boys stood in silence, nodding their heads politely as Reg shook their hands. These were the workers who would help keep the homestead running.

The head boy, Gadat, stepped forward, establishing his leadership, his well-spoken English allowing them to understand his welcome.

Inside the house they were greeted by three girls; house *meris* who did the chores for the household. Joanie was pleased she wouldn't have to cook or clean, instead these girls were paid to do it for her. The first two girls were shy, their dark eyes not meeting hers, their replies barely audible as she asked their names. The last girl who looked about the same age as Joanie, was more confident and their eyes met as they grinned at each other.

She spoke quietly. '*Nem bilong mi emi, Sissy.*'

Joanie listened intently before replying, 'Hello, my name is Joanie.'

The girls wore the customary colourful blouses with another piece of cloth wrapped around their hips. Joanie eyed them enviously, their clothing practical and cool. Various shell necklaces hung around their necks and they had different coloured flowers tucked behind their ears, the colours a sharp contrast against their hair.

The girls lived in separate rooms attached to the back of the house, returning to their villages on their days off. The boys' quarters were on the other side of the house and a couple of the single men also lived on the grounds.

Beautifully laid out gardens surrounded the house, the bright flowery shrubs and large leafed rainforest plants different to those that grew in the drier climate of Australia. A huge clam shell filled with dirt made a decorative container for a variety of ferns, their delicate fronds dripping over the wavy edges. Orchids grew alongside, the yellow and pink flowers a bright pattern in front of glossy palm trees and trees ferns. Inside a fenced off area, a large garden with neat rows, also grew plenty of fresh vegetables for the household, the vigorous bean climbers and winding passionfruit vines held up by a trellis, barely visible under the thick growth.

* * *

That night Reg and Joanie sat outside, relaxing after the long trip and busy day. Fragrances from frangipani trees drifted across the verandah and Joanie inhaled the mysterious concoctions of scents in the night air. The sky sparkled with thousands of stars and night parrots and owls called out across the darkness surrounding them.

'I can't wait to explore. We've only travelled from the town to here and already there's so much to take in,' Joanie said.

Reg wiped his brow, the humidity and stillness of the night air, thick and heavy, his shirt once again dripping with sweat. 'I'm interested to meet the different nationalities. Such a mixture of people, both in the town and then when we came through the markets.'

'I didn't realise there would be so many Asian people,' Joanie said. 'Isabel told me that Chinatown is the most exciting place to visit and the shops there sell everything you could ever want.'

'I've heard the Chinese people are well-regarded and run very profitable businesses.' Reg stretched his legs out, leaning back in the wicker chair. 'Isabel wasn't sure of the exact numbers living here, but she said there must be close to, if not more than a thousand Chinese adults in Rabaul. They do a good trade with the native people. Apparently the Chinese give them free cups of tea or cigarettes as well as rides in their cars. That's a good strategy, keeping on the right side of the local people who live here.'

'What's strange about picking them up?'

'Bill said we aren't to give the natives a lift or become too friendly with them. There are rules about how we interact with them and the Chinese.'

'Isabel said the Chinese are the backbone of the town. They send their children abroad to be educated so they can come back and work as professional people here in Rabaul. They set up commercial enterprises. It sounds to me like they're clever and good business owners.'

'I guess we'll soon work out who is who. Bill also spoke about the Chinese and how they own most of the building companies in Rabaul as well as providing the plantations with workers and trade. Their companies are also responsible for most of the government buildings being erected.'

* * *

It took Joanie a while to distinguish the different people, the town of Rabaul a melting pot of different backgrounds and nationalities. The local people were the most fascinating. They were the Tolai and Joanie was intrigued by their traditions and families. When she walked into town she encouraged the yard boys to talk, to let her carry her own bags and walk beside her. But their customs could not be swayed and they would stop and wait until she moved on, always making sure they were behind her.

There were fewer women than men in Rabaul, the men travelling into town for work while the women stayed in the villages. Joanie found much of her information out from Sissy who she spent many hours with, teaching each other their own language.

The house that would be their home for the next two years was as Bill and Leila had described. The building was elevated with several stairs at the front and a climbing mandevilla with bright pink flowers covered much of the stair rails and other parts of the house. Jasmine and flaming red bougainvillea grew along the front and Joanie soon learnt to keep an eye out for the snakes winding themselves around the vines, looking as if they were part of the growth.

The yard boys ensured that the lawns were manicured, the garden beds overflowing with vibrantly coloured impatiens and succulents that spilled onto the lush grass. It was a magical place to walk around, and was, Joanie thought, paradise. The entire area of Rabaul was like a Garden of Eden, a tropical utopia, and she had already decided she may never want to leave.

CHAPTER 35

Settling in – 1940

As the first few weeks flew past, Reg and Joanie were kept busy meeting other families and workers who called Rabaul home. There were dinners and long lunches with other Australian families who were all keen to meet the relieving manager of Burns Philp and his daughter. The town was small and isolated, but there were plenty of groups and activities to entertain them during their stay. Reg became a member of the Rabaul Club while each week Joanie joined with other women for a social, but competitive, game of tennis.

She also regularly met up with Jean, who was also getting used to the unusual ways of the local people, as well as trying to cope with the humidity and rain that bucketed out of the sky at any time of the day. The two had plenty to talk about and according to Reg, there was plenty of talk about them. Most of the European women in Rabaul were married and had come to the town due to the nature of their husband's jobs. The fact that two, attractive single women had arrived on the last ship from Brisbane, was noted by many of the younger men in the town.

The girls' jobs kept them busy though and although there were plenty of invitations, they tended to stick together, politely declining the single dates and instead enjoying the groups that joined together for social events.

Joanie took to her new role at the store with enthusiasm, although there had been a few arguments with a couple of the other workers. She made sure, right from the start, that she wasn't to be treated any differently, just because she was a young single woman or because her father was the acting manager. Sometimes the pace at work was too slow for her liking and she had ruffled feathers with her bossy nature. There were also some rules she didn't agree with and she had not hesitated in letting the other workers know.

She also surprised herself at her growing affinity towards the local people and the Chinese. Before she had come to Rabaul, she had held a superior notion, believing white Australians were smarter than those with different coloured skins or ethnicity. Now she was working and living amongst people from a variety of cultures, she began to realise her previous beliefs were not accurate.

The Chinese women who came to buy from the store appreciated that Joanie's attitude towards them was friendly and respectful. One of the regulars was Mi-Lee, who along with her husband owned one of the best eateries and trading stores in Chinatown. Joanie knew that as a fact, because Mi-Lee in her best English always made a point of telling her. The tiny woman was the same age as Joanie and had three children, who were always in tow.

'I am Mi-Lee and my eatery and trading store is best in all of New Guinea. Now what I need is pot that is very, very big.' Her hands demonstrated the size. 'The workers here tell me it is not available and I will have to wait until the next shipment comes in.'

'I'm sure I saw one of those cooking pots buried below these boxes.' Joanie moved numerous crates, stacking other items out of the way as she looked.

Mi-Lee stood close behind her, peering into the shelves, her hands grabbing the boxes that were passed back to her. Her newest baby slept in a sling strapped across her chest, and not even the excited yells as the two women located the item were enough to wake her. Joanie held the pot up high, checking for any scratches or faults. 'Here it is, Mi-Lee. It's the size you want, perfect condition and the only one left.'

'You tell your big boss father, the two men on the counter do not bother to look. Unless the item is in front of their noses, they say, no Mi-Lee, that will be on next shipment. You wait. You are best worker in shop, Miss Joanie, and you will have very good fortune in your life and very, very prosperous work.' Mi-Lee spoke in a loud voice, the two older men behind the counter rolling their eyes at her comments.

When Joanie repeated the story to her father, he smiled. 'It's an inbuilt mistrust of anyone who's a bit different. Our workers are friendly to the Chinese, but they still don't treat them the same as other Europeans or Australians. It's the same in other places.'

Another annoyance for Joanie, was the window down the side of the building where the local people waited when they wanted to buy from the store. Joanie had watched in confusion as a worker walked over to the window to ask what the person waiting outside, required.

She moved closer to see what was going on. A short line had formed outside the building, the customers waiting patiently. They were not allowed to walk in because the rules were that no one was allowed in the store without shoes or a shirt. That ruled out the local people, as the women did not wear shoes and the men did not wear shirts.

She had not been popular with the other workers when she had marched outside and brought three of the customers into the store, helping them locate what they wanted and then serving them up at the front counter.

'I don't get it.' Joanie was frustrated when relating the incident to her father that night, the two of them eating dinner together at the long dining table. Joanie fanned herself with a decorated Chinese fan, the windows closed to keep out the mosquitos and sandflies. 'The only difference is the colour of their skin or where they were born. They're the same as us. They like to run a business, they're always looking for new ventures and most of all they love their families. That's what their lives revolve around.'

'I know. I may be upstairs in the office, but I do know exactly what is going on down on the bottom floor. I've questioned the rule also, but I'm told it's always been in place. You can only enter the store if you're clothed in the appropriate attire and have shoes on.'

'They've only made that rule so it doesn't sound like, *no natives allowed*. But that's what they really want to say. The natives don't discriminate who they trade with at the markets. The white people are down there buying everything they want. Why is there one rule for how we trade with them, yet they don't have rules for how they trade with us?'

'Calm down, Joanie! You can't change practices that have been in place for years.'

'The local people have lived the way they do for thousands of years. Anyway, I'm ignoring the rule that they're not allowed in!'

Reg sighed. 'I know, I've heard. The men have already complained to me.'

'Let them complain. There's no way I'm going to treat anyone differently.'

Reg chuckled. 'I agree with you but it's the same throughout Rabaul and people are segregated, divided according to their culture. I'm not sure you'll be able to change the way people think.'

* * *

It hadn't taken Joanie long to step away from the usual treatment of other races. She often spent her time off work, with Sissy, who wanted to become a teacher in her village and was quick to pick up whatever Joanie taught her. One day Joanie gave her a thin silver chain with a small pendant of a kangaroo hanging on the end.

'This is for you, Sissy. Now we are sisters.'

The young Papuan girl grinned and nodded with excitement, returning the next day with a necklace made from a string of white shells. She placed it around Joanie's neck, her grin stretching across her face. 'You are sister also,' she said.

* * *

Reg watched the girls as they wandered around the garden practising English, Joanie often doubling over in laughter at something Sissy said.

In his letter home to Edna he wrote, '*The two girls have developed a firm friendship and have a great regard for one another. Even with their different skin and hair colours, they could be sisters and it is a wondrous sight to see them talk and laugh together. I feel perhaps when we come home there may be another daughter for you to take under your wing.*'

Edna wrote back. She was missing Reg and Joanie terribly, but knew the time would fly. '*It would be a great pleasure to welcome Sissy into our home. Perhaps she could be educated at the college and become a teacher. From what you both say, she would make a hardworking student. It will be something for us to think of once the year draws to a close. Life here is the same and the store continues to run well so do not worry, but rather enjoy the tropical life. I look forward to your return and the many stories you will have. I miss your tender touch and long for the nights when we can once again be together. I will let another two months pass and then I will plan a visit.*'

Reg was also missing being together and once the two years

were up, he would be ready to return home. As each day passed he missed Edna more. The heat was also playing havoc with his health. It left him weak and lethargic, his handkerchiefs always on hand to wipe the sweat continually cloaking his brow and neck.

The shaking that often woke him in the middle of the night was also a strain on his well-being and played on his nerves. He tried to stop looking up at the mountains, waiting for something to happen.

Reg found relief from his frayed nerves and separation from Edna, at the Rabaul Club; a friendly place in town where many of the men met to enjoy a quiet drink. The other men had laughed at his concerns. 'The big eruption has already happened,' one of the men, Stanley, told him. 'We aren't due for another one for forty years or more.'

Another added, 'You've got as much chance as that mountain erupting as you have of the German army marching here from across the sea.'

The talk at the club turned to the war, as it often did, averting his worries. At least Joanie was not perturbed by the instability of the volcano. The large tremors that sent the neighbours screaming and the dogs howling, often didn't even wake her up. The last one, however, had seemed to go on for eternity. The twittering of the birds for a long time after the rumbling stopped, were a background noise to Reg's thoughts and he lay on top of his bed, wondering if he'd made the right decision, bringing his daughter to such an isolated and sometimes dangerous place.

Pungent whiffs of sulphur drifted across the night air; a constant reminder they were living under the shadow of a circle of volcanoes. He closed his eyes, the scent from a magnolia tree, laden with flowers, wafting in through the open window, the smell and noises of the night sending him into a fitful sleep.

CHAPTER 36

Rabaul 1940 - 41

eeks turned into months, and soon a year had passed by. Customs that had seemed strange when Joanie first arrived were now commonplace and with each new experience, Rabaul became more and more like home. The native boys, bare-chested, their skin glistening with sweat as they worked in the garden with only a small lap lap on the lower half of their body, no longer caused her to blush and look away. Instead, she marvelled at their strength and ability to scale a coconut tree or carry a heavy load, with little effort.

One day Sissy sat with Joanie on the steps of the house watching the yard boys, including Gadat, at work.

'He is from my village and I have known him since I was a child.' Sissy giggled, her shoulders drawn back as she sat tall. Gadat continued to glance her way, his muscles bulging, the sweat on his body like shimmering oil as he moved rocks to create a pond and garden. Joanie picked up a tray holding a jug of cold water and glasses, motioning for Sissy to take it over to him.

The young girl hesitated, giggling again, before adjusting the bright hibiscus tucked behind her ear. The red petals were vivid against her skin and hair, the beauty in her face matching the elegant movement of her body. She picked up the tray and moved towards Gadat. Her curvaceous hips swayed a little more than usual and her smile was wide as she poured him a cold drink. Their voices lowered and Joanie was unable to hear what they were saying. She averted her eyes, instead watching a red and yellow lizard resting on the bottom step, its pink tongue flicking in and out as it sought out smaller insects. Eventually Sissy returned. The initial meeting with Gadat had been established and the two young people had become a couple.

* * *

The other woman with whom Joanie had become good friends, was Mi-Lee. It had become customary for Mi-Lee to bring the children to visit on a Saturday morning and a pot of tea and a tray of sweet biscuits, as well as a cool drink for the children was waiting for them when they arrived. The baby, Ah Lam, whose name meant, 'peace', was usually wrapped in a sling, asleep across her mother's chest. When she was awake she sat on Mi-Lee's lap and stared at Joanie through long eyelashes, her dark brown eyes set deep into her chubby round face.

After a while, Ah Lam, became used to Joanie and would hold out her arms, wanting to sit on her lap. Joanie had no experience with babies and at first it had been awkward to hold her. Ah Lam would try to grab her necklace or pull her hair, which was tied in plaits, hanging down like tempting pieces of braided rope.

Ah Lam's two older siblings looked like twins, both close in age but different genders. Mi-Lee took a deep breath, her voice tinged with sadness as she spoke about the children she had brought into the world. 'There is a year between them, Li is four and Chun is three. There was another baby born that should now be two, but he is buried on the hill in the Chinese cemetery. The doctor came too late and it is a miracle I survived. Next time my husband sent me to Brisbane one month before baby Ah Lam comes.'

Mi-Lee's words were fast and clipped and Joanie listened carefully for the different pronunciation of words, her friend delighting in telling how she came to be running a trading house and living in Rabaul.

'My family in China is very wealthy, and my father made sure all his children, that is me included, were educated and taught four different languages. That includes English, which you can hear I speak very well.' Joanie loved Mi-Lee's confidence and assured her that, yes, she did speak very good English.

Mi-Lee, and her husband Huan, owned one of the major hotels on Casuarina Avenue as well as a large trading store. Their comfortable house in Chinatown, with spacious rooms and wide verandahs, was always brimming with visiting relatives and friends, who considered Rabaul their home away from home.

Chinatown was one of the most exotic and exciting areas of Rabaul. The narrow streets with buildings crammed together, offered every type of goods Joanie could dream of. The bulging shelves overflowed with exquisite wares, ornamental brassware and lacquered teak oddments of every shape and size. Other shelves were crammed full of fabrics, silk scarves and garments, their vibrant colours cascading over the timber ledges.

The Chinese trading stores were often crowded with the local people and the constant bargaining chatter, along with the blend of different languages was a melodic background, muffling the noises of the families who often lived in cramped conditions above. The smells of vegetable and spices cooking in the kitchens wafted through the open windows, making Joanie think she was not in the remote town of Rabaul, but instead in one of the cities in China that Mi-Lee had described.

Rabaul had its own Chinese school, so many of the young people could speak fluent English as well a variety of other languages. This allowed them to work for the European trading companies in town. However, not everyone respected the Chinese and Joanie was horrified when Mi-Lee told her how some of her family had been treated.

'I can't believe it,' Joanie repeated the stories to her father. 'The Australian companies use the Chinese as workers for building, or in their stores, but they have this dreadful stand-off attitude to them and don't mix with them socially. They try to pay them less and often talk down to them. I feel ashamed to be an Australian when I see the way they treat the Asian people.'

Reg tried to explain the situation. 'Not everyone treats people the same way you do and it would do you good to remember the attitude you had before you came to live here. It's a shame, because they're wonderful people and on the same side as us. The Japanese are slaughtering them in their own country, taking over their towns and destroying their way of life. To add to it all, the Japs are on the same side as the Germans, but it seems like no-one cares what's happening.'

Joanie had also caused a few eyebrows to raise at the tennis club when one of the British ladies, Rose, mentioned it wasn't the done thing to socialise with the Chinese.

It was morning tea break in between games and Rose sipped her tea, holding the cup with her little finger pointed outwards, her nose pointed upwards. She wore a neatly pressed white dress, her matching white hat placed next to her as she sat up straight, her prim voice commanding everyone else to listen. Most of the tennis ladies were Australian, however there were some British ladies whose comments were often irritating.

Rose spoke in a haughty voice, a pious look on her face. 'You know they aren't clean and they are unkind people. Why sometimes they even sell their children. We should all stay well clear of them. Let them go about their business, but it's best to avoid talking or heaven forbid, having any of them as friends or members of our tennis club.' She looked down her nose straight at Joanie.

Joanie's reply was abrupt. 'The Chinese get along with everyone and they're part of the community. They build your houses and shops, and as for their children, you're absolutely wrong. They love their children. Your ideas are completely false, and I won't hear you speak badly of the Chinese people. There's no difference between them and us. Mi-Lee and her family happen to be our best friends and I won't listen to your nonsense.'

Rose tutted, a patronising smile on her face. 'We're lucky, my dear, none have actually asked to play tennis anyway. I doubt they'd know how to, due to being, you know, uncivilised.'

The conversation had become tiring and Joanie stood up. 'They don't play tennis because most of them work or are looking after their children. Tennis isn't a popular sport in their own country' The group had gone silent, only one of the other ladies following her onto the court.

Reg shook his head when Joanie recounted the conversation. 'I admire your fortitude, my dear, but I can't imagine you changed anyone's mind.'

'Of course not! They just all gave me that look, as if to say, you'll learn, you're new here. I don't care what the others think. Mi-Lee is my friend.'

Nothing was going to stop Joanie remaining friends with the young Chinese woman and the two became a common sight as they strolled along the main street of Rabaul. The wide awning of the pubs and stores offered shade and Joanie stopped to look in a window of a haberdashery store, taking off her hat, using it to fan herself. She pushed her hair back from her face, Mi-Lee passing her a handkerchief to wipe the sweat from her face. The humidity was stifling and Joanie was grateful for the light fabric of her clothes; a knee-length fitted dress with a curved neckline and short sleeves, light to wear and revealing her tanned skin.

Mi-Lee was barely visible under a wide Chinese hat, a high necked, long sleeved shirt and long straight skirt. As they moved away from the shade and walked towards Chinatown, the streets widened, with low houses to either side, their front verandahs shading children who sat on the rails, calling out and waving back to them.

Their conversation often turned to the fact Joanie was nearly twenty-three and was still single with no children of her own.

'Who will you marry?' Mi-Lee loved to ask.

'I have been close to Peter and Andrew for many years. They are brothers. Andrew is fun to be with and I love him dearly, but it is Peter who says he wants to marry me once the war is over and we're back home.'

'It is good you have a choice.' Mi-Lee's face was serious. 'Which one will you marry? Maybe you should go back home soon and choose one, because they may find another wife while you are here?'

Joanie linked her arm through Mi-Lee's. 'They're like family to me. I love them both, but not as husbands, just as friends.'

'How can you love two boys but only as friends? If you marry one of them the love will change. Then you will love one as a husband and have many children.'

Joanie laughed. 'No, Mi-Lee, I'm sorry, but at this stage there isn't anyone who I have fallen in love with.'

'But that is how it is done in China. The love will grow as you become husband and wife.'

'That's not how it works in Australia.'

* * *

There were quite a few single young men working in Rabaul and some had asked Joanie on a date or on a picnic. A couple of times she relented and went to the picture theatre, or walked with a young man to the area where couples threw a blanket down, sharing food and drink. The dates were pleasant, the backdrop of the bay with towering palms a relaxed shaded area and a perfect setting for a young couple to find romance and perhaps fall in love. But no one had aroused Joanie's interest and she was more than happy with single life.

CHAPTER 37

To celebrate Joanie's birthday, Reg invited Mi-Lee and her family to a picnic at Karavia Bay. Laughter filled the inside of the car as the two young women squeezed into the back, the children perched on their laps. Huan sat in the front as Reg drove, the car bumping along the dirt road until they arrived at a grassy area on the foreshore. Swaying palm trees and tall tree ferns provided a shaded area for their picnic lunch; a perfect setting for Joanie's twenty-third birthday.

Mi-Lee prompted her eldest child, Li, to present Joanie with a gift wrapped in red glossy paper. The paper was decorated with gold Chinese characters and Joanie laughed with excitement as she accepted it and shook Li's hand.

As she unwrapped the present, the children leaned forward to see what lay under the paper. A silk shawl fell into her hands, the glossy fabric catching the sunlight as she pressed the fine fabric to her face, the cloth smooth and cool against her skin. Holding the shawl at arm's length she revealed the hand-painted picture on its surface. Exquisite green and blue splashes of paint, formed brooding mountains and tranquil seas, the dense jungle and buildings of Rabaul positioned accurately beneath them.'

'It's beautiful.' Joanie's voice trembled and she spread the shawl out so they could all see. Thank you, Mi-Lee, I will keep this forever and think of you, Huan and the children when I look at it.'

* * *

Joanie lay back on the picnic rug, relaxing with Mi-lee as they watched the children rolling down the gentle grassy slope in front of them. The men's talk had of course turned to the war and the ongoing situation in China.

'So many of our young Australian men have already joined and gone to fight the Germans,' Reg said. 'This blasted war isn't finishing as quick as we thought it would.'

Huan listened carefully, his English, learnt at a foreign university, clipped and well-pronounced. 'Should your government be sending the Australian men so far, when Japan is more threatening and closer to your country?'

Reg explained that the Australian government wasn't that concerned about the Japanese but Mi-Lee who was also knowledgeable on the subject of war, disagreed. Her opinion was that the government should not be so worried about the Germans who were far away, but instead the actions and threats of the Japanese in their country, and in the future, the danger to Australia.

'That's crazy, Mi-Lee.' Joanie frowned as she folded the silk scarf, placing it carefully into her bag. 'Why would the Japanese ever want to invade Australia?'

Mi-Lee had numerous alarming stories from family in China. The Japanese armies were massacring her people and more and more Chinese people were leaving their homes and coming to Rabaul, where they felt they would be safer.

Joanie shook her head. 'The talk back home in Australia is about the Germans. Our government doesn't really consider Japan a major threat. Otherwise, why would they be sending all those young men over to Europe to fight?'

'I'm not sure,' Huan added. 'But like Mi-Lee said, the Australian government needs to be more careful and not so carefree just because they are far away from Japan. Their aggression is the same as the Germans and their tentacles are long and dangerous. They will let nothing stand in their way.' Huan raised his eyebrows as he spoke and then nodded his head, indicating for the others to look towards the thick jungle at the back of the clearing where they sat.

A large woman emerged from a path between the thick undergrowth. She bent down low, using a stick to support herself, walking slowly onto another well-worn path that followed the edge of the cleared area. She did not glance towards the group – which she would have heard long before she reached the area – but rather kept her head down and continued walking, veering away from the clearing when she got to another path, its direction back into the scrub and towards a nearby cluster of houses.

Mi-Lee called the children to come back from where they were playing.

Both children sat on Mi-Lee's lap, while Joanie held the baby who was fast asleep in her arms.

'What's wrong Mi-Lee? Why are you so worried?' Joanie asked.

'That is Mrs Schmidt. She lives further up the hill. It is said by others who observe her, that she walks through the jungle and climbs the hill at the top of the point.'

'I'm sure other people walk up there also. There is an excellent view over the entire bay of Rabaul.' Reg said.

'It is the best viewpoint in the area,' Huan added.

Mi-Lee had started to pack up, her face unhappy.

'It is time for us to go,' she said. 'The children are tired and we should return. I do not wish so see that lady again.'

Huan looked across the bay, his dark eyes serious as he used his hand to shield his face from the afternoon sun. His voice was stern. 'She is half-German, half-Samoan and has lived here for many years. It is spoken amongst our people that she walks up the hill to send information to the Germans and Japanese.'

Joanie laughed. 'Goodness me, what information would she send from here to the Japanese?'

'They believe she sends local information to the Japanese. She walks up that hill often and carries a large pair of field glasses.'

'You're all worried about nothing.' Joanie kept her tone flippant. 'It was only last week a small group of Japanese men came into the harbour. They walked around town, smiling at everyone. I served them when they came into the store. So polite and respectful.'

* * *

Joanie had been re-stocking the shelves when the Japanese men had entered the store. They had propped their pushbikes against the side of the shop, bowing deeply as they came in through the front door. One of them, who spoke English, asked Joanie if the store sold visitor maps; one they could follow as they walked around on an excursion, looking at the different trees and plants growing in the area. The men had bowed again and exited the store once she had been unable to provide them with what they wanted.

Huan had also observed the Japanese. He had been at the wharf when they disembarked from the *Takaichiko Maru*, a large passenger and freight ship, anchored in the harbour. So few men on such a large ship. He followed them at a distance, running to keep up with them, as they pedalled along the main road on the bikes they had brought with them. Field glasses and cameras hung from their necks and not long after they left the Burns Philp store, they were met by another Japanese man who worked at one of the shipping companies in town. The man had led them further up the road before they rested their bikes up against the trees, making their way by foot onto a narrow track. Huan had walked the track later when the men had left, their boot marks still discernible in the mud. The trail of prints led right up to the airport and then further onto the airstrip and other buildings.

Reg was puzzled. He didn't believe the Japanese would be so open if they were up to no good. There were a number of Japanese who traded in the town, so perhaps the visitors were looking at expanding business in the area.

Joanie looked across the bay as they packed up the picnic blanket and gathered the children ready to leave. The bay was sparkling, the small waves dancing over the surface, catching the glint of the sun. Foreboding clouds gathered on the horizon, readying themselves for the usual afternoon downpour. A shiver ran through her body as the breeze picked up, scuttling the clouds across the sky.

Australia and Japan traded with each other and Joanie had never given serious thought about the danger of their forces. Only last week one of the men at work had been reading a newspaper detailing the Australian government's hope to revive: *'The spirit of goodwill between Japan and Australia'*. She had read with interest, the declaration. *'We desire to live in peace with our neighbours in the Pacific, who are north of the equator. Insofar as the problems of the Pacific are concerned, we have no quarrel with the people of Japan ... We lay it down that what they do is their business and we feel that Japan will fully reciprocate in this connection.'*

There had been quarrels between the two countries in the past, but they were just that. Arguments about trade agreements.

Andrew had once said. 'Menzies took legal action against the Australian waterside workers because they've refused to load pig-iron bound for Japan.'

'Why didn't they want to load it?' Joanie had asked.

'I think the same as the workers and so do many others. We're handing over our precious resources to Japan. They'll bloody well use it to make their weapons. One day it might not just be the Chinese who feel their brunt. It could also be us.'

Joanie remembered Andrew's words now as she watched Huan and Mi-Lee pack the picnic items back into the car. She put her arm around Mi-Lee's shoulder. 'Don't worry, Mi-Lee. You're living in safety here and our government is not far away if anything were to happen. Hopefully the war will be over before long.'

Mi-Lee looked at Joanie. 'Let's hope so, for all of us and for our children.'

* * *

Reg followed up Joanie's story about the visitors. Up until recently the Japanese had been a threat in Asia, but his concerns had been more with the situation in Europe and Great Britain.

Now, Huan's and Mi-Lee's words niggled, and his uneasiness grew.

Next time he was at the Rabaul Club he made a point of talking to one of the government workers called Stanley, questioning him over the presence of the Japanese in town. Stanley clarified the officials were aware of the visit. 'Yes, old boy, we're aware some of them even came to your store. You're not the only one to let us know. They had a good look around and spoke to a few of the Australian traders. They're probably just looking at expanding their business ventures here, however we've let the appropriate people know back home in Australia.'

Reg also filled Stanley in on the suspicious nature of the lady they had witnessed on Joanie's birthday.

Stanley nodded. 'Yes, we're aware of the old German lady also. She's half-Samoan and not important enough to be relaying information back to anyone. We'll pass your information on though and send it all through to higher up authorities.'

'Thanks, Stanley,' Reg said. 'There are a few strange things going on. We're so far from the action, but it would be terrible if there was anything untoward going on right under our noses.'

'Never can be too careful,' Stanley said. 'Our government is making decisions about the outposts in New Guinea. The talk is they are going to fortify the communications up here. Send men up to build some new buildings and put extra communication stations in place. Not that they think the Japanese are a direct threat to us.' He chuckled, taking a large swig from his whiskey glass. 'And definitely not to Australia. They just think it would be worth their while to have some stations up here, in case there is a threat to our borders.'

* * *

Reg repeated the details of his conversations to Joanie. There was nothing to worry about and the Australian government and the authorities in Rabaul had been informed. Joanie felt at ease. 'Thank goodness our government looks after us and we'll never need to worry about a war in Australia. Let's hope for Huan and Mi-Lee's sake their government is as strong and trustworthy.'

CHAPTER 38

Arrival of Lark Force in Rabaul – March 1941

$\mathcal{S}$tanley's information had been correct and in early March 1941, a force of Australian soldiers arrived in Rabaul. They had been sent to fortify communications and erect essential buildings for the Australian government. The first of the men were part of a battalion known as Lark Force and they sailed into Rabaul on board the *SS Zealandia*.

The ship sounded its horn as it arrived in Simpson Harbour, the usual fanfare and friendly crowd, welcoming the vessel into the bay. Joanie and Reg stood together as the ship sailed slowly through the mouth of the cauldron, the dark waters parting in front of its pointed stern. The decks were lined with men, who gazed in awe at the scene, much the same as Joanie and her father had when they arrived just over a year ago.

Joanie was perplexed. 'Why are Australian troops being sent to such a peaceful place, especially when there're so many of them needed in Europe?'

'I'm not sure what's in the wind,' Reg said. 'Stanley says they're only sending troops here for a short while, to erect buildings and complete maintenance work. Your mother is still deciding about her visit. I know our last twelve months will go quickly but there's always the option of leaving early if there looks like any trouble brewing.'

'There's no way I'm leaving early. Rabaul is like home to me and I wouldn't mind staying longer after you go. That's if Burns Philp will keep me on.'

Reg's face was strained, his forehead furrowed with wrinkles. 'I'm watching it carefully. The Nazis are gaining strength in Europe and the Japs are becoming restless, plus they're tied in even more now with Germany and Italy. The more I talk to Huan, the more I see how they're not to be trusted and how aggressive they've become. I'm starting to have an uneasy feeling, what with troops coming and now there's even talk of creating a rifle brigade here in Rabaul.'

'What's that and who would be in it?' Joanie asked.

'They're going to train some of the natives and then civilians like myself. At least they'd have a brigade ready in case there was a breakout of violence.'

'I think it's all talk. The war in Europe is so distant. The Australian boys who have joined to fight over there will fix them. I wonder how Peter and Andrew are going?'

Joanie turned to her father, his usually cheery face, lined with worry. She usually liked to steer the conversation away from the war to lessen her father's anxiety about being separated from Edna. If Mother decided to take the trip and spend a few months with them, Father would be the happiest man in the world.

* * *

Reg gazed at his daughter. She had settled into life in Rabaul, however she had no idea about the repercussions of war. She hadn't experienced the horrors and aftermath of World War I. So many young men had joined up to see the world, to have a bit of fun and adventure. It had not been an adventure though, and had resulted in broken men, broken spirits and thousands who never returned to their families in Australia. Surely, the world had learned its lesson.

He had another year to go. The store in Rabaul was running as usual, the profits even up a little since they'd arrived. He'd love for Edna to visit, although the heat and distance were putting her off. Her last letter had said that the next year would fly past and then they would have the rest of their lives together. She would however, give it some more thought.

He stood next to Joanie. The pristine bay with its sparkling waters did not bring a smile to his face as it normally did. The Australian government had seemed confident with the movements of troops. They'd sent forces to support and fight alongside Britain in the Middle East and others had been sent elsewhere, to fight against the Germans and Italians. If they were worried about the Japanese, surely they wouldn't still be trading and sending valuable iron ore to them? And then, there was Singapore. The Australian and British governments touted the naval base at Singapore as, 'an impregnable bastion'. His thoughts flew back and forth in his head. Correspondence he'd received only last week, showed that the Australians thought of the Japanese as intimidating, but really there wasn't anything to worry about.

The paper clipping had been included in a letter from a friend in Queensland and showed the Prime Minister as declaring that all the difficulties between nations could be resolved by the, 'utmost frankness'. Surely if Menzies was not worried there was no reason for them to be.

He glanced at Joanie, pushing the worrying thoughts to the back of his mind. Her skin glowed with a healthy tan and her green eyes sparkled as she looked across the water. Her blonde hair was short and curly, and she looked very much like Edna. Now she stood on tiptoes, straining to get a view of the ship, above the heads of the locals who had gathered for the occasion. She wore a spotted cream dress, the dots brown, the same colour as her arms and legs.

He was a blessed man to have such a beautiful daughter, and such a close relationship. This trip had strengthened that even more. Thank goodness for her youthfulness, the way she viewed everything through an inquisitive mind. Her cheeks were flushed with excitement, and she laughed at the colourful and noisy scene of the ship arriving. Her arm linked through his and the moment was completed when she planted a firm kiss on his cheek.

'I love you, Father. This is the best thing we could have ever done together. I will always remember our time here in Rabaul.'

'It's exciting, isn't it.' He pulled himself out of his reverie as the men lining the decks, waved to the crowds. Joanie waved back, watching the ship as it came up next to the dock.

The ship's motors stopped and huge ropes were thrown down, their braided lengths tied to large wooden posts. A group of men started singing and clapping sticks, the women joining in, swaying and stomping their feet in unison.

Joanie had closed her eyes and he looked at her fondly. 'I want to remember this day forever.' Her words were muffled by the ship's horn, one last blast before the side opened up, allowing the men to put the gangplank in place. A band started up and a loud voice announced the arrival of the Australian troops to New Guinea. The 2/22nd Battalion, otherwise known as Lark Force, had arrived in Rabaul.

CHAPTER 39

Melbourne - March 1941

Gracie had stuck so many pins into the photo of her mother, Layla, that the picture was no longer recognisable. She liked it like that; crinkled and riddled with holes, spots of dust clinging to its dirty surface from where it had laid hidden under the lounge chair. She had pulled it out from the same spot where she had pushed it months earlier after ripping it in half. The other half of the photo had showed her father who had left to fight in the war. That well-worn part of the picture was tucked away, in a place where Layla would never find it.

Gracie felt better when she pushed the pin into the photo of Layla. Her mother's face was no longer visible, the lace dress now a smudged pock holed section. When she stabbed the pins in quickly it made her stop thinking about how hungry and cold she was, and when she pushed them slowly and twisted them through the picture, it made her forget her mother's cruel words that were flung at her every time they saw each other.

'Your father is nothing but a penniless drover who was just after a good time.' Her mother's voice was shrill and loud, and Gracie wanted to hold her hands over her ears so she could block the words. She stopped herself though; as to do so would result in further beatings.

'I was the star of the 1935 circus tour, the flying Layla, the most amazing acrobat Wirth's Circus ever had. And how did they thank me when you started to grow in my belly? My beautiful flat belly you made fat and left stretch marks across.' Her hand came up and slapped Gracie across the face. 'Answer me, you stupid brat.'

Gracie's voice was a whisper. She was only five-years-old, but she knew when and how she was expected to respond. 'How did they thank you?' her voice trailed off at the end, causing Layla to sneer and put her face up close to Gracie's.

'They sent me away. Told me to go and not come back. Your stupid father with all his honour said he'd support me. And so, . . .' She flounced off, as usual her moods swinging from low to high in a second. 'And so,' she repeated, 'we ended up here in this tiny Melbourne flat, with no room to swing a cat.' She danced like a wild woman around a chair, a crazy smirk on her face. 'But at least I'm in the right place for work. The Vaudeville shows all beg me to dance for them and the theatre group are my new family. The men there love me. And what did your father do?'

Gracie whispered again. 'What did my father do?'

Layla's laughter was jarring and high-pitched. 'He went off and joined up. Left us both. Lucky for me I get his pay, even though we were never married. Just a stupid drover from the bush, who didn't know a thing about women until I met him.'

Gracie wanted to ask when her father would come back. She needed him to look after her and read to her at night. Since he had left, Layla had become even nastier and left Gracie alone in the small flat for days on end with nothing to eat. She was hungry and cold, and missed her father terribly. She hugged her knees as Layla pranced and pivoted across the room. Suddenly her mother stopped, her face deep in thought. Gracie stayed still, knowing better than to draw attention to herself.

Layla came over to her. 'Stand up, miss.'

Gracie continued to hug her legs, only moving when Layla kicked her and yelled again.

'Stand up, you stupid skinny brat.' She grabbed Gracie's arm, digging her fingers into the skin, which was already sore from previous whacks. 'I have a plan. Turn around my little princess.'

Gracie did as she was told, bewildered by the changes in Layla's moods. 'It's time to put my plan into action. You're nearly six. The time has come.' Layla laughed and reached into her bag, pulling out a packet of biscuits. 'Here, eat up. You're too thin and things around here are about to change. I've had enough of this life here in Fitzroy.'

CHAPTER 40

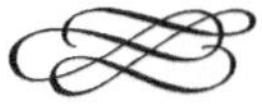

Rabaul – March 1941

The shoreline of Rabaul was a welcome sight to Michael. As they approached the harbour, the men on the boat were given a spectacular view of the bay and surrounds. Michael looked towards the tallest mountain, the view making him miss his step. A gentle jab in the back kept him going, his feet finding the gangplank.

'Hey mate, watch where you're going, I nearly walked over the top of you.'

'Sorry George, I've never seen a volcano before. There's smoke coming out of the top.'

'They did warn us about the smell,' George replied.

'It's the sulphur from the volcano,' another voice boomed behind them, 'now get a move on. We're supposed to look like a military group, not a bunch of drongos from the bush.'

Michael focussed on the bustling scene in front of where the ship had docked. The wharf was filled with people, the different groups gathering to welcome the new arrivals. They called out to each other in their own language, children hoisted on their hips or standing next to them, hiding behind their legs. The men looked strong, their upper bodies bare and bulging with muscles. Similar to the women, their hair was a mass of frizzy curls, some decorated with strings of beads and shells that wound through the spirals of dark ringlets.

The sound of women singing had been a heartfelt greeting as the ship docked and the group continued to welcome the arrivals with their music. They wore bright blouses, their bodies swaying and feet stomping as the men came down the gangplank.

To the side of the wharf, groups of Chinese stood, families, dressed for the occasion in their best attire. Other townsfolk waved and cheered, welcoming the group of Australian forces to the shores of New Britain.

For a moment he held his breath, the sights and sounds were so foreign. He was over two and a half thousand miles from home. And which home? Not only had he left Gracie, but now he was also further from his family in western Queensland. He had envisaged landing in a middle-eastern city, or perhaps being sent to fight in Europe, where so many other young Australian men were. But here they were; a town called Rabaul in New Britain, miles from home, and to all of them, also miles from the war.

'It's the greatest commitment to the Imperial Service you can make. To defend your homeland,' the commander had told them before they embarked on the *Zealandia*.

Now as Michael watched the festive welcome, he contemplated the work of building defences and protecting the seaplane base. He looked again at the celebrations on shore. If the government wanted to waste so many men in an area so far away from the war, then so be it.

The sound of a band playing broke his daydreaming and

George once again prodded him in the back. 'Michael, get your wits about you. You were a million miles away.'

'Sorry, mate,' Michael said, taking one last look at the terrain. A single wisp of smoke trailed out of the top of the highest peak, the curly tendrils spiralling upwards before disappearing into the crisp blue sky.

CHAPTER 41

$\mathcal{M}$ichael's battalion had formed, prepared and trained in Victoria. Now, just as they had in training, they helped each other settle into regular army life in Rabaul. Some of them, like him, had been brought up in the bush, their hands and bodies accustomed to long days and hard work. Others, who had lived a comfortable city life, had struggled with the earlier army training, unused to the rigour and exercise regimes demanded of them. It hadn't taken long for the city fellas to work out that the men from the bush were helpful and resilient when the going got tough. If they all worked together, they made a strong team.

George Lester was a city man. He was a red-headed Scottish lad, brought up in the suburbs of Canberra. After finishing school, he had been a clerk in a large office in the middle of the city, spending his days behind a desk, the flight of stairs leading down to the ground floor the only exercise he did. He had suffered terribly through the rigorous training, only surviving due to the support of Michael.

It was distressing to watch George struggle through even the easier drills and Michael ensured he was by his side, until he grew fitter and stronger. The young lanky Scotsman with piercing blue eyes, reminded Michael of his younger brothers and the two soon become mates.

Although George was a good talker and kept Michael entertained for hours with stories of Scotland, he was also a good listener; a sympathetic ear for Michael, who unburdened the weight sitting heavy on his shoulders.

'I was a drover. My older brother, Rory, and my twin brother, Dan, and I worked with my father. We moved cattle and horses up and down the properties from the top of Queensland to the towns down south. I should have stuck to doing that.'

'How come you didn't?' George was curious.

'Both Dan and I wanted to visit places further afield, experience life away from where we'd always lived. Away from the dust and cattle and the best Haggis stew you'd ever tasted.'

'Now that sounds like something.' George's ears pricked up at the sound of his favourite meal.

'I have four brothers. The younger two, Frank and Lachie would be twenty-one and twenty-two by now.' Michael sighed. 'I wanted to get back home. I missed the family like you wouldn't believe.'

'What happened? How'd you end up here in New Guinea if you want to be back out there?'

'It's a long story.'

George chuckled. 'We've got nothing else to do. I don't want to go to the pictures in town again. I've seen the same movie three times already. Tell me your story. I'm intrigued.'

Michael stirred a tin cup of steaming tea. He clinked his spoon on the side, the remaining drops falling back into the cup. He laid the spoon down on the table, taking a long sip before divulging his story.

George listened silently to Michael's tale of droving and family life on the property. He scratched his head, his eyes wide, when Michael repeated the part about Layla and the encounter in the bathtub. 'A naked acrobat in a bathtub! My God, I could only dream of it.'

Michael frowned. 'It sounds exciting, doesn't it? Every man's dream come true. And from what I can remember it was good at the time, but the problem was, five weeks later she was vomiting and the circus boss found out she was pregnant.'

'Did you marry her?'

'No. People just presumed we were. The night I slept with her, was the first and last time I was ever with her in that way. I never meant anything to her and now I'm at fault for leaving Gracie behind.'

George filled Michael's cup up again. 'That's a sad story.'

'Every night I would read to Gracie,' Michael said. 'She loved books and I'd taught her to read. I told her when she was alone to talk to a special star at night.' His voice became shaky. 'I told her I would listen and be able to hear what she said no matter where I was.'

'I've seen you go outside at night and look to the sky. I've often wondered what it is you're searching for.'

'It's Elizabeth's Star. My folks lost a little baby girl, Elizabeth, a year or so after I was born. They named the evening star after her and we all grew up knowing the story. I taught Gracie about the star and convinced her I would hear her wherever I was.'

'She won't forget you.'

'I hope you're right, George. Layla was always jealous about the two of us together. I'm not sure why, because she didn't appear to have any affection for either of us.'

'Aye, there are some mean women out there. You'd be best to steer clear of the women for a while.'

Michael laughed. 'Women are the last thing on my mind and besides we're off to fight a war. I don't think they're going to be too many women wherever we end up.'

'Don't be too sure. Have you seen the nurses at the hospital?

Long hair, slender legs. Oh my God, I swear they're angels sent from heaven. We're going to ask them to the movies.

'Leave me out of it. I'm not having anything to do with a woman ever again.'

'Aye, so you've been burnt, but you'll get over it. There's a war coming, Michael, we might die tomorrow.'

'You're on your own. My answer is no. Now get ready, we're going up to the airfield to do some work. You'd better stick with me because there're more snakes and bugs here, than you've ever seen in your entire life.'

* * *

Michael had seen the nurses when he'd been in town exploring on a day off. Thank goodness some of the huge trees had survived the 1937 eruption; the tree-lined streets were shady, a welcome shelter against the constant tropical heat.

The town was more civilised than he had imagined. The houses were comfortable and much like houses in the larger towns back home. The difference was the backdrop; a dense jungle flowing down from the mountains, forming a distinct line behind the town. From a distance the tangle of trees and undergrowth appeared impenetrable, although animals and the villagers frequently slipped off into its depths. For those who knew, there were small invisible openings, a way in through the dense wall of foliage.

The local people were at one with the land, much like the Aboriginal people back home. Their build was different though and they were a more solid physique, not as tall and lanky but rather shorter and more solid. They were warrior men with frizzy dark hair, their arms and legs, sturdy and muscly. Michael was in charge of a group of them who had been sent to help clear an area for a new defence structure. He was wary of them, sceptical they

197

would be able to understand his directions or have the knowledge to build what was needed.

The men though, irrespective of their ages, had the ability to lift the heaviest timbers and to position building materials wherever needed. They were the strongest men Michael had ever seen and skilful in clearing areas for new defence structures and locating local resources. Once the work was finished they'd stand around in groups, talking and partaking in their custom of chewing and then spitting out betel nut.

The Sergeant had warned that they were not to be trusted; their habits were uncivilised, and it was forbidden to mix with them socially or allow them to address the Australians by their Christian names. The troops were not allowed to gift them any food or liquor and discouraged from making jokes with them. That way they would work better and the results would be greater.

Michael side-stepped another patch of unwanted chewed up pulp from the betel nuts, reminding himself he would need to keep an eye on them, ensuring they didn't laze around when they were supposed to be working.

* * *

It had taken Michael a while to put the Sergeant's comments to rest and form his own opinions. At first, he had heeded the advice and spoken to them sparingly, saving his words for orders for the buildings they were erecting. However, a young man called Birri had begun to follow him around and always seemed to be there when Michael needed help with moving logs or directing the men about something they didn't understand.

Birri was strong, his upper body covered in a criss cross arrangement of scars and tribal markings. His lower body was covered by a piece of material wrapped around his hips, his broad chest bare, his arms and legs sinewy and powerful.

When Michael cut his arm on an axe blade, Birri bandaged it, applying a mixture that he made from the plants nearby. He spoke pidgin English and when he continued to check on Michael's wound each day, the two began to have long conversations, a mutual trust and friendship developing between them. The socialising rules were disregarded and the two soon became firm friends.

When one of the other men chided Michael about getting too friendly with the locals, he ignored the advice. The workers might be a different colour but if you made the effort to get to know them, they were really just the same as other men.

Birri taught Michael his language as well as taking the opportunity to improve on what he called his, 'Australian English.' He spoke this English well and it was only when he became animated or couldn't get his point across, he would break into pidgin English, and then his language; the language of the Tolai people.

When he was younger Michael had loved to sit with the Aboriginal people who lived near his parents' property. Much like he had done then, out in the paddocks or squatting next to a dry creek bed, he now sat with Birri.

Birri taught him the skills and culture of his people and the two often trekked through the jungle to the higher slopes behind Rabaul. Birri led him deep into the dense jungle, pointing out the secret trails and small clearings scattered throughout the mountains. He pointed out the food and shelter the thick growth provided and Michael was soon able to find his way along the seemingly invisible paths, weaving through the jungle interior.

Birri had taken Michael to visit his village; a cluster of huts situated in a small hidden clearing, high above Rabaul. The track there was well worn and Michael's boots sunk into the thick leaf litter as Birri led him through huge towering trees, their trunks covered in moss, their branches laden with clinging staghorns and ferns. Thick liana vines curled around the trees, spiralling like rope, their sturdy growth reaching for the canopies in search of direct sunlight. The tendrils of buttress roots stretched across the ground, a solid footing for the trees that soared hundreds of feet above. Tiny birds flitted in and out of tarantula-like orchids, their vibrant hues matched by the myriad of parrots and brightly coloured birds that called out to each other through the heavy growth of the jungle.

Birri slowed every so often to point out a plant or small animal to Michael, stopping when they approached a clearing, allowing Michael a first look at his home village.

The village was a cluster of huts on short stilts, their walls and roofs woven from palm fronds and branches, the frames built with logs cut from trees growing higher up the slopes. Small pigs and chickens roamed around the huts and children ran back and forth, their naked dark bodies leaping and jumping as they played in the dirt and amongst the vegetable plots.

A small group of men greeted the two men, their excited conversation a friendly welcome to Michael, who suddenly found himself surrounded by giggling children who grabbed at his hands and gathered around him as he squatted in the dirt to talk to them. They touched his hat and squealed with delight when he took it off and placed it on the head of one of the smallest boys. The women had also gathered and chattered loudly, laughing and pointing at the small boy who strutted around, naked, except for the hat which covered not only his head but also his face. One of the women called out to the boy. She lifted the hat off and returned it to Michael. Her smile was wide, her round face attractive and Michael nodded as he took the hat.

Some women sat on the floor at the front of their huts, their legs swinging over the edges as they talked, babies suckling on their breasts.

It was a hive of activity and Michael joined the men around a firepit. He held his hand out to accept a mixture of meat and vegetables that had been divided out onto banana leaves, the smooth green surface as enticing as a fine china plate.

It appeared to be an idyllic existence and he relaxed as he sat with the men, the sound of women singing and children playing a homely noise. As he listened to the men talk, he thought of how they had everything they needed. Their houses were strong and a dry haven from the torrential rain that fell, not in drops, but like someone was tipping out buckets from above. They had fruit and vegetables to eat and meat from the pigs they kept and small animals they hunted. Rabaul was not far and wares and vegies were bartered in the market, the villagers procuring other items in exchange.

He squatted next to the others, a calm warm feeling enveloping him. Birri and his family lived in paradise, a tropical utopia where everyone appeared to be happy and content with their homes and way of life.

***

The sun was low in the sky when the two men returned to Rabaul and they talked only for a moment before they parted ways.

Birri hoped, even with all the talk of the Japanese to the north and troops arriving, that nothing would change. 'We live a good life but now there are more newcomers and new buildings going up. I hope with this talk of those to the north and the Australians coming, nothing will change for my people. Do they send soldiers here to protect us, our people, or is it to defend your own people?'

'I'm no expert on this, but from what I can gather they're just trying to show the Japanese we're in the area and they can't intimidate us. It's a precaution and once the buildings and communications are built, we'll be taken back home and then sent to the Middle East or Europe.'

Birri frowned, the wrinkles dark and thick on his forehead. 'The Chinese are worried. We do business with them in Chinatown and they tell us the Japanese are killing their brothers and sisters in their own country.'

'Yes, that's right.' Michael said. 'My friend, George, has news-paper cuttings from back home. The papers are old and dated, well before we left Australia, but it keeps us informed.'

Birri leaned on the long stick he always carried. 'Our people are a peaceful tribe. Sometimes tribes from other areas want wars with others, but not us. We are at one with our families, our land and the waters where we catch fish.'

'Why is your English so good?' Michael asked.

'The missionaries teach us, at the native school. Only our people from the villages can go there. They teach me English and I learn very quick because I am very smart.' He tapped his head and talked slowly, making sure his words were as he wanted them to be. 'But my true strength is in here.' He pounded his chest showing Michael it was his heart that was the strongest. 'My family, and now you, my friend. You are Birri's friend.'

The two men laughed, and Michael patted Birri vigorously on the back. 'Yes, you are my friend also.'

ichael strolled along the wide streets, a long list from the camp cook in his pocket. He smiled at others he passed, before stopping under a large weeping tree, the shade a welcome relief from the heat of the day. A flock of king parrots screeched in the branches overhead, their vivid reds and green feathers making them easy to spot in the dense canopy.

He watched the birds for a while before continuing, slowing his pace as he passed an empty sports ground. The laughter and excited yells of ladies playing a game on the tennis courts over further, drifting across the nearby streets.

The town was busy, and men went in and out of the pubs on the corners, the buildings with shady verandahs framed by lattice-work, reminiscent of the pubs in Broken Hill. Their windows were flung open to catch the breeze, their timber counters wide and worn, smoothed by arms of the men who sat and drank a cold beer on a hot day.

As smartly dressed businessmen passed by and a well-dressed man in a suit doffed his hat in a polite welcome, Michael asked himself the same question he had pondered, over and over again.

Why had the Australian government sent troops to such a peaceful town and why did he feel like he was just out for a morning stroll, rather than off to fight a war?

He rolled his sleeves up higher, making sure the shirt was tucked in firmly as he made his way through the centre of town, past more houses until he approached the bustling area of China-town. People hurried past him, a polite bob of their head in greet-ing. A variety of decorative signs hung from shops lining the street, and he looked up and down until he spotted the one he had been looking for, *Mi-Lee's Trading Store.* The sergeant back at camp had told him that this shop stocked the best herbs and spices, their prices fair and service second-to-none.

A bell attached to the front door jingled as Michael entered, the wide timber floorboards creaking beneath his boots. He looked around, fascinated at the collection of goods for sale. Colourful lanterns hung from the ceiling, swaying back and forth in the warm breeze filtering in through a side window. Fine china jugs and vases filled the shelves lining every wall, and wooden chests of every shape and size were stacked neatly on the floor, their tops stacked with timber cases full of a variety of smaller ornaments. He walked past large cane baskets overflowing with fruit and vegetables, and more shelves, stacked with spices and herbs, bottled in glass jars.

There was a sweet aroma of exotic foods and he tried to deci-pher what it was as he made his way towards an ornate timber counter stretching across the entire breadth of the shop. The front was made of glass and the shelves behind the glass held containers and bric-a-brac of every description. The timeworn timbers on the top of the counter were smooth under Michael's fingers, the dents and scratches testament to the transactions that took place across its surface.

Hundreds of small timber drawers with metal handles lined the wall behind the counter, above them, a glass compartment filled with more china vases and ornaments.

A table filled with an assortment of children's' toys caught his eye and he rested his hand on a colourful metal spinning top. He held it up by the timber handle and used his other hand to spin the bottom part around. The scene painted on it was of a circus. He watched the horses and elephants swirl past his eyes, the cages, tents, and circus people blurring as the top spun around.

Laughter from behind a curtain at the back of the counter broke his daydream and he remembered what he had been sent for. He looked up as two young women came from behind the counter. An elegant young Chinese woman welcomed him with a bow. She was tiny, her dark hair pulled back neatly, a bun perched perfectly on top of her head. A long skirt covered her slender body, a short-sleeved shirt sitting immaculately over the top. She pulled the curtains back to allow herself and the woman behind her to come towards where he stood. Her voice was clear when she spoke.

'I will be with you in a moment, sir', she said as she bowed her head towards Michael.

'No hurry,' Michael replied, his eyes turning to the woman who came out behind her.

This woman was tall, with blonde curly hair and green eyes that held his gaze. She wore a floral dress, the waist drawn in tight by a red belt, accentuating her slender body.

Michael caught his breath as she spoke, her beauty and poise mesmeric. 'We're sorry to keep you waiting. Mi-Lee and I don't stop talking once we start.' The beautiful young woman kissed the Chinese woman's cheek and took the basket filled with bottles containing herbs. 'Mi-Lee's shop has the best herbs in all of New Britain. Everything you need to make your food delicious.'

Michael stood tall, his eyes never leaving those of the blonde girl. 'That's just what I've been sent for. The sergeant over at the mess tent has sent me with a list.' He turned to Mi-Lee. 'He said the herbs from here are the best his cook has ever used.'

The blonde woman smiled again as Mi-Lee turned to the

sound of children giggling from behind the curtain. She spoke to the children in her language, her speech quick and direct. Michael's smile was wide, as first one, and then another small face peered around the edge of the fabric. Two sets of dark, almond-shaped eyes peered at him with curiosity and the two children jostled each other to push past the curtain to get to their mother. The tallest child held fast to a spinning top, similar to the one Michael had looked at.

'I was just looking at one of those. Can you show me how it works?' He directed his question to the children.

Mi-Lee translated what Michael asked.

The older girl walked from behind the counter and placed the spinning top down on the timber floor. Michael squatted down so he was on the same level. She pulled the timber handle of the top upwards before giving him a cheeky grin and pushing the handle down hard. They all watched as the top twirled on the spot, the girl grabbing it quickly before it stopped and fell down.

'Well done.' Michael held out his hand, requesting a turn.

The girl held the top out towards him and he took it, his voice shaky as he thanked her.

Even though her face looked nothing like Gracie's, she was a similar size, the tiny hands offering him the top, much the same as the ones which had often clutched his own or stroked his face when they read books together. A dull ache in his chest tightened. It didn't matter what he did or how hard he berated himself, he could never shake it off. Although thousands of men had also left their families and joining up was an honourable action, the guilt never left.

When night came and he lay in his narrow bunk, his thoughts turned to Gracie. Sometimes while the others around him slept, he would get up and walk outside, looking for their star. If he closed his eyes he could imagine he was lying next to her, reading *Black Beauty*. Sometimes in his dreams he heard her voice, but the words were jumbled and all he could hear was her calling his name. That upset him even more and although he felt like he was letting her down, sometimes it was easier not to look at the star or think about what she was doing.

Now, he realised he had been holding the top and staring at it for quite a while, his mind not here in the room of the Chinese traders in Rabaul, but thousands of miles away, remembering the times when he and Gracie had sat and played with a spinning top.

The little girl looked at him suspiciously. She was probably worried he had held the top for too long and might not give it back. He pulled the handle up and down a few times and then let it go. The top spun wildly, cavorting and dancing across the floor. It spun around in a wide circle, the two women stepping back to let it continue its circular path. When it neared Michael, he swung his hand underneath it, causing it to flip over and land back down before continuing on its final spin. The children gasped and clapped their hands, excited by the new trick. He handed it back to the little girl. 'This is a very fine spinning top. You will have to teach it some new tricks.'

Mi-Lee interpreted again for the children and they both nodded. Michael stood up, the little girl's smile almost too much for him to bear. He steadied his voice before speaking to Mi-Lee. 'I have a list here. I better get these items, otherwise they'll be wondering where I am.'

The blonde woman bent down and gave both the children a kiss. 'Be good for your mother and I will see you soon.' She nodded at Michael before saying her goodbyes. 'Come and visit soon, Mi-Lee, Father would love to see you.'

Mi-Lee answered, 'Thank you, Joanie. We will all visit soon.' She said something to the children in her own language, the two of them giving Michael one last cheeky smile before disappearing behind the curtain.

CHAPTER 43

The sergeant soon realised Michael was a reliable person to send to town for supplies. He knew exactly where to get the best food and was quick to find his way around the markets and stores in town. Today there were several errands to attend to, which suited, as it was a chance to post his regular weekly letters to Layla.

Hopefully Layla was reading the letters to Gracie. So far, he had not had a letter in return. When the bag came through with mail for others in his regiment, he stood to the back, waiting.

One day he had been excited to hear his name called out when the mail bag arrived. There it was, his first letter since he had arrived in Rabaul. He had walked away from the camp, finding a cool and isolated spot to sit. The letter hadn't been from Layla though. It was from Dan, who wanted to check how he was going and to bring news of their family.

It was fortunate Michael had walked a fair distance from the camp, because when he finished reading the letter, he'd cried. Not just a quiet cry, but heart wrenching loud sobs, muffled by his arms as he buried his head in them. He sat for a long while, clutching the letter as he read it over and over again, the tears still wet on his face.

Dear Michael,

We received the letter from you saying you were being deployed overseas and also the news about your young daughter, Gracie. I hope this letter finds you, as when you wrote you didn't have a forwarding address. I travelled to Melbourne, to where another girl from the circus told me Layla was working. I tracked her down working in the theatre. I spoke to her after the show and she told me you had left for the war. She wouldn't allow me to see your daughter, Gracie. She said the child is doing well and is much better behaved now you are not there. Unfortunately I argued with her and then had to pay her money before she would give me your address. In her bag she had an envelope which she said had only just arrived. It was lucky she still had it because she said she had thrown your others away and never read them. Mother and Father have been beside themselves about what has happened and father blames himself, as do I, for your misfortunes. They want you to know they will support you and your family. They love you and when you return from the war they hope you will come back home, with your Gracie.'

Michael had broken down when he read that part and it was as if his mother's arms were wrapped around him, consoling him as he finished reading the last part of the letter.

Young Frank has joined the Australian army and has been deployed to North Africa. Lachie has also enlisted and is waiting instructions to begin his training. I am with the circus still and Audrey and I married two years after you left. I tried to contact you but was unable to locate you.'

When he regained his composure and wiped his eyes, his gaze travelled up to the brightest star he could find. The faces of Gracie and his family swirled in front of him. No matter what happened in the years ahead, he would return to look after his daughter and to see his parents.

He would write back and let his family know he was in the safety of Rabaul and would be home as soon as the war was over. They would be relieved his duties entailed building a few shelters at the airfield and running errands for the officers. At least that would give them comfort, to know he was safe and a long way from the war.

CHAPTER 44

Rabaul - August 1941

Michael loved the walk down to the township of Rabaul. His battalion was stationed a mile or so up the road from the main street and there was always plenty to see on the way back and forth.

Bungalow houses dotted the road, their crisscrossed verandah rails a safe perch for the variety of colourful parrots flitting from the trees to the shaded area. Large mango trees that had survived previous eruptions spread their branches across sections of the road, providing fruit in the season and a welcome shelter from the heat.

Occasionally a car beeped as it passed or stopped to offer a lift, but Michael always declined, enjoying the time to think and be alone.

It was an easy stroll compared to the treks he did with Birri.

* * *

One day they had left before daylight, not returning until after dark. They had trekked further than Michael had been before, witnessing small eruptions of steam and smoke from where they sat in a cave, carved high up in the side of the mountain.

Birri had pointed with his stick, his voice serious. 'The mountains are unstable but we have learnt to live with them over us. They give us lush soil and vegetation, but they can destroy our villages. When they choose, they rain fire and rocks on us.'

The jungle grew so thick around the cave it was amazing how anyone could find a way through. But Birri followed ancient invisible trails, bringing them to a clearing where the sun's rays filtered through, only in the middle of the day. They sat in the middle of the grassy clearing, peering upwards at trees so tall they reached the heavy clouds above. Michael gazed around the perimeter of the clearing. They were surrounded by a solid fence of tall jungle scrub with sinewing vines twisting from one plant to the other.

Birri had laughed at the look on Michael's face. 'There are many clearings such as this, that only we who live in the jungle can find. The secrets of the trails has been passed down from generation to generation.'

Michael was intrigued. 'It is the same for the Aborigines in Australia; their knowledge has been passed down for thousands of years. They too have sacred spots only they know about and the ability to find water where no white man could. They can find their way through the deserts and across the vast plains, following invisible trails to waterholes, surrounded by paintings of their forebears.'

Birri listened with interest, the two men exchanging knowledge, both interested in the ways of the original people of two islands that lay not far across the ocean from one another. One was the largest island in the world, arid in many places while the other was smaller and covered in thick vegetation with many places inaccessible, leaving it as one of the least explored places in the world.

When they went to leave the clearing, Birri didn't hesitate and walked to what appeared to be a solid wall of jungle. He guided Michael behind a tree, its trunk as thick as an army truck was wide. The tree's web of branches entangled with others nearby, their surfaces cluttered and covered in a variety of plants. Behind the tree was a small gap, an entrance only visible when Michael and Birri stood in a particular spot. After passing through, they continued to traverse upwards, hanging onto the vines and twisted tree roots as they went.

The path narrowed before opening up to another clearing, a burial ground and special place to those of Birri's village. They didn't enter, but rather skirted the perimeter to get to where they needed to go.

They talked as they walked, feeding on the fruits Birri picked. He pointed out other plants to Michael, explaining why not to eat certain fruits, which could make a man sick and sometimes bring on death.

Birri's knowledge was endless. He was only young, but it was as he said, tapping his head, 'all up here.' His job was to pass the traditions and life skills on to his sons and they in turn to theirs. It was his pleasure to also pass it onto his new friend.

Now as Michael walked along the road towards Rabaul, he looked up towards where Birri had led him through the maze of trails and secret clearings. He remembered what he'd been taught and looked for the plants he'd been shown. There was the tree whose bark could be ground up and eaten for tummy upsets and the root plants providing year-round food for the people of the surrounding villages.

Michael passed local women gathering fruit growing alongside the road, huge baskets balancing on their heads. Groups of children, with yellow frizzy hair, ran after them, a few of them looking back and waving to Michael.

Today he would make his way to the post office and post letters for the other men as well as his correspondence to Gracie and Layla. There was banking to do for some of the officers and a small list of items to be purchased from the Burns Philp store in the main street. The cook was after another stewing pot, as the word was out that other Australian troops were coming to join the 2/22nd Battalion in the months ahead.

* * *

Michael stood on the footpath and straightened his uniform. He re-adjusted his wide leather belt, ensuring his shirt was tucked in, fixing the collar so it sat flat. His khaki shorts came to just above his knees and he pulled his socks up, his boots scuffed and scratched, but without any mud. The Burns Philp building was the largest in the street and its prominent sign made it easy to locate.

The stairs creaked as he walked into the store and he stepped lightly. It was lunchtime and most of the general public were enjoying their lunch at one of the clubs, or those who were able to, had headed home for an afternoon siesta while the day was at its hottest.

The heat, although a different type than he was used to, didn't bother Michael, and the tropical downpours arriving in torrential flows, passed over as fast as they arrived. He marvelled at the amount of water deposited in such a short space of time. If only that amount of rain was available on the properties back home, what a different landscape it would be. Even the constant rumblings and spitting of the mountain did little to unsettle his nerves and he often found amusement in George's reactions to the unstable earth they lived on.

At first, the movement of the ground and shaking of the earth had stopped Michael in his tracks, but now it was a routine part of daily life.

'You're so calm when the earth shakes,' George said, his eyes wide, his feet rammed apart. 'I feel like the earth is going to open up and swallow us.'

'It's just the volcano,' Michael explained. 'There's a new testing centre up the mountain. They'll keep an eye on it and if it's ever ready to go again, like it did in '37, there'll be plenty of time for warnings and evacuation.'

'And where the bloody hell do we evacuate to from here? You'd have to go by sea because there's nothing but jungle, malaria and steep mountains up behind us. I tell you if we ever had to get out of here in a hurry, unless there was a massive ship to take the lot of us, we'd be doomed,' George said.

'The natives know how to get away fast. It's only because last time they didn't realise what was happening and how bad it would be. If they'd known, they would have packed up and travelled over the ranges to the sea on the other side.'

'And then where?' George asked. 'There's no escaping this little place, unless you go back out over the crater that's covered in water in front of us.'

'Hopefully we won't need to think about it. They say the volcano won't happen again for another forty years. We won't be here that long.'

'I'll tell you right now.' George scratched his arms and legs. 'I hope we won't be here long because these mozzies are driving me mad. We'll get this airfield secured and a few other buildings in place and I reckon we'll be gone by Christmas time. Back home and see the family and then unless we've already finished up the Germans in Europe, I'm planning to be over there fighting by the New Year. Mark my words, we won't be here too long.'

CHAPTER 45

ichael looked around the Burns Philp Store. The arrival of more Australian troops would be good for businesses in the town and no doubt the clubs and pubs were looking forward to the extra income. He wondered why the government was sending more men, when there wasn't much to do for the ones already here. He looked at the shelves lining the walls. Everything one needed was available in Rabaul and life was civilised. His was an easy role compared to being in the real war, fighting the Germans. His mind turned to his younger brothers. Where were they and what were they dealing with? Surely they weren't wandering around a trading store looking for a cooking pot.

'Hello.' A voice broke his thoughts and he turned from the shelves to look straight into the eyes of the blonde girl he had encountered the previous week at Mi-Lee's trading store.

He stared hard, captivated by her smile and full lips, touched by the hint of pale-pink lipstick. She wore a similar dress to last time he had seen her; fitted and floral, the skirt straight and coming down to below her knees. When she spoke the dimples on her cheeks indented and he smiled back, charmed by her friendly manner.

'Hello,' she said again. 'Is there something in particular you were looking for?'

Michael stuttered. 'Um, yes, well no, but yes, I, well not I, but the sergeant, um, he was after a lipstick.'

'He wanted lipstick?' She giggled as she pushed one side of her hair back behind her ear.

Michael took a deep breath, drawing himself up and looking her straight in the eye. Her eyes twinkled mischievously, and he could tell she was amused he was having difficulty getting his words out.

The girl held out her hand, 'I'm Joanie, and I believe we've already met. I saw you at Mi-Lee's shop last week.'

He laughed and relaxed a little. 'I'm Michael.'

'Pleased to meet you, Michael. You must be with the second, twenty-second, up there on the hill.'

'Yes, that's us.'

'And the sergeant who wants the lipstick, is he also with you on the hill?'

'The sergeant, oh no, he doesn't want lipstick. I'm not sure why I said that. He's after a large cooking pot for making stew.'

They stood facing each other, their eyes locked as they smiled at each other. Narrow shafts of light filtered in through the frosted glass windows and outside, muted car horns sounded in the distant. The clanging of logs being unloaded further down the street faded away, the muffled noises of a busy town street disappearing into the background as time stood still.

A booming voice from the back of the shop broke the moment. 'Joanie, where's that docket I asked you to bring me?'

Michael looked down at his feet and then back up again, making sure the beautiful girl with the vivid green eyes was still standing there. His voice was steady. 'I'm pleased to meet you,

Joanie. I'll have a look around while you do whatever you need to do.'

'Oh, that's Father,' she laughed and then called out. 'I'm over here. Come here, Father, and meet one of the men from the camp. He's after a stewing pot.'

'I've been looking high and low for the paperwork for the new typewriter. I can't find it anywhere,' Joanie's father said as he walked towards them. He stretched out his hand in welcome. 'Good morning, young man. I'm pleased to meet you. I'm Reg Black.'

The older man's facial features, although weathered and masculine, carried a resemblance to his daughter and the same dancing eyes looked out from beneath bushy eyebrows. Michael shook his hand; Reg's grip was firm and friendly.

'Please to meet you, sir. I'm Michael McTavish.'

'And where are you from, Michael?'

'Originally I'm from Bundeen Station, but more lately from Melbourne.'

'And where the hell is Bundeen Station?'

'It's in the Channel country, about three hundred miles north of Birdsville.'

'And how has a young fellow like yourself ended up such a long way from home?'

Michael sighed. 'That sir, is a very long story and not always a happy tale to tell.'

Reg wrapped his arm around his daughter's shoulders. 'You fellows get leave passes every now and then, don't you?'

'Yes sir, we're allowed to come down into town when we have a pass.'

'You're a long way from home, so perhaps you'd like to join us for dinner one night. Bring one of your mates with you, we'd love to have you visit.'

'Thank you, sir,'

'Oh please call me Reg, and this is my daughter, Joanie.'

'We've met, Father,' Joanie chimed in. 'We were both at Mi-Lee's store last week. Michael was showing Li and Chun how to race the spinning top around the room.'

'Well, Michael, how about Wednesday afternoon? Come when you can and you can have a good look around the property where we're staying. We'll have early dinner and I can drive you back to the base when we're finished.'

'Thank you and I do have a friend who would appreciate a good dinner, rather than dining at the mess tent. He's a city fellow and he's missing the more civilised aspects of life.'

'We'll see you Wednesday. It's the least we can do for you young fellas. Now Joanie, find this young man the best stewing pot you can and make sure to throw in a good ladling spoon for free.' Reg turned and began walking back down to the back of the shop. 'And Joanie when you're finished there, I need that darn docket for the typewriter.'

* * *

Michael and Joanie stood looking at each other, both smiling as Reg's voice bellowed from the back. 'A stewing pot, Joanie, show the young man the stewing pot.'

Michael chuckled, causing Joanie to laugh out loud also.

'He's the boss,' she said. 'The workers here love him, because even when he tries to sound angry, they know he's not.' She looked up at Michael. 'What's it like to join up? You know, to sign up, to go off to war?'

'There's not much of a war happening here, although they say the Japanese are starting to move around a bit more than what they were.'

'Father was told there's another ship bringing more troops next month.'

'Yes, we've been told the same. They'll join with us. We're known as Lark Force.'

'Are you all from the same area?'

'Most of us in the second, twenty-second, are from down south, near Melbourne. These new fellows though, they're coming from a variety of different places and battalions. That's what we've heard anyway. They don't tell us too much.'

They stood and chatted for a long while, Michael asking Joanie where she had lived and what she had done before she came to Rabaul. She was easy to talk to and he was intrigued by her story. His voice had regained a steady composure, although his heart thumped when she looked straight at him and gave him the most beautiful smile he'd ever seen. She had been in the middle of answering his question about the rose brooch she was wearing when the banging of the shop door startled them both. Michael was reminded of where he was and what he was supposed to be doing as Joanie's father reappeared. He rolled his eyes at them. They were both standing in exactly the same spot he had left them over an hour ago.

'That stewing pot must be hard to find and don't forget the ladling spoon. Goodness Joanie, it's nearly time to start doing up the register.'

CHAPTER 46

Rabaul - August 1941

Joanie's head had been full of thoughts of the handsome Australian soldier. His deep-set eyes had looked straight at her when he spoke, his face, tanned and rugged. He was tall, with a strong physique and although his hair was short, blonde curls sprung up in an unruly fashion. She had tried to stop herself staring and to instead listen to his words, his deep voice mesmerising, his manner relaxed and friendly.

There was something about him, something that made her want to know more. She had wanted to keep him talking, to store the sound of his voice in her mind, but her father had interrupted. Thank goodness he had asked Michael to come to dinner, at least that would give her a chance to get to know him better.

Wednesday couldn't come around quick enough and she had already worked out what she would wear. She had tried on three different dresses, before deciding on a dark green skirt and white blouse. She would wear a small red hibiscus flower behind her ear and pin the other side up with the silver hairclip Mi-Lee had given her.

* * *

On Wednesday, Joanie had gone to Mi-Lee's to buy condiments that her father wanted for their dinner. She explained to Mi-Lee who was coming.

'You sound excited, Joanie. I've never seen you so interested in visitors your father invited.' Mi-Lee pulled a quizzical face.

'Mi-Lee, if I tell you something will you promise not to laugh.'

'Of course.'

'Do you think it's possible to fall in love at first sight?'

'You mean to catch another's heart when you first meet?

Joanie's face flushed. 'Yes. I've never felt like this before. When I spoke to Michael in the store, I didn't want him to leave. I keep hearing his voice in my head. Plus he's very handsome, he's a bit taller than me and I would say he's about the same age, and his eyes … they're dark brown and it's as if they look straight into my soul, and his arms are strong and tanned, and they're …'

She stopped, surprised at herself and aware not only Mi-Lee was listening, but both Li and Chun were holding their stomachs, laughing and rolling around on the ground.

'I thought they couldn't understand English,' Joanie said, trying to look stern as she frowned at them.

'They can pick up on some words and sentences now. They're teaching them English at the school. The nuns are very strict and that is why they are learning quickly. They seem to know exactly who and what you're talking about.' Mi-Lee spoke to the children in her language, giggling with them as they replied.

'What did they say?' Joanie asked her, scowling again as the children broke into more loud giggles.

'They are saying Miss Joanie is in love with the soldier man with the spinning top.'

'I'm not in love. Well, I'm not sure. But he's very nice and yes, I am excited about him coming to dinner. Now quickly find me these condiments Father wants, otherwise he'll be cranky with me for taking so long.

CHAPTER 47

Rabaul – August 1941

Michael and George arrived on the dot of four, both dressed in their army uniforms, khaki trousers and shirts, neat and formal for the special occasion. Joanie and her father greeted them and they chatted for a while before Joanie gave a tour of the property. The two young men were good friends and their banter about country versus city life had Reg laughing so hard that at one stage he lost his breath.

'I haven't had such a good laugh for a long while,' he said, as he sipped a glass of water Joanie rushed to get him. 'Good for the soul and beats off all this hearsay of the Japs and the war coming our way.'

* * *

The talk continued long after dinner and into the night. When George and Reg got into a long-winded discussion about the events of the war in Europe, Joanie found herself talking to Michael, who she had made sure to sit next to once they left the dining room.

The wide verandahs provided a cool, relaxed place to sit and Joanie plied Michael with questions about his life, when it had been simple and a matter of droving cattle and horses from one station to the next. His answers were short and she detected a sense of wariness, of not wanting to divulge too much. He had been comfortable talking to her in the store but now he shifted in his seat, looking towards the other men, as if he would have preferred to talk to them rather than her. She slowed her conversation and stopped with her questioning, instead, talking about her childhood in Woombye. She told him about her friend's ponies she had ridden, their pet dog Raj and the bantam hens she'd often smuggled into her bedroom to play with.

He smiled and relaxed when she talked about the green rolling hills near to her home, the cold winter mornings and the fat dairy cows that grazed on the lush pastures. She continued to talk softly, every now and then, answering a question he asked.

'I've never been further west than where we live. I can't imagine what those vast plains look like in Western Queensland,' Joanie said as she picked up her fan, waving it slowly in front of her face.

They both looked up at the night sky. 'The stars are even brighter than the ones above here,' Michael replied, his voice deep and slow as he looked towards the brightest star, briefly closing his eyes.

There was something about him, a melancholic loneliness. A sorrow, under the joviality he showed on the surface. He was young like she was, but in some ways he seemed older.

'You were saying, Michael?' she prompted him.

He opened his eyes, wiping his hand across his brow. 'The stars out west cover the entire sky. They stretch from the horizon and up to the highest reaches, where they blur into a cluster of diamonds, millions of specks lighting up the outback sky.'

Reg and George both stopped talking and listened.

'At night when you're on the track, you can lie on your back and look at the sky for hours. It's your own light show, a million miles away.'

'Is it a hard job, being a drover?' Joanie asked, her mind full of visions of swirling dust and stampeding cattle, like in the paintings exhibited at the local show in Woombye.

Michael swivelled his body in the cane chair, so he was looking directly at her. 'The drovers not only stock all the runs, but they're also responsible for moving the cattle and horses hundreds of miles to the markets. Some may think it's a hard job but when you've been brought up with it, no, it's not hard.' He smiled. 'There's nothing better than being out on the track.'

She leaned back in her chair, meeting his gaze as she turned towards him. The way he looked at her made her stomach do strange little flips and she took a deep breath, determined to keep her voice steady and not sound like a love-struck teenager. 'Is it mainly young men who do the droving? It sounds like a tough job.'

'There are a lot of us young ones coming up, well there were before this war. But there are as many of the older blokes, and those boss drovers are the toughest workers you'll ever find. They make sure we're doing everything right and everyone is safe and the drove is going the way it should. It's a heavy load for them, worrying about the stock and the workers out on the track. Some of them can tell you stories of droving stock right down from the Gulf Country up in Northern Queensland, straight down the middle, over thousands of miles to the New South Wales area near Bourke and then further down to Adelaide.'

'What makes a good drover?' George piped up.

'Firstly, he needs to know the route. It's the opposite of here.'

Michael swung his hand around, pointing towards the jungle, a dark blotch on the mountainside. 'There have been men who've died because they've lost their way or missed a watering hole. A good drover knows his cattle and horses, he knows how to keep them satisfied, rested, watered and fed as well as checking the pace he travels at.'

'Young man, you sound like this droving is a great passion of yours.' Reg said.

'Aye sir, it is, well it was. I was brought up on the properties and my father was one of the best. He taught my brothers and I all we needed to know.'

Joanie was curious. 'Yet you said you joined up down in Melbourne. What were you doing down there?'

Michael looked down at his empty glass, the relaxed tone gone from his voice. 'That's another story and it's late. We'll be in trouble if we get back after the curfew.'

George added, 'Jeez they'll have our guts for garters if we're late, although a few of the officers are down at the club tonight so maybe they won't even miss us.'

The young men took their slouch hats from Joanie, shaking her hand as they thanked her and Reg for the night.

'It was a grand night,' Reg said. 'You'll have to come again. We'd love to hear more of your droving stories.'

'He was in the circus also.' George joined in.

'It's time for us to go,' Michael said, cutting George short. 'Thank you both. It was a lovely evening.'

* * *

Joanie and her father sat on the front stairs for a long time after Michael and George left. The two soldiers had declined Reg's offer to drive them back, happy to walk back along the road, through the town and up the other side of the hill.

'What are you thinking about, Father?' Joanie asked.

He hesitated, looking out across the yard to the dark silhouette of the mountains in the distance. 'They're nice young men, Joanie. It would be good to be young again. Like you, they have their whole life in front of them. Sometimes I feel like I'm running out of time.'

'You're not old. Please don't talk about running out of time. I always think you and Mother will be with me forever.'

Reg took a while to answer. 'I miss your mum. It's been an experience for us both, but I don't think I want to be away for too much longer.'

They sat together in silence, both gazing up at the stars. Joanie eventually broke the quiet, her words soft. 'How did you know you were in love with Mother?'

Reg sighed. 'It was a feeling, like my heart was full and I didn't want to let her out of my sight. She said it was the same for her. We were meant to be together. It's been thirty years now and we still love each other as much as the day we were married. I still think of her as my English Rose.'

'Do you think she'll come up here? Bill said there'd be jobs for both of us if we wanted to stay once he returns.'

'I'm not keen on it. I'm not sure your mother would cope, plus the malaria, the bugs and the smell from those wretched volca-noes. Once Christmas and New Year is over, we'll have to head back home.'

Joanie wrinkled her nose at the acrid smell of sulphur pervading the still night air. 'But it's already nearly September, so it only leaves us a few more months. I love it here.'

'I know you do.'

Joanie cuddled into him, his arm coming up and folding around her shoulders. He kissed the top of her head. 'Enjoy the next few months, because I've already promised your mother we'll be back there for her birthday in February.'

Joanie sighed. It was only fair considering Mother had been

such a good sport. She promised herself though, one day, she would return to Rabaul, even if it were only for a visit. Maybe the two young soldiers they had entertained would also be heading back to Australia. After all there wasn't much for them to do here.

CHAPTER 48

Woombye – 1941

hile Reg and Joanie had been busy settling into their new life in Rabaul, brothers Peter and Andrew had also been busy tying up loose ends with their jobs, before signing up in Brisbane. The sergeant behind the desk had methodically raised his arm and brought the inky stamp down hard on their forms; *Taken on Strength.*

Peter's occupation was recorded as, *fitter and turner* and Andrew, *labourer.* Bags were packed and goodbyes said and with only a small amount of training, they were told they would be moving out. There had been another short visit back to Woombye to say their last goodbyes.

There was plenty of backslapping, hugs and tears as their brother and sisters gathered to say their goodbyes. and the brothers were surprised at the emotional farewell from their father. He hadn't spent much time with them over the years, as his job at the Post Office as well as the long list of jobs Ethel always had for him, took up every spare second of his day. Now his voice shook, and he tried hard to remain stoic.

'You both come back here now, you hear me. I've never told you this before but I'm mighty proud of both of you.' He peered around making sure his wife wasn't in earshot. 'Let's just say you haven't bowed to the pressures of your mother. You've carved your own lives. Now keep your heads down and look after each other.'

Their younger brothers and sisters gathered around as Ethel gave them both a long hug, declaring how proud she was for them to be fighting for God and country. Her words rang in their ears as they made their way up the main street to the train station.

'Who knows when we'll be back,' Peter said, throwing his bags up to Andrew who was already waiting on the step of the carriage. They stood in the doorway of the train, leaning outward, excited with the anticipation of where they might be headed. Their family gathered at the back of their house, which butted onto the railway line. They waved and blew kisses, a few of the younger ones running alongside the train as it chugged slowly past the last of the houses in town. Peter and Andrew called out, waving until the family, the backyard and their house was no longer visible.

* * *

There had been confusion to begin with, not only for Peter and Andrew, but also for many of the others in the battalion when they found out where they were being sent. They would sail for overseas duty on the *SS Neptuna,* departing Brisbane on the eighteenth of September.

When they signed up it had been with the expectation they would join the Australian forces in Europe, to fight in the trenches alongside the British, against the might of the German army as they marched across Europe. But now they were on a ship, the nose pointed to the north, the next stop, a town few had heard of.

'You're going to be setting up communications and buildings in Rabaul. We're unsure of the movements of the Japs in Asia and we need some monitoring systems set in place. You fellas are to be working on that. It won't take long and you'll be back home in a few months when it's all finished and then sent out to further areas where there are Germans who need to be dealt with.'

Peter was furious. 'I didn't sign up to go to some backwater, mossie infested area where the most dangerous people will be the natives. The only good part of this is that I might run into Joanie.'

Andrew, however, was happy with the situation. 'Jesus, this is suiting me, it sounds a bit more like a holiday than a war.'

And so the two boys boarded the ship, its horn sounding loudly as it sailed through the mouth of the Brisbane River. The sun rose above the ocean in front of them, the safe waters of Moreton Bay glistening, dolphins dancing alongside the bow of the ship. The horn sounded one more time, and Peter and Andrew looked back to get their last glimpse of the coastline of Australia, the men and cargo gliding across the calm waters of the Pacific Ocean towards the islands of New Guinea.

CHAPTER 49

September - Rabaul 1941

On September 29[th,] 1941, the last of the men who would make up Lark Force, disembarked from the *S S Neptuna*. Joanie was working, so was unable to be at the port with what seemed like everyone else in the town. Reg had gone with two of the other workers from the store and stood with hundreds of others who lined the street, waiting to catch a glimpse of the new regiment.

The group of newly arrived soldiers clustered on the wharf, milling in small groups, the noise from a band warming up and the shouts of workers and traders, adding to the confusion. A whistle sounded and the soldiers sorted themselves into lines, eventually ready to march. The band gathered momentum and soon loud marching music filled the streets as the troops gathered their belongings, marching past the gathered crowds and towards the town.

They stopped to shake hands or bob their head in greeting to the spectators, who cheered and clapped their arrival.

Reg was taken by surprise when a young man broke ranks and bounded towards him. There was no mistaking the cheeky grin and boisterous manner of Andrew O'Rourke, who shook Reg's hand and patted his back, before loudly stating that Peter was up ahead and had already gone past. His words were rushed and he gave a quick wave of his hat before jogging back alongside the group and slotting back into his original position.

Reg kept his eyes on Andrew's hat for as long as he could, his mind reeling as he took in the fact that both the boys had arrived in Rabaul. Wait until Joanie found out!

* * *

It had been quiet in the store that morning and Joanie had kept busy, rearranging the shelves and waiting patiently for her father to arrive back from the wharf. When he finally appeared, his face was red and his breathing short, as if he had been walking fast.

'Father, whatever is wrong? You look like you're ill. Why are you in such a hurry?'

He sat down and tried to get his breath, holding out his hand as Joanie poured him a glass of chilled water.

His sips were long and he looked over the top of the glass at Joanie, his bushy eyebrows moving up and down, as they did when he was excited about something. His breathing evened as the water cooled him down.

'Well, young lady. A new ship came to port today.'

She rolled her eyes and went back behind the counter, continuing to sort out the money in the drawer, relaxing now he had regained his breath. 'I know, Father. It's nothing new. It was the *Neptuna*. Even the locals who came to the side window an hour ago told me. I'm sorry but it's old news.'

'You would never guess who arrived with it.'

'The King of England, he's come to visit us.'

'No, you'll never guess.' He took huge gulps of water before plonking the glass down on the table beside him.

'Do tell me,' Joanie said, not even bothering to look up.

'The boys are there. They marched right past me.'

'I know there are new soldiers who've arrived with the ship.' She looked at her father. Perhaps the heat was getting to him.

'I said the boys have come with the new regiment.'

'What boys?'

'Peter and Andrew O'Rourke.'

'What!'

'Now you're listening to me.'

Joanie moved quickly from behind the counter, standing in front of him, her hands on his shoulders. 'Are you sure you're not affected by the heat? You're not making sense.'

'Remember the boys said they were going to join up. Well, here they are.'

* * *

It was only a matter of days before the brothers found an excuse to come to the Burns Philp store. There was boisterous hugging and laughter and Peter and Andrew had plenty to tell as they exchanged news on what had happened over the last year. The conversation turned to the topic of what the Germans were up to and how the boys, particularly Peter, were annoyed they were missing out on the action.

'I can tell you right now, if they think we'll be fit to protect this place were anything to happen ...' Andrew laughed, 'I mean, you don't have to be an expert to see the shortage of decent weaponry and the amount of terrain we're supposed to be defending. It's a bit of a joke!'

Peter butted in. 'This is between the four of us because you're not supposed to be repeating this, Andrew.'

'I couldn't care less. You only have to walk around to see what's happening. If they were serious about securing the island of New Britain, or for that matter New Guinea, they should ask the Yanks for help.'

'They wouldn't like the rotten egg smell,' Joanie said.

'We're all safe here,' Reg added. 'The talk is the Japanese have exhausted all their supplies and overextended themselves in China, so they've nothing left in their barrels for a war in the Pacific.'

'They'll have to rest up and build up their men and armoury before they even think of heading this way. Anyway, who'd want these islands?' Peter said, wrinkling up his nose.

The war was always on the tip of everyone's tongue and Joanie was getting tired of it. She was young and in love. At the moment, all she could think about was the next time she would see Michael.

The boys hugged Joanie before they left and shook Reg's hand. 'We won't be here for long,' Peter said. 'The Japs aren't coming this way. McArthur himself, is optimistic about the war in the Pacific and if he believes everything is alright, then that's good enough for me.'

The boys had taken a while to leave and Peter had tried to have a quiet conversation alone with Joanie, leaving Andrew and Reg to talk war. But Joanie made sure she kept the conversation general. She could tell from the way he looked at her nothing had changed and he probably thought Rabaul was as good as place as any to win her over. She smiled as they said their goodbyes, her mind still thinking ahead to the next outing with Michael.

* * *

The *Neptuna* had brought mail and although the arrival of the brothers had broken Reg's gloomy mood, he hadn't been himself since opening a letter from Edna.

Joanie sat silently, her heart sinking, as he read parts aloud. Edna was worried about the increasing hostilities in Asia and was spending a lot of time listening to the radio reports and reading the newspapers, both about Europe and the areas to the north of Australia.

Her apprehension was evident. *I have always encouraged you both to pursue your dreams and adventures, however I have started to have an uneasiness about the months to come. To my darling Reg, I miss you with all my heart and my sadness at your absence is overwhelming. I rarely ask for much, but this time I am asking you to return a little earlier so we can all be together again.'*

Reg had penned a response. He would appease Edna's concerns. His mind was set, and they would return in January, two months earlier than intended.

Joanie resigned herself to their imminent early departure. She sensed her father's angst. 'I'll be sad to leave, Father, but I also understand. I'll return one day.'

'Perhaps you will come back to Rabaul one day,' Reg said. 'But for me, once I return to your mother, I have no inclination to leave her side again. I am suffering from the separation and if it weren't for the fact I've given my word to Bill White to stay on until January, we would be leaving, perhaps on the ship in the harbour now.'

'I'm happy to stay until after Christmas. It only cuts our time here short by three months.' Joanie said.

'And are you pleased to be staying because of one handsome young drover, who has asked my permission to escort you to the movies tonight?'

Joanie blushed. 'It will be hard to leave Michael, but I'm a great believer in fate.' She gave her father a quick kiss on his cheek, her mind already on what she was going to wear tonight.

Joanie rustled through her wardrobe. She wanted to look her best and she laid four dresses out on the bed, trying to decide which one would show off her figure the best. She held them up to her body, one by one, peering at herself in the small mirror above the dressing table. She flattened her eyebrows, pinching her cheeks for the desired look. Never before had she been so intent on impressing someone. She laughed out loud, spinning around, the chosen floral dress held tight to her body. It was magical being young, living on a tropical island and meeting a young man who caused her heart to beat faster and butterflies to flutter in her stomach.

CHAPTER 50

Over the next month, Peter and Andrew settled into army life in Rabaul. Their camp was a short distance from town, and when they could get a leave pass they'd come in to visit Joanie and Reg. Although Rabaul was spread out and the boys were kept busy with their duties, it had not escaped Peter that Joanie had been seen around town with another young man from Lark Force.

He comforted himself with the fact that she'd been out with other men before and this was most likely someone to fill in the time with. It was an unexpected opportunity to land in the same town as she was, although his plans of courting her were being foiled because every time he asked her out, she already had other plans.

Peter had encountered the young man Joanie was friends with when he visited the store.

* * *

He'd hesitated only briefly once he reached Burns Philp, straightening his uniform before striding confidently up the front steps, his hand raised to push open the front door. At the same time another man came from inside the store, swinging the door open and nearly running straight into Peter.

They looked hard at each other. The man who had come out of the store stretched out his hand, a friendly smile on his face. 'G'day you must be one of the brothers from Joanie's hometown. I'm Michael.'

Peter was lost for words for a moment, trying to work out who he was talking to.

He put his arm out and the two men shook hands, both of their grips strong, neither of them letting go. 'Pleased to meet you, Michael.' Peter said. 'How did you know who I was?'

'Joanie saw you coming through the window. She told me your name.'

'That's right, we've known each other for many years. I'm very close to her and her father.'

'She said you were. It must be great to catch up again. Such a small town and so many of us stationed here.'

Peter relaxed a little as they stood and chatted. Michael explained what he'd been working on for the last few months while Peter asked about some of the other military buildings on the island.

'You know the area well,' Peter said.

'The war is a long way off and sometimes you need to pass the time. I spend a lot of my spare time up in the hills. There's a lot to explore and some magnificent views.' He looked at his watch. 'I'll need to get going. There's been complaints about the poor discipline in our group, so we're all trying to be more orderly.'

'That sounds like our crew. Most of the men can't even get to the afternoon parade on time and there's been a complaint about the drunkenness of a few of the fellows who came into town last night.'

* * *

Inside, Joanie kept busy, rearranging items on a shelf. She kept checking on Michael and Peter through a slit in the curtain. For goodness sake, what were they talking about and why was Peter being so friendly? She hadn't counted on the two of them meeting each other. Surely in a town, thousands of miles from home, she could go unnoticed having a romantic relationship.

Michael and Peter talked for a bit longer, their conversation audible through the open windows. 'Camp duties can get a bit boring and then there's the terrible food they serve up,' Peter said.

Michael laughed. 'The markets are the place to go for the fresh food or even better, the restaurants run by the Chinese.'

'I know,' Peter said, his laughter causing Joanie to look out through the curtain again. 'My brother Andrew opened a tin of biscuits the other day and the label was from the Great War. Now I'm not sure how long biscuits keep, but there was no way we were eating them. We fed them to the chooks out the back who weren't keen on them either. One of them kept spitting out the crumbs.'

'It would be good to have one of your brothers with you.'

'He's the younger one. Getting into trouble without even trying. Why he's down at the swimming pool right now, running bets on the swim races he's organised.'

'I have a twin brother, Dan, and he was always the one to get in trouble in our family.' The two men talked some more and then shook hands.

'I'm likely to run into you back at camp but if I don't, we should all meet up for a feed somewhere,' Peter said.

'We could meet in one of the pubs in town. They're double the price of the army canteen, but it's cool in there and the seats are a sight more comfortable than those benches we normally sit on.'

Joanie quickly pulled back from the curtain as the two men parted, the frown on her face disappearing as she busied herself behind the counter.

* * *

Peter watched Michael walk back down the main street. He seemed like a good bloke and if he took Joanie out a few times while they were all stationed here, he wasn't that worried. Joanie had probably dated a few of the soldiers in Rabaul but she had never been serious about anyone before. Once they were all back in Woombye, Peter knew he would be the one to win her over. Dates with blokes like Michael were just giving her something to do to pass the time until she returned home.

He turned and walked into the store. Perhaps it might be a good idea for him to hold back from her, to pretend he didn't really care who she went out with. If he didn't act interested in her, then she would want him more and worry she might have missed her chance. To arouse her jealousy, he might even ask one of the nurses out from the hospital. He ran his hands through his hair, put his shoulders back and walked confidently towards the counter. There was plenty of time and he had lots of ideas to play on. He would win Joanie in the end and once they were back in Queensland everything would fall into place.

CHAPTER 51

Rabaul - November 1941

Peter was not happy about being sent to Rabaul, however Andrew was having a ball. Over the last two months he had visited every shop in Chinatown and was a well-known character at the 'Bung', which was the busy market, right in the middle of the town. He loved nothing more than to barter with the women and tell jokes to the men. One of them wrapped a traditional sarong around Andrew's waist, the onlookers clapping hands and laughing at him as he swayed his hips and danced.

Peter was not impressed with his younger brother's behaviour and one afternoon he related some of Andrew's antics to Joanie and Reg. They sat together in the cool of the verandah, the house *meri* bringing them a cold drink each. 'He takes all his money to the two-up game he runs and then spends all his winnings on Castlemaine Beer.'

'There's nothing wrong with supporting a local Queensland

business,' Reg said, laughing and shaking his head. 'What's wrong with spending a penny or two?'

'It would be alright if it was just one penny, but he spends a lot more than that. The canteen is making a fortune out of him, that is his winnings. Last night he was like a performer. Someone pulled out their mouth organ and another bloke banged on some saucepans. Andrew was up on the table dancing, moving his hips around and swinging wildly. I don't know where he picked up such behaviour.'

'Oh, I've seen him dance like that.' Joanie said, realising too late she had said too much. She sat stony-faced as both her father and Peter looked her way. 'Sometimes when he came to Brisbane we'd go out dancing, that's all. There's nothing wrong with that, is there?'

Joanie walked away from them to stop further discussion. Peter had been polite to her after meeting Michael on the steps of the store the previous week. Before that he had continually asked her out, but she had always declined, telling him she had a lot on at work or needed to be at home with her father. Now it was as if he was resigned to the fact she was being taken out by someone else. His behaviour was confusing and she was suspicious about why he had given in so easily.

There had been another awkward meeting when she had gone with Michael to watch some of the servicemen play cricket against the civilian workers in the town. The cricket match was in full swing when she and Michael arrived. It had been a highly competitive match and most of the town had turned out to watch the two sides play. She had spotted Andrew first, collecting bets on the far side of the field. A noisy bunch of young men who had arrived, caused her to look around and straight into the eyes of Peter. Once again he had been friendly and appeared not to worry that Joanie and Michael were there together.

When he left, his parting words to Michael were to not forget to catch up for a beer with him and Andrew. Joanie was quiet as they sat and watched the end of the match. She was confused by Peter's attitude. Had she imagined it or had Peter declared his love for her before she had left for Rabaul. Now he was acting as if he was resigned to the fact she had met someone else and wasn't at all worried she was avoiding going out with him.

'Past boyfriend?' Michael interrupted her thoughts.

'Not really, well only when we were teenagers. I'm good friends with both Peter and Andrew. They're like my brothers. And speak of the devil.' Joanie moved quickly out of the way as Andrew came flying out of nowhere and plonked himself on the picnic rug between them.

'Ah, the beautiful Joanie. And who do we have here? You appear to be on a date, young lady. I hope your father knows about this.' Andrew shook hands with Michael, leaning over to give Joanie a kiss on the cheek. He sent a cheeky wink her way, his speech jovial and a little slurred. 'This here is the most eligible and gorgeous young lady, not only here in Rabaul but also in the entire southern hemisphere. I hope you treat her well because you'll have to deal with me if you don't.'

'Oh for goodness sake, Andrew, how many beers have you had?' Joanie asked.

'Not enough, my dear, there's still more money to be won. Look at those office fellows toss the ball. Half of them have never played cricket before.'

Andrew placed his arm around Michael's shoulders, as if he had known him for as long as he'd known Joanie. 'Are your intentions honourable?' He tried to look serious, nearly falling sideways as he tried to keep his balance.

Michael laughed back and pretended to punch Andrew in the arm. 'She's safe with me and yes my intentions are sincere. You're putting on a good show of protecting her, but I hate to say it, you're very wobbly even when you're sitting down.'

Andrew looked down at his feet, his body swaying unsteadily as he tried to get up.

Michael took his arm and manoeuvred him back onto the rug. 'Sit with us for a bit longer. Here.' He pulled out his canteen of water. 'Have some water and finish off this food. You'll thank me tomorrow morning.' Andrew took huge gulps of water and scoffed down the sandwiches Joanie had made for the day. He laughed and chatted with them, and after a while he put his head down on the rug. 'I'll have a kip. Five minutes will fix me up.'

Joanie looked at him as he slept, placing her hat over his face to shield him from the sun filtering through the canopy of the trees above.

'He gets himself in trouble,' she told Michael. 'He's the wilder of the two.'

'He reminds me of my brother, Dan. So full of energy and that big happy grin lighting up his face.'

The three of them had stayed on the rug until the last ball was bowled and the sun started to sink behind the mountains. Joanie nudged Andrew to wake him, both she and Michael laughing as he shook his head and looked around, for a moment lost as to where he was.

'Aha.' He pulled his hand through his thick hair; much the same way Peter always did. 'Just had a short nap. It's been a big day.' He jumped up, hugging both Joanie and Michael. 'I'll leave you two young lovers, now I'm off to collect my winnings. By the way, who won?'

CHAPTER 52

Over the next few weeks, Joanie and Michael took every opportunity to be together. Sometimes they would walk a short distance into the jungle, Michael pointing out the different plants and trees Birri had shown him. One afternoon Michael led Joanie down to the waterfront, the narrow path leading them to a quiet secluded area behind the rocks and trees. They sat together on a blanket Michael spread out on the sand.

The surface of the ocean sparkled with the last rays of the afternoon sun and seabirds called out to each other, their squawks echoing across the beach as they dived and plunged into the dark water. The pristine waters were brimming with fish of every variety and Joanie and Michael watched the birds resurface with shiny silver fish dangling from their beaks.

'They make it look so easy.' Michael said. 'Maybe we should get some rods and try fishing ourselves one day.'

Joanie turned her gaze away from the birds and towards Michael. 'Father and I are booked to leave not long after Christmas. I'm not sure when I will see you again after that.'

Michael reached over and stroked her arm, his brown eyes

dark in the afternoon light. 'I want you to know I care very much for you, Joanie. You've become a special person in my life and I won't want to say goodbye. But I will also leave here soon, and who knows where I'll go next.'

Her voice was a whisper. 'There is so much uncertainty.'

She looked up into his eyes and her body ached as he bent down and kissed her. His lips were soft and she kissed him back, his strong arms wrapping around her.

This time her voice was strong and steady. 'I will wait for you. I haven't known you for long, but I will wait until you return or a time when we can be together.'

He caressed her arm, his tender hands playing with the edges of her sleeves, his eyes never leaving hers. He stroked her cheeks and they kissed again, their arms entwining around each other. Above them the squawking of birds blended into the background, the continual wash of the ocean waves onto the beach, a soothing dreamy sound.

When they finally drew away from each other and their lips parted, Michael spoke softly. 'I have something to tell you. I haven't been completely honest with you, but I'm in love with you and this is probably going to wreck everything.'

'What is it, Michael? Nothing is that bad. What could possible destroy the way we feel about each other?'

He cleared his throat before speaking. 'I have a daughter, a small daughter who is six-years-old.'

'You mean you're married.' Joanie pulled her arm away from his, the tone of her voice changing, a shocked look on her face.

'No, oh, my God, this sounds so terrible. But no, I'm not married. I've separated from her mother and we were never married.

* * *

The moon had started to rise over the ocean, a golden beam of light reflected across the glossy water. Joanie was glad she'd told her father they would be home late, because once Michael started telling his story, he couldn't stop.

The droving, missing his family, the circus, Layla, the disgrace and guilt he carried with him always, and then...Gracie. It had been a long story and Joanie held his hand as he spoke, wanting him to continue.

When he finished talking, he reached into his pocket, pulling out a small leather pouch that held some black and white photos. He flicked through them until he found the one he wanted and passed it to Joanie. It was a photo of Gracie, smiling, holding tight to her favourite doll. Dark curly hair framed a chubby face and cute dimples were indented either side of her mouth.

'She's adorable and so little. You have many reasons to return home, Michael. No matter what happens, remember that.'

'And now there is you. But how will this work? I've made a mess of life, let down my parents and left Gracie behind. Perhaps this was an escape.' He waved his hand around, his voice shaky.

'You haven't made a mess of your life. We all make mistakes at one time or another. And all of this has led you here to Rabaul, and,' she leaned over and stroked his face, 'it has led you to me. It will work out.'

'You sound so sure of that.'

'Of course I am. If you believe in something, you'll get there in the end.'

Michael didn't sound convinced. 'I'm sorry, Joanie, but life doesn't always go how you want it to. Believe me, I know.'

A dark cloud drifted across the moon and when they finished talking Joanie wrapped her arms around him and held him close. His lips pressed against the softness of her face and they kissed passionately, only remembering where they were and how long they'd been there, when the water started lapping at their toes.

'Whatever happens, wherever we go, I will wait for you,' Joanie reassured him. 'I will help you with Gracie and together we can raise her.' She stared at the small photo. 'I love her already. She's your baby. When the war is over and we meet up again, I want you to have Gracie with you. Bring her to me and from there everything else can be worked out.'

Michael tucked the worn photo back in the leather pouch. 'Layla may not want to part with her so easily. I'm not sure why, but she would never let me take her back to my family. Even though she was so harsh towards her, she didn't want me to have her.'

'Maybe it's a mother's attachment, I mean what mother would not want a beautiful little girl like that?'

CHAPTER 53

Melbourne - November 1941

In Fitzroy, the moon rose high above the red rooftops. Gracie sat at the window, her tiny face turned towards the sky. She closed her eyes and talked to her absent father, telling him what she had been doing. Turning towards the brightest star, she pressed her face up against the cracked window pane. Her mouth made a foggy mark on the glass and she wiped it with her hand. 'Mother said we're going on a holiday. She said she'd written to you and told you that. I asked her if you wrote letters to me and she said no. I guess you're busy being a soldier.'

The sound of her own voice was comforting, and she talked non-stop, telling her father everything she could think of. She hated it when mother left her at home by herself like this, locking the main door after she left. On those nights when she was alone, Gracie cried or spent most of the time at the window talking to her father, wishing with all her heart he was lying next to her in bed, reading her favourite book.

She pulled out the book, *Black Beauty*, the story tumbling off her tongue. *'I hope you will grow up gentle and good, and never learn bad ways; do your work with a good will, lift your feet up well when you trot, and never bite or kick even in play.'*

Blustery clouds raced across the night sky. The moonbeam disappeared, leaving Gracie alone in the dark. Mother had said the lights wouldn't work because they hadn't paid their bills. Mother said it was Father's fault and he'd left them with no money and they were poor because of him. Gracie wanted to speak, to defend her father, but she knew better than to incur Layla's wrath. Why, if they were so poor, did Layla have new clothes and also new jewellery, draped around her arms and neck? Sometimes she was so angry with her mother, that in her mind she called her Layla. Once she had spoken the name out loud, the result a quick slap across the face, her mother's hand always finding its mark.

Gracie sat still in the gloom, her body rigid, the closed book now abandoned on the bed beside her. She looked up to the bright star, shining beyond the edge of the clouds. Like so many other nights she clenched her eyes tight and concentrated, thinking of her father and wishing he would come back and take her away. She didn't want to go on a holiday and Mother said she was only to take a few clothes. She had said she wasn't allowed anything else and had grabbed Gracie's doll from under her arm. 'We need to get rid of that before we go. You're a big girl now, six-years-old. We don't want people thinking you're a baby. And only talk to people when they ask you a question.'

'What people?' Gracie asked. Layla never took her anywhere or let her see visitors who came to their home anyway. 'Father taught me the best manners ever.' She had stopped talking immediately, when she saw the savage look in Layla's eyes at the mention of her father.

'Your father has gone away. It's best you forget about him,

young lady, because he told me he's not ever coming back. He doesn't care for you, and I can tell you right now it would be better for you if you wiped him from your memory.'

Gracie felt like she wanted to vomit, but she bit her lip and stuck her chin out. Even when Layla's flat hand stretched out and then drew back before the usual slap, she stood without flinching, staring into her mother's mean face. That was the other strange thing. In the last couple of weeks, Layla had stopped hitting her. Some of the recent bruises, caused by her mother's dreadful temper, had healed. She liked the way her arms and legs looked without the red and blue patches on them.

When her father had been with them, Layla had not hit her, instead pinching or digging her long fingernails into her flesh when he wasn't looking. She told Gracie if she spoke to her father about the pinching, she would have her sent away to a children's home, where she would never see him again.

Once Father had left, Gracie had copped it. It didn't matter how quiet she kept or how much she tried to please Layla, the swinging hand or sometimes her mother's pointy shoes would find a place on her body. The last time she had been hit was when she asked when her father was coming back. Layla had gone red in the face and lashed out, striking Gracie hard in the middle of her back. She had fallen forward into a wooden chair, the corner of it tearing a small strip of skin from her face. It had been hard to breathe, and she sat still gasping for air. Layla had thrown a wet cloth at her and told her to clean her face up.

'You're winded. Pretend he's dead,' Layla snarled at Gracie. 'Because he's never coming back here.'

Layla went out after that, the front door slamming shut behind her, the key turning in the lock. Gracie was left sitting on the floor, holding the damp cloth to her stinging face. The room spun around her and the sounds of her mother's high-heeled shoes, clip clopping over the cobbled footpath resonated in her ears. When it became dark, she went to her bedroom, the middle of her back throbbing and her face stinging, even with the washer held tight. She sat at the window for a long time that night, looking at the star.

At first, she sat silently, the tears rolling down her face, little sobs making her shudder. After a while the star shone brighter, and the light from it pointed straight at her. In her head she heard words.

'You never take the trouble to see if he will go without it; your whip is always going as if you had the St. Vitus' dance in your arm, and if it does not wear you out it wears your horse out.'

Gracie wiped her eyes. They were the words from her book, *Black Beauty*. Stars didn't normally talk. She squeezed her eyes shut and listened hard. She jumped up and found her book, using the glow from the streetlight opposite to read. She read out loud, remembering the words she had read so many times with her father.

'You know you are always changing your horses; and why? Because you never give them any peace or encouragement."

Well, I have not had good luck, said Larry, that's where it is.'

Gracie stopped and waited and sure enough, other words came into her mind.

"Good Luck is rather particular who she rides with, and mostly prefers those who have got common sense and a good heart; at least that is my experience."

She started to forget about Layla's beatings and her stinging face, instead concentrating on the story she read. Now, she was calm, the words soothing and the light from the star consoling even after the book was finished. She pulled herself up onto her thin mattress and pulled the covers up, tucking the book in beside her to keep her company during the night.

* * *

Layla did not come home that night or the next. Perhaps she was dead. Maybe they'd never get to go on that holiday. Now it didn't even matter what Gracie was allowed or not allowed to eat. Pangs of hunger stretched tight across her stomach and for the next two days she ate whatever she could find. She ate the last of the biscuits in the tin, screwing up her nose at their stale taste. An orange that had found its way to the back of the fruit box made for lunch. At night she wet a washer with some water and scrubbed her face and hands, before getting into bed and pulling the covers up high so she didn't feel scared.

When she woke up after the second night she could hear Layla in the kitchen. The unusual sound of her mother singing filtered up to her where she lay in her bed. Gracie closed her eyes tight. Maybe her father was in the kitchen, making her eggs for breakfast like he used to do.

But it was not so and before long Layla came to the door, her shrill voice sounding the same as always. 'I'm taking you to get a haircut and we need to buy you a hat. Get out your clothes. Show me what you have.'

Gracie got out of bed. Layla didn't say where she'd been and there was no way after the last beating she was going to ask any questions.

Her mother yelled loudly, 'I said, get out of bed.'

Gracie tried to move faster but her body shook. She kept her eyes down, her feet cold from the bare floorboards. Her stomach growled with hunger and she cringed, waiting for Layla's hand across her face or body. But Layla was busy looking through the timber crate where her clothes were kept. 'There's nothing suitable in here for you to wear. I'll have to buy a dress and hat for you.' Her voice changed and took on a sickly sweet tone. 'Come here, my lovely little girl, let me look at you.'

Gracie stood still while Layla turned her around. 'You look fine. Now make sure you don't fall over anymore, I don't want any marks on you.'

'I don't fall over.'

Layla scowled and brought her hand up to slap her. Gracie pulled back, turning her head to the side. But Layla drew her hand back and clenched her teeth. Her voice took on a different tone. It didn't sound normal and Gracie wondered if her mother was ill. 'Hurry up and go and get your breakfast, I can't do everything for you. You and I are going to go on that holiday I told you about.'

'When?'

'We'll go in a day or two. I need to get a dress and hat for you.' Layla said, a strange sneer plastered across her face. 'Now practise your best behaviour and use your manners. Stand up straight and remember, don't speak unless you're spoken to. Pack your bag because you're going to have a wonderful time.'

CHAPTER 54

It was exciting to be going on a holiday, but Gracie was curious as to why Layla was being so nice. When she saw her mother throwing her doll into the metal rubbish tin outside their house, she became even more worried. Once Layla went out, Gracie crept downstairs and retrieved the doll from the bin. Luckily nothing smelly had been tipped in after her and she only had to brush some dirt and leaves from her clothes.

Father had bought the doll for her and they had named it Suzie. Gracie had become clever at hiding items she liked from Layla, and as soon as she retrieved Suzie from the bin she crawled under her bed, sliding on her stomach to find a hiding place to keep the doll safe. She pushed the old boxes and suitcases away that were stashed there. Behind them, and in amongst the dust was a small tin that even at an early age she had been smart enough to hide from Layla's prying eyes. Father had told her to hide it before he left and had shown her how to push it right to the back, where Layla would never look or clean.

Inside the small tin were photos of Gracie and Father, and Gracie looked at them as she lay in the dim light under the bed.

Because of Layla's violent and often unpredictable nature, Gracie had learnt to be cunning and was careful to protect herself and the things she loved. She learned not to answer back and no matter what, to never show her the tin box or to talk to her about anything she and her father had discussed before he left.

She held a small black and white photo up close so she could see it properly. It was a photo of her father taken in front of a big circus tent, the big banner saying, 'Wirth's Circus.' Her father had taught her the words. Together they had practised the sounds the letters made and she whispered the name now, remember the sound the 't' and the 'h' made when they were next to each other. She kissed the photo before carefully placing it back in the tin.

There was another photo in the tin and this time her father was holding her in his arms. She was a baby and his arms were wrapped around her, her head snuggled into his shoulder. She stared at the photo for a long time before putting it back. She had to wriggle out backwards to get out from under the bed, her dress picking up all the dirt as she edged out holding fast to the tin.

She placed it under the lining of her small suitcase. The doll would have to take its chances, wrapped up in one of her knitted jumpers and pushed to the bottom. Gracie wondered if they were going on holidays or if they were going to move. She had heard a conversation between Layla and the lady downstairs a few weeks ago. Layla had told the lady the flat might become empty as a friend of hers from the theatre had asked her to come and live with him.

Maybe they were going to move somewhere else and perhaps the man from the theatre would be nice and help her write a letter to her father. She hadn't met any of Layla's friends when they came to visit, because Layla always locked her in her bedroom before her friends arrived. She could hear them when Layla first let them in and then when they were in the small lounge room. It would have been exciting to sneak out and see what they looked like, but Layla always made sure her key was taken away.

She should have been able to spy through the empty keyhole, but there was a little metal latch that swung down once the key was removed, blocking her vision. There was however a crack in the timber of the door and if she put her face right up close, she could catch a glimpse of the men who arrived to visit Layla.

The men were always happy, laughing and talking loudly. They liked to dance and sing and drank out of bottles that were always scattered around the room in the morning. The friends never stayed long in the lounge room though and Gracie couldn't work out where they went. The only other room was Layla's bedroom and no-one, not even Gracie or her father was allowed to go in there.

Sometimes she could hear muffled sounds, so they must still be there. She never met any of them because her door remained locked until they left the next day. This wasn't a bad arrangement though, because in her room she could sit at her window or read her book for as long as she liked.

CHAPTER 55

One morning Layla yelled at Gracie to get dressed and have her bag ready. They were leaving. Going on a holiday. Gracie wore a new dress, hat and shoes. When they left the flat, Layla held her hand, pulling her along and making her walk fast. The small suitcase swung at her side as she tried to keep up with her mother and they made their way out of their street and towards the tram stop. A red tram was waiting and Layla pulled Gracie up behind her, both of them stepping onto the carriage.

Gracie sat still, curious and excited about being on a tram and going somewhere for a holiday. The tram stopped and started, metal wheels clattering along the lines crisscrossing the streets of Melbourne.

Eventually they pulled up outside a building with huge rounded domes on the roof. A large clock peered down and she stared back at it, hoping the hands would move as she looked. But they didn't and Layla pushed her along in front of her, pressing through the throngs of people who, like Layla and Gracie, crowded onto the corners waiting to cross the busy streets.

Gracie had to do little skips and sometimes run to keep up with

Layla who gripped her hand and pulled her next to her. Her mother wore her best dress, pretty gloves and a new hat to match. She also wore make-up. This holiday must be at a nice place, as both she and Layla wore their best clothes. She asked numerous times where they were going, but her questions were ignored and after a while, Layla's cutting looks kept her silent.

Inside the train station it was just as busy and hundreds of commuters hurriedly made their way to their designated platform. Layla seemed to know where she was going and Gracie waited in line while her mother bought their tickets. She was surrounded by tall people. Ladies and men who didn't even look down at her, their faces staring straight ahead. The men looked smart, dressed in dark suits and straight ties, leather briefcases at their sides. Their hair was slicked back and they didn't smile but instead looked at where they were headed. The women wore long dresses and large hats, their hair piled up high on their head, their elegant shoes shiny and pointed as they walked along the platform.

She found herself staring at their shoes. It was better to look down, as her neck ached from staring upwards at so many different people. It would be easy to get lost amongst the crowds and for once she was glad Layla was hanging onto her as they approached the platform. Her mother gripped tighter as she pushed Gracie in front, up onto the train that would take them on their holiday.

* * *

The leather seats on the train were hard and people sat upright, moving quickly to fill the last of them. When there weren't enough, they leaned against the walls or hung onto the grips swinging from the ceiling. Layla sat straight, her face stern, her voice terse as she told Gracie to sit still and behave. Before long the train began moving, easing out of the chaos of the station, chugging through a tunnel and out into the sunny streets of Melbourne.

Layla was not likely to hit her with so many people around, so it was worth the risk of getting up on her knees, perching on the seat and looking out the window of the train. The streets of Melbourne were full of cars and people, pedestrians weaving their way through the traffic and trams, everyone in a hurry. Tram lines criss-crossed the wide streets, and red trams wove their way down the middle, the wires attached to the top of them, guiding them and moving them along. A policeman stood in the intersection of the road, his uniform dark and distinguished as he blew his whistle. He stopped some cars and waved others through as Gracie pushed her face harder against the window, trying to look back at him for as long as she could as the train moved onwards.

The train chugged through stations crowded with people, perhaps waiting to go on holidays just like her. A small boy on a platform in amongst the adults stared at her, the carriages clattering as they passed slowly through the station. She peered back through the splotchy window, waving at him until he smiled and waved back.

Soon the streets became less busy and the large city buildings were replaced by rows and rows of houses. Some of them looked like the one Gracie lived in, while others were bigger houses, joined together and painted in different colours. Their gardens were beautiful, brimming with tall roses and climbing bushes that rambled over wooden arches, introducing the home to the pavement. She saw a lady in a long dress, sitting on a bench in a back yard, reading a book to a girl. The pair looked up as the train passed, both laughing as the girl waved to the people passing by. Gracie put her hand up to wave back, but Layla pulled it down, hissing at her to sit still.

She pushed her face against the cold glass, peering at the different yards. Picket fences bordered grounds filled with flowering trees and shrubs, their colours bright against the backdrop of the houses. The street they had lived in was grey and dirty and there weren't any flowers growing, only a floor of concrete and an occasional weed pushing its straggly head up through the cracks. The houses they passed in the train were pretty and if she craned her neck she could watch the people who walked along the road. The streets narrowed again and the train moved through areas with high fences running alongside the railway line. The houses here looked a lot more like the ones where she lived, darker, drearier and no flowers or ladies in pretty long dresses in their back yards.

Soon the houses became even older, their fronts boarded up, their windows covered with cardboard or cloth instead of glass or timber. The train slowed as it approached a crossing. There were groups of children playing in the streets, their clothes even older than hers, their hair standing up like it hadn't ever been brushed. They stood together in a ragged bunch, their legs and faces covered in dirt. One of the small boys poked his tongue and Gracie did the same. Her tongue pushed up against the window and Layla who had been watching, pulled her back down into her seat.

She whispered in Gracie's ear. 'If it wasn't for me, that's where you'd end up. Dirty and hungry, like those brats. Now sit down and behave.' Gracie's eyes flicked back and forth around the train, watching the other people who weren't paying any attention to anyone else anyway. She wanted to look out the window, there was so much to see, but Layla's hand rested on her leg and she could feel her nails digging in. A warning, to do as she was told.

When it was dinnertime, Layla placed a small box on Gracie's lap. Inside was a sandwich and biscuit which she ate quickly, picking up even the smallest crumbs that managed to escape her mouth and fall into the box.

'At least you eat like an adult,' Layla spoke for the first time in many hours. 'Your father did one thing right.'

Gracie didn't answer. She wanted to ask again, if her father knew where they were going on holidays. But the threat of Layla's quick hand silenced her and she continued to eat, looking through the window at the suburbs changing from rows of houses and streets to farms with old buildings and hills, dotted with sheep and cows. Before dark she thought she could see the ocean, but the light was fading and the movement of the train made it hard for her eyes to stay open. She looked at Layla whose head was tilted to one side, her mouth wide open and a tiny bit of dribble running down from her mouth. Gracie giggled and then put her hand over her mouth as Layla stirred and moved a bit in her seat.

The best times were when Layla was asleep. That was when Gracie could concentrate and talk to the sky, to her father. Tonight though, she could not find her star. She needed to be on the other side of the train. That would involve climbing over Layla and she didn't want to run the risk of waking her. She closed her eyes, picturing the star in her mind and saying silently the words of her *Black Beauty* book. Soon she fell asleep, her head resting on Layla's shoulder. For anyone looking on it could have been the perfect picture of mother and daughter love.

The noise of the train slowing in the early morning woke both Gracie and Layla. 'We've stopped,' Gracie said, pushing her hair back from her eyes and stretching her legs that had been tucked underneath her through the night. She turned towards Layla and laughed.

Layla's eyes narrowed and she glared at Gracie. 'What?'

'That black stuff you wear on your eyes is all over your face. It looks funny.' Gracie giggled again, drawing back when she saw Layla's hand come up. Once again though, her hand stopped and instead she smiled, pulling out a small mirror from her purse. By the time they pulled into the station, Layla had fixed her hair and face and she led Gracie off the train and along the platform until they came to a restroom. She made her change into her best clothes and put her new hat on. 'We want you to look your best and remember to sound grown up, we don't want you to be a baby.'

'I'm not a baby. I'm six-years-old and I can read.'

Layla frowned and grabbed her hand, walking to the area outside the station where she hailed a taxi. They sat in the back seat and although Gracie asked a couple of times where they were going and were they nearly there, no words came from her mother's tight lips.

The taxi wove through the streets, stopping outside a tall house. The house they had pulled up to and those next to it, had front yards full of pretty flowers and plants, their fences painted in clean colours. She clung hard to her tiny suitcase, wondering if this was where they would spend their holiday. Following Layla through a fancy gate and then along a concrete path with rows of white flowers either side, she stopped suddenly, causing Layla to pull at her hand. This garden had a small statue of a girl holding a bucket, with water coming out of the top it. Its gurgling noise reminded Gracie of the sound of the water when it went down the plughole. Layla leaned down towards Gracie, straightening her hat and then her clothes. She even pulled Gracie's socks up. 'Where does the water go?' she asked. Her mother didn't even turn to look at the statue, her dark eyes narrowing as she glared at Gracie.

'Don't ask stupid questions. Just keep your mouth closed and only talk when you have to.'

Layla stood up tall, adjusted her hair and hat, before knocking with the big brass handle attached to the front door.

It didn't take long before a lady opened the door. She was very tall and graceful, her stylish clothes matching the elegance of the house they entered. She introduced herself as Dawn and smiled at Gracie before ushering them into a room full of heavy wooden furniture. Gracie's didn't know what to look at first; there were so many beautiful things. She stopped to look at ornaments that caught her eye, china animals filling the shelves of a large glass cabinet. But Layla pulled on her hand, nearly making her trip. She scowled, annoyed Layla wouldn't let her stop. What sort of holiday was this if she couldn't even look at the pretty things in a cabinet?

A man with a large moustache sat in one of the red velvet chairs, the arms and legs of rosewood timber carved with intricate patterns. Gracie looked down at her feet, her polished brown shoes, plain against the pretty red and pink patterns of a large rug. She couldn't help herself and stared hard at the chandelier hanging right above where she and Layla stood. Hundreds of tiny crystals hung in patterns, the sunlight from a nearby window passing through them, creating rainbows that filtered across the floor near to where the man sat.

'And this is Henry,' Dawn introduced the man who held out his hand to Gracie. Layla took the small suitcase from Gracie and pushed her forward, causing her to stumble a little before regaining her balance and going over to the man. He had large bushy eyebrows that went up and down every time he spoke and his moustache was long and wispy.

'What is your name, young lady?' he asked.

'Gracie.'

'And how old are you?'

'Six.'

Gracie looked straight into his eyes, which were brown and set deep in his face.

He looked for a long time at Gracie and then smiled. 'Welcome, young lady. Welcome to Rosewood House.'

Gracie wanted to ask him about the fancy light, but she remembered Layla's warning about not talking, so nodded instead, her eyes still wandering over the room at the objects that filled it.

'Would you like to look in the china cabinet? I could see you wanted to when you passed it,' the man said.

He stood up and Gracie followed him back to the cabinet, where he turned a small key, opening the door so she could see the ornaments up closer. 'Perhaps Dawn can show you some of the precious things while your mother and I talk.'

A variety of ornaments filled the cabinet and Gracie sat on the soft rug as Dawn passed them to her to hold. Layla had disappeared with Henry although after a short while he returned by himself. His voice was gruff and he squatted down next to his wife.

He held up a china horse, turning it around, examining it for chips or breaks. 'This one is perfect,' he said. 'It can be yours.' He passed it to Gracie whose mouth was wide open, her hand closing around the ornament.

'You'll have to choose a name.' Dawn's voice was soft. 'What would you like to call him?'

'Black Beauty,' Gracie whispered as she stroked the mane of the horse, which she held with both hands.

Dawn and her husband stood up, watching as she stroked the smooth back of the china horse. Henry's arm wrapped around his wife's shoulders. He whispered to her, however Gracie had sharp ears and she could hear what he said. 'She didn't even look back. She took the payment and left.' His voice was one of disgust and he shook his head, his words silenced as his wife hushed him.

Gracie stared at them, their faces unfamiliar, voices that she didn't know. Her eyes flitted around the room looking for Layla. She hated her mother, but at least she was a connection to her father. She couldn't see her, and she sat rigidly, her stomach swirling, a strange sensation, a tightness in her head. She had become used to being left by herself at home but she had never been left with people she didn't know.

She stared at the horse, not knowing where else to look as she waited for Layla to reappear. Her thoughts were broken when Henry crouched down next to her. 'Now, how about some ice-cream and jelly to start the holiday. Your mother has gone for a while, so we should go into the kitchen. Elsa is our cook and I know she's been getting lots of yummy food ready for you to eat.'

Gracie didn't speak. She took Henry's large hand and grasping onto the horse with the other, followed him into the kitchen.

CHAPTER 57

Gracie didn't speak for the first few days. She wanted to ask when her mother was coming back and was this where they were staying for holidays, but Layla had said not to talk too much, so she remained silent. Even when she was shown her bedroom and her feet sunk into the plush carpet, she never uttered a word. The room smelt like the roses in Dawn's garden and she stood and stared at pictures of other pretty flowers that hung on the wall. Her bedspread was soft, like a puffy cushion and patterned with pink kittens, each one in a different position of play. She particularly liked the one lying on its back, its soft padded paws reaching out from the fabric to her.

***

Soon she settled into her new life. There was a white dressing table with a matching white chair. When she sat in the chair she could see herself in the mirror. On the dressing table was a tray with a small mirror, a brush and a comb, the handles and backs inlaid with a white patterned stone. Dawn told her it was called ivory. Pretty new dresses filled a wardrobe, their patterned flowery fabric hanging from coat hangers that were covered in the same fabric as her bedspread. A chest of drawers stored more clothes and Dawn said they were all for her and she could choose whatever she wanted to wear each day. Flannelette pyjamas were folded neatly under her pillow and a thick pink dressing gown and matching slippers hung on the white wicker chair next to her bed.

There was a large window next to her bed, and she could look out across the large backyard, its borders lined with tall trees, their leaves littering the yard in the cooler months. Henry helped her climb one of the big trees in the backyard and made a timber platform that stretched across the lower branches. He'd asked her to help him with the hammer and nails and together they'd made a wooden ladder she could climb up to reach the platform more easily. She could sit on the platform and watch the tiny lizards running up and down the bark, their suction feet scampering upwards into the higher branches.

One afternoon, Henry and Dawn sat on white iron chairs under the tree and passed her up lemonade and biscuits. They'd also passed up the Black Beauty ornament to sit with her on the platform. Gracie felt good that day and now it didn't worry her that Layla had left her to holiday here by herself and not even said goodbye. She forgot about not talking and called out to Henry and Dawn to look at the little lizard she'd caught, its tiny head peering out from beneath her chubby fingers.

The couple laughed and watched her as she let it go, the lizard scampering across the timber platform and up into the safety of the branches. Henry came over closer so she could show him a stick insect, clinging with sticky feet to her dress. Together they put it on the bark of the tree, Henry explaining how the tiny barbs helped the insect to latch on and how their colours worked as a camouflage against birds and other predators.

She wanted to know what camouflage and predator meant and

Henry explained the meaning and then they practised saying the words together.

They talked for a long time and every now and then they turned to wave to Dawn, who sat watching the two of them. Dawn kept wiping her eyes, as if she was crying; yet she was smiling as she waved back.

Eventually Gracie wanted to get down from the platform, so she passed the horse ornament to Henry.

'Jump and I'll catch you,' he said, his arms held out. Gracie bent down for take-off and Henry counted, 'One, two, three and jump.' It was such a good feeling to leap through the air and she jumped off into his waiting arms. Dawn stood up, laughing and Gracie laughed also as Henry's moustache tickled her face. He spun around with her in his arms before placing her back on the platform. She climbed up and down, jumping again and again into Henry's arms, her squeals of delight filling the usually quiet backyard.

CHAPTER 58

Gracie began to feel more and more comfortable with the couple and soon knew every area of their home like she'd been there for ever. She loved her bedroom, particularly the shelf Henry had built for her not long after she arrived. Each week Dawn would present her with a new book, the two of them reading it together before Gracie put it in its new place on her bookshelf.

The bedroom was large and full of natural light from a wide window that faced the right direction for her to see her star. Each night she dragged a chair next to the window so she could sit and look out.

'Why is the chair always under the window each morning when we come in to say good morning?' Henry asked her, his voice as always, soft and kind.

'I like to look at the stars and the moon when it comes up over there.'

'What do you like about them?'

She wanted to tell him about her father and Elizabeth's star, but she was worried if she told him, he might send her back to Layla.

* * *

Dawn could tell that there was something about the night sky that intrigued Grace and she'd talked to Henry about the fact that something was obviously worrying her.

'Just let her be,' Henry said. 'She was bound to come with some sort of affects from living with that woman.'

'She's everything we ever dreamed of. I can't believe how well she's fitted into our life and we just all seem to go together, an instant family.'

Henry hugged Dawn. 'We waited for a long time for this moment and I'd have to agree, it's worked out better than I ever imagined. It's as if she's always been with us, not just this past year. It was meant to be.' He cleared his throat. 'I didn't realise I could ever love a small child so much, so quickly.'

'We have been blessed.' Dawn reached up and stroked his face. 'After a while she'll forget why she looks at the sky.'

Henry built a long wooden seat below Grace's window. Dawn padded it with a soft mattress and scattered bright soft pillows along it, making it a cosy warm place to sit.

'She always ends up there asleep.' Henry once again brought up the subject.

'She says she likes to watch the stars, but she still won't tell me why,' Dawn said.

'That dreadful mother of hers didn't tell us much, only that her father left before she was born,' Henry replied. 'I don't know why she is so obsessed with the stars.'

'She's settled in quite well, not any of the problems I thought we'd encounter with adopting,' Dawn said.

'Thank goodness the solicitors did what the mother wanted and changed Grace's name on the adoption papers. By giving her a different surname, not hers or the father's, there's no way anyone can trace her back to Layla.' He shook his head. 'She didn't want any connection left between her and the child, or for anyone else to be able to track her back to her.'

Dawn patted his shoulder. 'At least now she has our surname. It's for the best,' she said. 'It's legal now, the paperwork's submitted and the extra money her mother asked for, will keep her happy.'

'I'm glad we could quicken the process and deal with her directly. It's amazing what having the right contacts and some extra money will do. God only knows where the poor child would have ended up otherwise,' Henry said.

Dawn closed her eyes. 'It just doesn't bear thinking about. It's fate that she came to us.'

The government department Henry worked for had been looking into adoption for him when a work colleague told him about a lady who had been in to make enquiries. She was going to put a young girl up for adoption. The arrangement sounded perfect and his high position at work helped to speed up the process and cut some corners. He had contacted Layla in person and she had been most accommodating, saying she would deliver the child to them, sign the papers and they could have Gracie even before the paperwork was finalised. She'd been keen to speed up the usual process and when she'd asked for more money and received it, she left without a backward glance.

The arrangement was perfect for the older couple, who had spent years trying to conceive a baby with no success. In time they would tell Gracie, or Grace as they preferred to call her, that she was adopted. For now though, they wanted her to enjoy her new life without any complications. She had been through enough.

They watched her now, through a window in the kitchen. She had quickly filled out and her skin had a healthy glow from the hours spent playing outside in the yard. Henry placed his arm fondly around Dawn's shoulders. 'Thank goodness she's carefree and happy, too young to worry about where she's come from, or the war.'

Dawn stood on her tiptoes to get a better view of the yard. 'Look at her with those animals. She has a natural way with them.'

Grace swung down from an upper branch of a tree before landing firmly on the ground. Her two pet dogs jumped around and licked her face as she lay on the ground. She rolled around with them before making them both sit. When she held out her hand they put their paw on it and on her command, rolled over in unison, three times before they stopped. Their reward was a kind pat on the head, before she let them chase her back to the house.

Dawn opened the door for her. 'Goodness me, you gorgeous little thing.' She picked Grace up and hugged her tight, 'Look how dusty you are.'

Henry came over and picked some leaves and sticks from her hair. 'I don't know how you've taught them those tricks. You certainly have a way with animals,' he said, the fondness evident in his voice.

'It's easy, Papa, it just takes patience.'

He ruffled her hair and took her from Dawn, placing her down on a wooden chair. 'Right, time for some morning tea, scones and cream this morning. What do you think about that?'

* * *

Grace's former life with her mother became a distant memory. She had asked Papa and Mum, as she now called Dawn, if she could live with them for a long time. They'd looked at each other and asked if she would be happy to live with them forever. Gracie wanted to say that as long as her father knew where she was, she was happy. She bit her lip, still worried if she brought up the subject of Layla or her father that her new family might send her back. Instead, she told them she wanted to stay with them forever. Well, she thought, until her father came home.

Gracie called Dawn, Mother or Mum, and Henry, Papa. At

night she curled up in his arms, the end of his moustache tickling her face as he ran it over her forehead. 'Ah you're the best thing that ever happened to us, Grace. God gave us something special the day you arrived.'

She snuggled close, happy and settled in with her new parents.

CHAPTER 59

Rabaul - November 1941

Reg celebrated his fiftieth birthday by inviting some friends over for dinner. It was November and hot winds pushed across the valley, the smell of sulphur ever present. Joanie set the long table on the verandah, wishing the toxic smell would disappear.

She was filling the vases with sweet-smelling Jasmine when the ground started to shake. The earth was jittery today and she grasped the verandah rail, pressing her feet down hard as the whole house shook on its foundations. When the shaking stopped, dogs resting in a shady spot away from the heat, came to life, their barking echoing throughout the valley. Birds chirped noisily, their typical melodious chorus now a crescendo of panicky calls, a muddled mixture of bird noises making Joanie even more apprehensive.

She turned as a familiar voice called out and her heart beat faster as Michael bounded up the stairs. He wrapped his arms around her and kissed her passionately. She lost her breath, the intensity of his kisses catching her by surprise.

Michael pulled away, his hands holding her arms. 'I couldn't wait to kiss you. It must be the tremors. They're making me jumpy.'

'You're very bold today,' Joanie said, wiping her lipstick off his lips.

'Sometimes that old volcano and its shakings make me feel like it could be the last day on earth. It's as if it's just waiting to blow and I want to make sure I get all the kisses in before it does.'

She laughed and pulled away. 'There are others about to arrive. I can hear the car coming up the road.' She looked up into his eyes. 'I love your boldness.'

'Look at you two.' Reg's voice boomed along the wide verandah. 'Were you hanging onto each other in case the house falls down?'

* * *

Joanie stayed beside her father for most of the night, her arm tucked in his, making sure she was always there to talk to his friends and their partners. When he said he was tired, she walked with him inside, the party continuing on the wide verandah, some guests spilling out onto the neatly mowed front lawn.

'Thank you, Joanie, this has been a night for me to remember.'

'It was a wonderful night and you've made so many new friends here in Rabaul.'

He looked at her, his eyes tired. 'I'm ready for bed, my dear.'

She could sense his sorrow. 'We will be home very soon and then you don't have to leave mother ever again.'

'You will be sorry to leave young Michael though.' He raised his eyebrows at her, looking out through the window at Michael, who was deep in conversation with Peter and Andrew. 'You're lucky they all get on; they have become good mates.'

She sighed. 'I know. I'm worried about Peter though. He still believes that once the war is over and we're back home that I'll be ready to make decisions about the two of us.'

Her father's voice was stern. 'Have you been honest with him?'

'He hasn't asked me any questions. He's stepped back a bit, but I know him well and I can tell he thinks, that what I feel for Michael is going to disappear once I leave Rabaul.'

'And it won't, will it?' His bushy eyebrows moved high on his forehead.

'No, Father. It's not ever going to go. I know that. But I also know we can't stay here.'

Reg kissed the top of her head and they hugged, neither wanting to let the other go on this special night.

* * *

There had been eight of them left celebrating. Joanie stood arm-in-arm with Jean. Unlike Joanie, Jean had no plans to leave Rabaul. The two of them chatted between themselves, leaving the talk of war to the others. It was an exciting night, because Jean had leave for the entire night and was staying in the visitors' bedroom.

The moon was high in the sky when all the boys left; piling into the two cars they'd come in. Michael gave Joanie a wave, any chance of being alone or sneaking a goodnight kiss, impossible with the others around. Joanie and Jean waved them off, noisy laughter and raucous goodbyes coming from the departing soldiers. Dogs barked and the girls giggled at the sound of the car's horn as it made its way onto the road leading into the town. The silhouette of the mountains was large and imposing, a million stars above them decorating the vast expanse as they stood staring out into the night sky.

'It's a beautiful town,' Joanie linked her arm through Jean's. 'I'm going to be sad to leave.'

'I know,' Jean leaned in against her. 'I've also fallen in love with the place. Not only the mountains and the bay, but also the people. Especially the Aussie boys. They're great fun.'

'You're keen on Andrew, aren't you?' Joanie asked.

Jean laughed. 'How could you tell?'

'I've known those boys for a long time. I saw Andrew watching you. I've not seen him look at anyone like that before.'

'You can't talk.' Jean banged her hip into Joanie's. 'What about you and Michael? Why, it's plain to see you've both fallen in love.'

'I've never felt like this. I want to be with him all the time, but there's a stupid war getting in the way. It's not long until Father and I leave.'

'Your father is pining for your mother. I talked to him tonight and he talked about nothing else, except going back home to her. I hope when I'm their age I'm still in love like that with my husband.'

Joanie sighed. 'Michael's much like Father. He's romantic, compassionate and has everything in a man I love.'

'He's also very handsome,' Jean added. 'That blonde hair, even when it's so short you can still see the curls.'

The girls laughed loudly, excited about their romances and impatient as to where their lives were headed. 'Maybe once the boys leave I'll go back to Brisbane. I mean if Andrew isn't up here, I'm not sure I'll want to stay. I want to be wherever he is,' Jean said.

'I feel the same.' Joanie replied. For a moment neither spoke, steadying themselves as the timbers under their feet shook and the windows and doors rattled. They gripped each other's arm, shocked at the ferocity of the quake and the way the night sky had begun to light up.

The volcano known as, Matupi, had been dormant for four years, its bubbling centre hidden and thought to be asleep. Tonight, on Reg's birthday, it had decided to wake and now the two girls looked up, transfixed at the fireworks shooting out of the mountain's crater.

The ground continued to shake as bright red splashed like splattered blood across the darkness. Strips of white light streaked across the sky, the glow of a yellow ball of fire near the mountain's top lighting up the entire area.

Her father appeared behind them, still tying up his dressing gown as he looked towards the mountain. 'Fireworks for my birthday.'

'It hasn't done this for a few years,' Jean said. 'I hope it's not going to be a big one like in '37.' Her voice was nervous, and Joanie put her arm around her.

Every few minutes incandescent orange and red lava burst forth from the mountain, the glow remaining long after the liquid either retreated back into the crater's mouth or trickled down the slopes now littered with glowing fluid and rocks.

Jean hung tightly to Joanie. 'Do you think we should evacuate?'

'There's no need to worry.' Reg's voice was shaky as he watched the light show in front of them. 'The observatory would have picked up if it was going to be another huge eruption. This is only a small show.'

Thick clouds suddenly covered the sky and wafts of hot air blew across where they stood. The rumbling increased, a swell of noise gathering until it sounded like a train thundering across a bridge. The noise pushed up the valley towards them, louder and louder, causing the three of them to hang onto each other. The commotion eventually quietened and then stopped. They waited silently for the next round, but there were no further sounds or rumblings.

'It's very late,' Reg said, breathing a sigh of relief. 'We should go to bed and get some sleep. It's been one hell of a day.'

CHAPTER 60

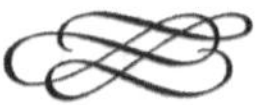

No-one felt comfortable that night and like many others in Rabaul, Joanie lay awake, listening to the noises and waiting for the intermittent shaking of the earth to stop. The next day the volcano continued to spew noxious fumes over the town and she kept herself busy at the store, trying to ignore the unsettling movement of the ground.

Another week passed before she finally had the opportunity to catch up with Michael. With her father's permission, they travelled to a small bay that lay to the east of the town, accessible only by foot. It was peaceful once they moved onto the jungle trail and they stopped to watch tropical birds flitting from branch to branch in the towering canopy above them. Michael moved quickly through the jungle maze, not hesitating once about which direction to take.

She hung tightly to his hand as he led her along an even narrower trail, dense foliage closing in on them as they ducked under huge boughs and sidestepped holes full of murky water.

Joanie stopped in her tracks.

'Why have you stopped?' Michael pulled at her hand.

The jungle pressed in on them, the dark green tunnel they stood in, dripping moisture from every leaf. A tingling sensation ran over her body and she looked into Michael's eyes as she took a step towards him. She stared hard at him, her heart thumping. 'I was thinking how I would follow you anywhere in the world. Wherever you go, I'll follow.'

He stopped and reached for her other hand. 'You mean it, don't you?'

'Of course I do. I wouldn't have said it otherwise. I've never wanted to follow anyone before. I've always wanted someone to follow me, but with you, it's different.' She looked upwards, a narrow sliver of sky visible through the canopy of the trees. 'We are in the middle of the jungle, next to a volcano that could erupt again any second and there is a war not far away. Yet I feel happier and safer than ever before.'

Michael pushed a strand of hair from her forehead, tiny beads of sweat trickling down her face as the heat pushed down on them. 'I could get lost in your green eyes.' He stroked her cheek, his hands rough against her soft skin. The ground beneath them trembled and shook and they hung onto each other's arms until the vibrations stopped. Both of them burst into laughter. Michael grabbed her hand again and pulled her along, eager to get to where they were headed.

The path ended, the shadowy dim of the jungle opening up to bright sunshine, soaking the white sand they stood on.

'I'm going to call this Joanie's Bay. The green of the ocean matches your eyes.'

'Oh, Michael, it's beautiful. Look at the colour of the water. It's so clear.'

Birri had shown Michael the area, a favourite place for his people who went there to collect shellfish and oysters. Caves that could only be entered at low tide pockmarked the low cliffs and today the beach was deserted, belonging to just the two of them.

For a while neither spoke, the sparkling waters of the bay a mesmerising moving canvas stretching endlessly in front of them. Joanie lay on the beach, tall palm trees throwing shade across her as she enjoyed the cool sand on her back. Michael bent down toward her, gently running his fingers around her face and then across her lips. She looked straight into eyes, longing to feel his arms around her. Reaching up she pulled him down towards her, their lips meeting as his body pressed hard against her.

A tingling sensation filled her as their skin touched and when his hands held her waist, her breaths became short and she reached up and stroked his chest. The weight of his leg lay across hers and her body tensed with excitement as he kissed her face, his lips moving down her neck.

When he stopped, she opened her eyes and looked at him; his face serious, his eyes wanting.

'I love you, Joanie. I've fallen in love with you.'

She smiled and spoke softly. 'I love you too, Michael. There's just something so right about the two of us together.' She closed her eyes as Michael kissed her again.

Suddenly, Michael sat up and straightened his clothes.

She reached out to him. 'It's okay, I'm not afraid of going further. I don't know how long until we will see each other again once I leave.'

'I don't want it to be like that. I want to ask your father for his permission and then the first chance I have to come back to Australia we can be together.' He stood up and then got down again on one knee, next to where Joanie was sitting.

'Will you marry me? When I come back and the first chance we have, will you marry me?'

Joanie leant over and caressed his arm. 'I will, Michael McTavish. I will.'

Michael reached into his pocket and pulled out a woven ring. 'I made this last night. It's from the grass growing closest to Birri's village and I want you to take is as a symbol of marriage and being together forever.'

She held out her hand and he slipped the plaited tiny circle onto her finger.

'I want to grow old with you,' Joanie whispered, as they kissed and held each other tight.

Suddenly she pulled away and sat up straight, turning the ring on her finger. 'There is one condition, Michael.'

He held her hands and they gazed into each other's eyes. 'What is it?'

'That once Father has given his blessing and you have returned to me, our main priority will be to re-unite you with your daughter. I want her to come and live with us. I will take her on as if she was my own.'

Michael took a deep breath. 'You have made my world complete by saying that.'

'You and Gracie are a package.'

'I know she will love you, just as I do.'

They sat and talked for a long time, discussing plans for their future together, where they would live and how they would bring Gracie to be with them. It wasn't until the sun started to sink behind the jungle, that they realised how late it was.

Michael jumped up and gazed across the ocean. 'We'd better get back. Even though I know my way around these tracks, I wouldn't like to be out here once it's dark.' He pulled her up by her hands and together they packed up the picnic basket.

Michael bent down and kissed her again and again. The day was perfect; the food, the wine, the grass ring and now the promise of the three of them becoming a family once Michael returned to Australia.

She held out her hands for him to lead her back along the tracks. 'Let's get moving,' he said, 'I need to practise what I'm going to say to your father.' Joanie laughed as he led her away from their beach and back through the jungle, its depths already darkening with the fading sun.

* * *

That day would stay in her mind for many years. Even when she was old, she would take out that tiny ring, the grass frayed and only just holding together. If she lay on her back, it was as if she could still feel his soft kisses and the texture of the sand between her toes. When she closed her eyes she could feel the dampness as they had entered the jungle and the musty smell of the wet leaves and mulch underfoot. She could hear the sounds of the birds making their last calls of the day and the rustlings in the bushes that had made her jump, and Michael laugh. It was to be one of her last happy memories of her time in Rabaul.

CHAPTER 61

From his cane chair on the front verandah, Reg could see a section of the road and he observed Michael walking briskly towards the house. There was a purpose in his stride and Reg's eyes narrowed. Perhaps he was going to ask if he could take Joanie out again.

The two had become quite an item and it was lovely to watch their romance blossom.

Joanie was open about Michael's previous circumstances and although Reg questioned her on how she really felt about Michael having a small child, she remained adamant that it did not make any difference to their relationship.

There was also another obstacle, or interference in this new relationship. Peter had talked to Reg on the quiet, a couple of times. His feelings for Joanie were also strong and once the war was over and life settled back to normal, he was hoping she would realise and appreciate what he had to offer her. Reg had been upfront and even though the boys were like his own family, he would not come into any discussions about Joanie's feelings towards Peter. His daughter would make her own decisions. Now as Reg watched Michael walk up the path towards the front steps he pondered, knowing that Peter would not be happy about the recent advances in the romance. Two young men, both in the prime of their life and both chasing the same dream—Joanie.

Michael appeared to be in a hurry and took the steps two at a time. He was startled when Reg stood up and greeted him.

'Good afternoon, Sir, I mean, good morning.'

'That's a formal greeting, what happened to calling me Reg?'

'Good morning, Reg. It's a beautiful day.'

'Yes, the sun is bright and not a cloud in the sky.'

'Even the dust has settled today. No smoke from the mountain.' Michael sat down next to him and he settled back in his chair. They were silent, both looking across the manicured front lawn to the road, a few locals talking and laughing as they walked back and forth. Michael sat upright and tapped his feet, his hands clenched and resting on his knees.

'Did you come to talk about the weather, Michael?' Reg offered.

'The weather, yes, well no, of course not.'

'It's a long way to walk to tell me it's a fine day.'

Michael took a deep breath, his shoulders straightening as he sat up tall and turned towards Reg. 'I'd like to ask you something, Sir.'

'Only, if you stop with the *sir*. You know I like you fellas to call me Reg.'

'Yes of course.'

There was silence again as Michael looked down at his feet.

'What was it you wanted to ask me?' Reg prompted.

'Well, sir . . . Reg, I'm not sure how to go about this, but it's to do with Joanie and me.'

Reg laughed; a deep guttural laugh that startled a couple of green parrots feeding on the berries of a tree next to the verandah. 'I figured it might be.'

'I know we haven't known each other for long and at the moment I don't have a great financial backing or much to offer, but—' He stopped and looked out across the lawn before looking straight into Reg's eyes. 'I wanted to ask you for Joanie's hand in marriage. When the war is over, or if we can be back together in your home town, we'd . . . um . . . I'd like to ask if we could get married.' Michael wiped sweat from his brow. He sat up straight, waiting for the reply.

This was not what Reg expected and he took a deep breath, surprised the two had reached this point in such a short time. He gave Michael a sharp look, their eyes meeting again.

'You have spoken to Joanie about this?' Reg asked. 'She is an independent young woman with a mind of her own.'

'We have talked, and she feels the same way I do. I have also told her it would only be with yours and Edna's blessing. I know Joanie has told you I have a young daughter, however there is no other woman in my life and,' he paused, 'there never really was. What occurred was an unfortunate night that changed my life.'

'And the young child would live where, if you were to marry Joanie?' Reg asked.

'Joanie has said once we are married, that, Gracie, that's my daughter, if we were to try and make arrangements for her to live with us.'

'It may not be an easy road for Joanie, bringing up another woman's child. What is the situation with the child's mother?'

Michael's face fell and his voice trembled. 'The mother does not care for the child at all, she never has. My hope is that once I'm back and settled, she will give Gracie into my care.'

'And may I ask what your main reason is for wanting to wed my only daughter?'

This time Michael's face did not go red. His eyes were bright and there was a steadiness and calm in his voice. 'I love her. I have loved her from the moment we met, and I know she is the one I want to marry and grow old with.'

'Agghhh,' Reg sighed, as he leaned back in the wicker chair, his body relaxed, and feet stretched out in front of him. There was something about this young man that made him happy, excited, for the years to come. He possessed honesty and a quiet strength, and it was easy to see how he had captured Joanie's heart. Reg smiled. 'It was the same when I met Edna. From the moment I laid eyes on her, I knew, I knew straight away. It's a strange thing, a love between a young man and woman. It's stirring, it's romantic, it's the start of new lives.'

Michael also leaned back in his chair. 'It is exciting, how we feel about each other and amazing how in a place like this and in these times when the world is so unsettled, we have met and fallen in love.'

'Different times indeed, and we cannot determine what is on the horizon for any of us, but Joanie and you are young, and many obstacles can be overcome. We just need this damn war to be over.'

Michael's voice was deep, his face serious. 'I feel it may creep closer before leaving us. The news through today is that all military leave has been cancelled. They're starting to take the Japanese threat more seriously.'

'I'm also worried about the recent threats,' Reg said. 'As you are aware, Joanie and I planned to leave early in the new year.'

'Even though it will be hard to say goodbye to you both, I'll feel happier when Joanie is back on Australian soil.'

'I'm of the same mind. There has however been a change in our plans and the new advice has only come through to me this morning. Joanie is at work and I haven't even had a chance to talk to her about it. I've managed to get us on a ship that will depart from here within the month.'

The two men sat for a moment, watching groups of villagers walk past, a procession of women and children, many of them balancing baskets of fruit on their heads. Reg knew that Joanie would not be happy about the early departure, but the passage was booked and paid for and there was nothing that would deter him from getting on a ship and sailing home to Edna. He glanced at Michael, trying to read his thoughts.

'They're a happy bunch of people,' Reg said. 'I will be sad to leave it all behind, but it has been a great experience. And now to top it off, Joanie has also met you.'

'Thank you, Reg,' Michael said. 'I also have become attached to the people who I have met here in Rabaul. I must say though, that it is good news that you have managed to gain a passage home and I will do my best to placate Joanie, reminding her that leaving early is in both your best interests.'

Reg stood up and tipped the remnants of a cup of tea he had been drinking over the verandah. He leaned back on the rails, facing Michael, his face stern. 'So, what is your intention, if I was to give my consent and Joanie and you were to marry. Once everything settles back down and life resumes to normal, what are your plans?'

Michael added, 'I am aware Joanie is your only child. I wouldn't take her away from you, but rather live our lives so you and your wife are part of it.'

Reg nodded, relieved Michael had not stated his intention to return to the life of a drover.

'You have made me happy to hear that, young man, but it does not make any difference to my decision to your question. If Joanie has already said she will marry you, then she has made up her mind. It will also be my greatest pleasure that you wed whenever the chance arises, and I know Edna would think the same.'

Michael stood up, his grin widening. Reg gripped his hand before placing his arm around the young man's shoulder, squeezing him affectionately. 'You do indeed have my blessing.'

There had been little chance for Joanie and Michael to see each other over the next couple of weeks. Michael called into the store a couple of times, but they were only quick visits between errands. One night he managed to slip away from the barracks and visit

Joanie at home. The three of them shared a meal and Reg opened a bottle of wine he had been saving for such an occasion.

As her father had anticipated, Joanie had not taken the news regarding the early departure kindly. She tried every persuasive excuse she could think of and had argued for days about her father's decision. In the end she had given in. He was not looking well and every day away from her mother seemed to make him more distant and unhappy. Michael also took her father's side, arguing the same points and re-iterating that before they knew it, they would be back in Woombye, planning their wedding and life together.

'To the two of you.' Reg raised his glass, clinking against Joanie's and Michael's. 'A toast to your marriage, once you are both back in Australia. Let not distance deter your love for one another.'

'We will write every week.' Joanie said, refusing to let the separation interfere with their romance. 'And it won't be long, Father. We have it all planned.'

* * *

Reg left the two of them together on the verandah. He was tired and counting down the days and nights, relieved the position at Burns Philp was ending. It had been one hell of an experience, but he was well and truly ready to go home and gaining the early passage on a ship that would take them directly back to Australia was indeed a bonus. His and Joanie's time in Rabaul was coming to a close.

He sat at his oak desk in the office of the house they had called home for not quite two years. He would miss the place, the business and the people. Bill and his wife, Leila, would return on a ship to Rabaul not long after he and Joanie left. They would slip back into their roles at Burns Philp and Reg, in turn, would return to the store in Woombye. Edna had been a stoic trooper to run and maintain the business while him and Joanie were absent, but thankfully now he could go back and pick up his old life as he had left it.

Joanie had already told him that she would work in the Woombye store while she waited for the war to finish and Michael to come home. She had no desire to live in Brisbane and would be safe and kept busy, hopefully the time passing quickly until the two of them could be re-united and plan for their future together.

Picking up his pen he prepared to write to Edna, imagining her delight when she opened his letter that would tell of his early homecoming. Everything had fallen into place and once the war was over their lives could return to some sort of normality. Peter and Andrew would come back to Woombye, they'd find new jobs and work out what they wanted in life. Michael also would return and become part of their family, hopefully bringing his young daughter to join them. The young soldier and Joanie would marry, right under the huge Jacaranda tree in the front yard and then they'd live nearby and… he sighed and put his pen down. Perhaps one day they would even bless him and Edna with grandchildren.

Dreaming about the cool winter days in Woombye, he smiled and closed his eyes, imagining the fresh smell of the bread that Edna loved to bake, the sound of kookaburras cackling in the trees nearby and languid afternoons relaxing on the verandah with his beloved wife by his side. Australian shores were beckoning him home. It had been one hell of an adventure, but their stay in Rabaul had come to an end.

~~~
~~~

ABOUT THE AUTHOR

Rhonda Forrest is an Australian author who juggles writing and publishing, alongside teaching high school students. She writes captivating contemporary and historical/romance fiction about relationships, family life and social issues, set amidst beautiful and uniquely Australian landscapes.

After bringing up three daughters and traversing several careers, Rhonda went on to teach creative writing, English and history. Her passion for literacy, history and travelling around Australia fuels her novels. Along with her husband, she divides her time between Tamborine Mountain and a century-old cottage with a rambling garden overlooking the waters of the Whitsundays.

Recent novels bring to life the remarkable characters and settings that make up the unique Australian heritage and take the reader on a journey from bush to beach, with steamy romances, riveting history and eclectic characters.

Rhonda's books are available in audio and large print and you can also find some titles available in Portuguese, Publisher-Leabhar Books Brazil.

If you enjoyed this book or any of Rhonda's other books, you can make a big difference by writing a review, or leaving a star rating on Amazon, Goodreads or Bookbub. A personal recommendation to family, friends, libraries and book clubs is another great way to share the books with others. You can also follow the author on Facebook, Instagram, Goodreads and Bookbub.

Author's favourite - sample chapters from *Silkworm Secrets* are in the back of this book.

Website - https://www.rhondaforrest.com/

ACKNOWLEDGMENTS

A completed manuscript is a fabulous feeling. You've really put yourself out there, exposed your soul to anyone who reads the words that you've spent years writing, editing and sculpting into the story you want to be told, the emotions that you want to evoke and the characters that you want to introduce. My husband and three daughters—all avid readers —have loved my stories from the very first book. They have given me continual support, listened to my endless ideas, helped me with covers, technology, editing and most of all always been there to listen to me during the highs and lows of writing and publishing. My husband, Terry, has as always, encouraged me to pursue what I want, to continue writing and to follow my dreams. He has spent many hours, sometimes in a tent in the middle of nowhere, reading and editing my manuscripts, correcting errors and writing hilarious comments and helpful ideas.

Thank you to all of those who have read and made suggestions, not only for this book but also my previous titles. Without your support, I would not be still writing. Thank you to Sue Curran, Maree Page-Gear, Jill Agnew and Nicole Forrest for your patience and editing with proof copies. Annie Seaton for her continual support and advice, Colette Weeden for her local book launches, Maree Rowell for advice on covers, Sean Doyle for appraisal guidance and Ethel Beckett for creating my covers.

I have an incredible circle of friends and family, who have given me continual support over the years. They too have read my uncorrected proofs, offered advice, edited manuscripts and encouraged me to continue writing. They have hosted book launches, talked books over wines at Clancy's, analysed covers, attended book signings, taken my books on planes and trains all over the world and then sent me photos, emails and texts to say they've loved the stories. They have harassed me until I used social media for marketing and then helped me promote my books and spread the word. They are the best friends and family anyone could ever wish for.

Through the world of books, I have also met and become firm friends with a tribe of book lovers both here in Australia and overseas. To the book reviewers, readers and other authors who have supported me and helped promote my books, I give many thanks. Your kind words and friendship have encouraged me to keep writing and publishing.

To my mum, Margaret – Thank you for sharing your stories with me about your dad; not only his time in Rabaul but also about the years that your family spent waiting to hear of his fate. In your 94th year, your practical, *get-on-with-it,* attitude is a grounding stability for all of your family who are inspired by your resilience and outlook on life.

I hope that Elizabeth's Star enlightens readers about the tragic events that occurred in and around Rabaul, and of the fate of the Montevideo Maru. These fictional stories are a poignant reminder of the very real sacrifices made and the hardships endured by the men and women who were involved.

***

My research for Elizabeth's Star has involved many different sources, a list too long to include. I would, however, like to acknowledge the use of the books below, which give accurate facts and make for interesting reading on life in Rabaul, before and during WWII.

Hostages to Freedom – Peter Stone

Darkest Hour: The True Story of Lark Force at Rabaul – Bruce Gamble

Rabaul 1942 – Douglas Aplin

Malaguna Road – The Papua and New Guinea Diaries of – Sarah Chinnery - Sarah Chinnery

He's Not Coming Home – Gillian Nikakis

James McGowan Mackay
1939

**James McGowan
QX64913
Lark Force   AAOC**

James and eldest daughter
May, Brisbane 1940

Chief in Rabaul - 1941

Rabaul - 1941

Fish
nets
Rabaul

James and local kids -
Rabaul

Police Boys

UNTIL WE MEET
by Rhonda Forrest

'When you go home, tell them of us and say, for your tomorrow,
we gave our today.'
John Maxwell Edmonds 1918

In early 1940 Bud joins the United States Navy, his aim, to become a US Submariner. Less than two years later, Japanese forces bomb Pearl Harbour. Those living on the islands of New Guinea lie directly in the path of the oncoming enemy.

Along with other Australians, Joanie prepares to depart Rabaul, leaving behind her fiancée, Michael, her father, and many others she loves.

As the volcano, Tavurvur, gathers its forces and bursts forth from its crater, the ill-equipped, small Australian defence known as Lark Force is left to secure the small town. Overwhelmed by the large enemy forces, the order is given, 'every man for themselves.' Although some will survive, over a thousand men lose their lives when a US Submarine sinks the POW Japanese ship, Montevideo Maru. The seeds of destiny are sown and the lives of Bud and those in Rabaul, intrinsically linked.

Will Michael return to fulfil his promise of marrying Joanie and what will be the fate of his young daughter, Gracie, who still turns to the evening star for guidance, for her questions to be answered, and above all to be reunited with her father.

Until We Meet is an epic war saga based on actual events that continues the story of Elizabeth's Star. A tale of survival, love and family, set amidst the backdrop of World War II.

Happy Valley BooksRead

Prepared to be wowed again as the plot unfolds in this wonderful historical fiction of love, hope, courage, determination and strength in the midst of World War Two.

Rhonda has creatively taken actual events and inventively weaved and webbed a juicy, dramatic and entertaining tale that's original, fresh and interesting.

A vivid, strong and honest insight into the horror of war, the effects on family and war torn friendship this generous storyteller has yet another hit on her hands with a tender, moving and real novel.

WE'LL MEET AGAIN - 2022
by Rhonda Forrest

'My troubles are all over, and I am at home; and often before I am quite awake, I fancy I am still in the orchard at Birtwick, standing with my friends under the apple trees.'
~ Black Beauty

The 1950s are a carefree time for a young woman like Grace. The war is over and when her family moves to Brisbane, plans are made for her to complete her studies at the University of Queensland.

Ewan is also studying the same course and when he meets the

beautiful, head-strong Grace, the differences in their backgrounds are pushed aside as they plan their future together.

However, not everyone is happy with the romance and when the young couple are forced to separate, decisions are made that will determine their path in life. Will the path taken, lead Grace to the story behind a star she knows as Elizabeth's Star and will a fortune teller's prophecy 40 years prior, be proven.

We'll Meet Again is a story of devotion and family, a connection between those who suffered loss and separation and a sweeping tale of hope, chance and love.

Review - Chapter Ichi

The writing is superb, as are all of Rhonda's novels.

As a reader, I was emotional throughout this novel. If you're looking for a novel that will find a way deep into your soul, this is it. I would highly recommend We'll Meet Again and the series as a whole.

SALTWATER ROMANCE SERIES

SALTWATER ROMANCE SERIES

From the wild freedom of 1970s Australia to the tangled emotions of the present day, the Saltwater Romance Series delivers three powerful love stories.

Set against the rainforests of North Queensland, the Whitsundays, and the golden shores of Stradbroke Island, these novels explore first love, rebellion, second chances and the journeys that lead us back to ourselves, and to the ones we can't forget.

<h1 style="text-align:center">WHITSUNDAY ROMANCE - YOU MAY NEVER WANT TO LEAVE!</h1>

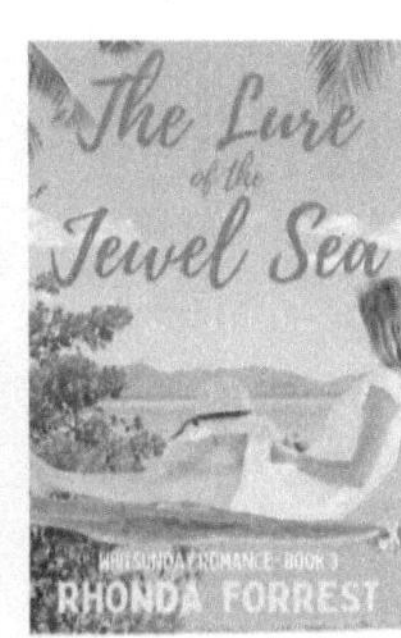

Love by the Jewel Sea - Book 1

Summer by the Jewel Sea - Book 2

The Lure of the Jewel Sea - Book 3

BINDARRA CREEK ROMANCE

BEYOND THE GATE - Mystery Romance at Bindarra Creek

CHRISTMAS AT FORREST GLEN - A Bindarra Creek Romance

A MAGICAL SUMMER - A Bindarra Creek Small Town Christmas Romance

THE SHACK BY THE BAY - Whitsunday Historical Romance

Romantic and purely Australian, *The Shack by the Bay* captures the pristine beauty of the Whitsundays and the wartime memories of older Australians while introducing an eclectic blend of friends and family.

ALL MY HEART - A Tranquil Bay Romance

A small town and school - She only had to last six months.

KICK THE DUST - Contemporary Romance

'If I close my eyes, it's easier to hold onto a memory. When I open them, I think it might really be there in front of me.'

SILKWORM SECRETS

SAMPLE CHAPTERS

'*The ancient trees with their rough bark wrap around me like silk cocoons. Their solid trunks and tendril roots grip the ground as if to say, I will hold you, I will not let go.*'

CHAPTER 1

There had been great excitement the day the silkworms first came to the treehouse. Walking knee-deep through the dense covering of ferns and bushes beneath the mulberry tree, Bobby had announced that he had a surprise for Ruby in his satchel. It was dim and cool under the tree, the knotted branches and canopy forming a shady, secluded area, only a few frilly-necked lizards and the occasional brown snake sharing the space with the two of them.

She had tried to get him to stop and open his bag, the suspense almost too much, but he kept walking, determined for once not to let her win.

'Wait, Ruby Rose. Just wait until we climb up and then I'll show you.'

'But what is it? Can't you tell me? I'll die of curiosity.'

Ruby liked to be in charge and know everything. The suspense made her climb erratically, stopping and starting,

continually looking down at Bobby climbing steadily below her.

'Just get up there and I'll show you,' he said.

Standing on her toes, she balanced on the rungs leading up the tree. He noticed the bottoms of her feet, dark purple colours mixed with dirt from the earth below. Her flowery cotton dress was also stained purple from where she had sat on some of the thousands, perhaps millions, of berries that had dropped from the tree during the fruiting season.

Above them, the trail of timber blocks, like steps, wove their way up into the darkest reaches of the tree. Nails that had long ago been hammered into the rough, textured bark held the timber secure, and as they climbed higher, tiny glimpses of the sky became visible; a blue backdrop to the thick branches that reached upwards, their tops covered by the dense canopy of weeping smaller branches and leaves.

Perched amongst the thick foliage of the massive mulberry tree

the treehouse was obscured, a safe haven, a place no one else bothered with, tucked away in an overgrown corner of Ruby's backyard. The two best friends considered the spot to be the best place
in the world, and its location among other large trees—figs,
mangoes and a towering pine tree—provided them with their own
secret corner, a safe house with no adults, just the two of them,
talking, laughing; conspirators.

'Hurry up.' Ruby used her bossy voice as she held up the canvas
for Bobby to enter the treehouse.

Once inside he had reached into his satchel and presented
Ruby with a number of pieces of cardboard, all covered in multi-
tudes of silkworm eggs. She was ecstatic and caused him great
embarrassment by continually hugging him and then jumping up
and down, making the treehouse creak and shake a little.

It had been school holidays and they had watched every day,
Ruby recording in her notebook when the tiny, grey eggs stuck to
the cardboard had lightened in colour.

Finally the day they had both waited so patiently for: tiny silkworms, hundreds of them, wriggling, squirming and climbing over
each other, filling an old school port, safe in their new home.

Although Ruby had only been eight, she was fastidious about
keeping records of events that occurred in and around the
mulberry tree. She left her small notebook in the treehouse, only
removing it when she needed to record major incidents. Today she
wrote: *143 healthy silkworms. All eating leaves.*

The silkworms grew quickly, fattening on the never-ending
supply of leaves from the mulberry tree that seemed to be at its
best, the thick canopy dripping with the heaviness of its foliage
and fruit. The job of picking the greenest leaves from the tree and
making sure that all the worms were fed had been allotted to
Bobby. Bobby's other job was to clean the droppings from the
boxes so the silkworms would have enough room to move around.

They had found extra boxes, the original school port now overflowing with fat silkworms that quickly ate through the leaves. Their droppings were bright green, an indication, Ruby told Bobby, that they were happy and healthy.

Once, when Ruby was not around, Bobby had carried the largest container, the school port, down the tree and into his bedroom at home. Plugging in the vacuum cleaner, he had tried— just using the pointy end of the vacuum and not the brush part as he later explained to Ruby—to suck up the droppings and give the container a really good clean.

Ruby had not been impressed and had efficiently recorded in her notebook:

September 24, 1968, 54 large fat silkworms. Now only 12 surviveing. Bobby and vacum encident.

Now she needed to make more notes regarding the latest incident. Bobby stood beside her as she recorded in her neat handwriting:

March 4, The accident, 1970.

School port moths, 17 healthy moths, now only 7 surviveing, 2 of those are injared becous of falling from tree.

Bobby and Ruby falling over encident acident.

' What?' Ruby said as she looked up at Bobby, his mouth opening as if to speak.

Perhaps it 's not the best time to point out her spelling mistakes, he thought, as he closed his mouth, instead smiling and shaking his head. ' You're the best club president,' he said, 'and at least we still have some moths, even after the accident yesterday.'

The small girl rolled her eyes at him, an indication that she was not impressed with the situation.

He had long ago decided to ignore Ruby's habit of eye rolling, as well as to go along with most of the ideas she came up with. The time he spent with her was his only sliver of happiness in amongst the misery of home and school, and he would do anything to keep the peace between them, whatever it took to stretch out the time before he had to return home. Even though the happenings of the day before had been calamitous to Ruby, they hadn't even rated in his own list of personal disasters.

Ruby was oblivious to the situation at his house. Although he sometimes longed to tell her what was really happening, he had decided that for now it was better to keep it that way, to keep it all to himself. Just try not to think about it, he told himself.

CHAPTER 2

The accident had happened the day before, on what had started out as a typical afternoon but had quickly gone wrong; a disastrous chain of events resulting in their moth tally decreasing to just seven.

As usual, they had both rushed home after school and made their way up into the treehouse as quickly as possible. They lay side by side, enjoying the cool of the rough timber flooring in their meeting area.

Bobby was happy to lie still and listen to Ruby as she chattered on about making a new area that she wanted to call the sitting area. Although there were many sections to the treehouse, designated and specified, it was, after all, not such a big structure. They had drawn boundary lines for the different areas on the floor with white chalk, the faint lines invisible in places where their bare feet or bodies had rubbed over them.

Now they sprawled out with their heads in the spying area, feet pushed up against the stump of the activity table, their bodies stretched across three areas—spying, meeting and activities.

Bobby, being the elder and taller of the two, lay contorted, with his knees bent high and his neck twisted slightly so he could fit across the largest flat area of the treehouse. He tried to stretch out his long legs, sinewy from years of school sport and running, before resigning himself to the cramped conditions. Turning his head, he looked through the slits in the timber walls. His intense brown eyes were set deeply, and his tousled dark hair, springy with the Queensland summer humidity, framed his squarish, still boyish face.

Ruby was stretched out fully beside him with her shoulder jammed up against his, her bare feet nowhere near the stump-table that hindered the comfort of the taller Bobby. Conspirators; two sets of eyes flickering back and forth, lying deathly still as if their lives depended on invisibility.

'I told you it was a good idea,' Ruby whispered, indicating the rolled-down canvas across the doorway. ' There's no way anyone can see in now.'

'You're smart for a girl. Sometimes.'

Bobby's chuckle was cut short by the cutting look, a savage glare as the small girl turned towards him, glinting green eyes scowling, her scrunched-up face willing him to remain silent. They stared hard at each other and Bobby concentrated on her face as he counted the biggest freckles, a smattering of cute brown spots across her nose that faded into each other as they ran across the top of her somewhat chubby cheeks. There were a couple of gaps in her teeth where adult incisors had failed to come through quickly enough to mask the fact that she was still young enough to be losing baby teeth.

Knowing better than to tease Ruby about still having teeth like a baby, he kept his quick words to himself rather than incur the wrath and sharp retorts that would flow forth from her; so young but already more than capable of sticking up for herself.

Wavy blonde hair spread out beneath her, so long that it reached below her red cotton shorts. Her thin brown legs were stretched out beside him as she tried to match the length of his own. Ruby didn't like to be far behind Bobby in anything, and she was always measuring her height, telling him that one day they would be the same size.

'But you'll never be as strong as me,' he would say, flexing his muscles, thinking that one day he would have muscles as strong as Popeye in the cartoon pictures.

'My dad says that I can do anything a boy can do,' Ruby said. 'Just because I'm a girl doesn't mean I can't do stuff. He reckons I can do whatever I want, and if I want to be the strongest person, well, I can be.'

'Girls can't do some things that boys can.' Bobby looked at her, suspicious of her confidence and confused about her ideas, so different from what was promoted in his house.

'Of course they can. I can be whatever I want. If I want to be a doctor, well, I can.'

'That's not right. Girls should be nurses or mums.'

'My dad says if I want to be an astronaut like Neil Armstrong then I can be. He says I'm really smart, and when I grow up I can be whatever I want.'

'Bet you can't be a concreter like him.' 'Bet I could.'

'Girls are supposed to get married and have babies. They look after the kids and cook, clean the house.'

'I don't like cooking and cleaning. I hate cleaning the bathtub. I'm going to do something else when I'm grown up.'

'Like what?'

'I'm going to be a lawyer.'

' You mean like on *Homicide*?' he said, referring to the popular television show.

'Yeah, you know, they solve crimes.'

'I thought you weren't allowed to watch those shows. How do you know what a lawyer is when you aren't allowed to watch it?'

'Silkworm secret,' Ruby said. 'If I lie in bed with the door open, I can see the TV screen reflected in the big mirror on the sideboard. My dad's a bit deaf so he has it up pretty loud. I get to see most TV programs, but you can't tell him or Mum.'

'Lawyers are always men.' 'I watch *Matlock Police* too.'

'Your dad would be really angry if he knew you were watching those programs. You'll get in trouble if you get caught.' 'Bobby, I won't get caught. Besides, they're really scary, so most of the time I put my hands over my eyes.'

'You're so lucky that your mum and dad care about you. I wish my parents were like yours. The other day Theresa asked me how you get a new mum and dad. She's tired of all the trouble at home and the way Sally doesn't get looked after properly. I didn't know what to say. I wish I was older, then I'd run away and take them both with me.'

The two best friends stared hard at each other as they talked. It was a game they often played: who could go the longest without blinking. Both blinked sharply, however, when a loud voice bellowed up from under the tree.

'Ruby, you climb down here this minute. I know you're up there. I wasn't born yesterday.' Footsteps scuffed through the thick layer of fallen leaves, moving closer, the voice booming out again. 'You get down here *now*. I've got jobs for you to do and you're not supposed to play until your homework's done.'

The two conspirators, who had no intention of moving or answering, pulled faces at each other, imitating the adult face below.

'Your father will clip you across the ears when you come down and there' ll be no ice cream for you tonight.' Mary, Ruby's mum, waited for a reply. ' You're wasting my time, Ruby. I've got better things to do than look for you. I'm telling you now, though, if you didn't change and you've got mulberry on that school uniform there'll be hell to pay.'

The exasperated voice faded away as Ruby's mum made her way back to the house.

'She's not really mad,' Ruby whispered. 'She just likes to sound like she is, making out she's the boss.'

Bobby looked worried. 'Are you sure your dad won't thrash you?'

The small girl's laughter resounded off the rough timber walls. 'Are you joking? My dad loves me too much. He would never hit me.'

'Does your mum ever hit you?' Bobby was trying to manoeuvre his neck, which was starting to feel like it would be attached sideways on his body permanently.

Ruby's little face scrunched up, her eyes narrowing.'She loses it sometimes, especially when I keep going on about something. Because I'm more stubborn than her, she knows she can't beat me. I can always tell when she's really mad because her face goes red and her eyes … it's like she's a dragon and there's flames coming out of them, red flames licking out of her green eyes. And sometimes her lips go real thin and mean, like this.' Ruby sat up and gave a demonstration.

' What does she do? Does she use a belt?' ' Worse than that.'

'A cricket bat? A broom handle?' 'Don't be silly.'

'I know,' Bobby said, 'the whippy wire out of the curtains.' His curiosity was aroused as he imaged the horrendous punishment her mother might inflict.

' Way worse.' Ruby loved having Bobby's full attention. 'She goes all quiet, then she starts whispering all the angry things she wants to say to me.'

'You mean she doesn't scream or yell?'

Ruby rolled her eyes. 'No, she goes quieter and quieter, telling me off, saying she's going to tell Dad all the bad things I do.'

'Then what?'

'She snaps off a branch, a thin little branch from the wattle tree out the front. She sort of tests it in the air and then real quick, before I can run away, she twitches me with it.'

'Across your face?'

'No, stupid, across the back of my legs, and it stings like crazy and sometimes it leaves a red mark. If I rub it really hard I can make it stay there until Dad gets home and then I tell him that she whipped me with a thick tree branch.'

'Is that it? A bit of a whack from a wattle twig across your legs?'

' Well, it stings.'

'That's nothing, a little wattle twitch.'

'If I put it on real good and make out it hurts a lot,' Ruby said, 'when I sit with Dad at night he rubs it for me. Then he sort of lectures me, tells me how to get around Mum, how not to annoy her. You know the sort of stuff: "Your mother loves you, you need to be nice to her, don't bite the hand that feeds you." Dad reckons she's the boss.'

Bobby lay without speaking, staring up at the patchy tin roof. 'Bobby, are you listening to me? Do you reckon your mum's the boss?'

A lengthy silence followed before he spoke. ' There's no way Mum's the boss. You know my old man; you've seen what he's like. He's not kind like your dad.'

'Your dad's always nice to me,' Ruby said, 'and he gives me a little sausage when we go to your meat shop, and sometimes he makes Mum laugh. He always chats to her, tells her she has a pretty dress on, says he can smell her dinners cooking and that she must be the best cook in the street.'

'Ha.'

'Mum says that your dad has done really good to have such a big shop, and Dad reckons your dad is a good butcher giving us the meat cheaper, and he says that your sister Theresa works hard, she does really good at school, and Mum and Dad think you're smart, and your Uncle Mike, well, Mum says, "Fancy having an uncle that knows the prime minister, real high up in the government he is, and he has so much money and—"'

Bobby cut her off, wondering how she could speak for so long without a breath. 'You know things aren't always what they seem to be.'

'Like how?'

'Just … never mind.' He stretched out his stiffening muscles. 'What do you mean? Don't start something and not finish it.' 'I mean sometimes things look good to other people, but

they're only seeing what's on the outside.' ' Well, what's on the inside?'

'Forget it. I'm going to get your stupid records book so you can write up the tally.' Bobby sat up suddenly, signalling an end to the conversation.

'Hey, I'm the boss.' Ruby grabbed Bobby as he tried to stand up, his long legs wobbly and unsteady after lying cramped and still for so long. 'Just because you're older—'

And that was when, in a split second, it happened: 'the accident' as Ruby liked to refer to it.

It was like watching a slow-motion movie. Ruby gasped out loud as Bobby's legs became tangled, his body twisted, and he lurched unsteadily towards the table in the centre of the treehouse. The piece of fibro that made up the top of the table rested on the stump of a huge branch. Apart from the way the tabletop crumbled a little around the edges from time to time, it made a perfect flat surface for many of their activities.

That day a number of containers were lined up neatly across the table: an old school port with broken hinges, its stickers peeling; two shirt boxes, the colours on their sides faded and blurry; and two smaller shoeboxes. All the lids on the containers had been punched with multiple holes, providing air for the tiny creatures within.

Ruby's eyes widened as Bobby stumbled and fell forward, one arm reaching out to steady himself and stop his face smashing into the boxes on the table. His hand made contact and he grasped wildly at the closest object. Before their eyes, the largest container, the school port, turned over, the lid going one way, and the rest of the port flipping forward and landing upside down in the reading area.

'Shit.' Bobby gathered himself, standing steady, looking from Ruby to the school port.

They both knew. They knew that below that port, which was now lying lidless in the centre of the reading area, were gaps in the timber floor that opened to the ground far below. This was serious. Bobby registered the fact that Ruby hadn't reprimanded him for swearing; rule number five on the list of Silkworm Club rules.

Ruby crawled slowly over to the port and waited for Bobby. Together they lifted it, cautiously moving it straight up and not sliding it, or allowing it to have any more contact with the floor than necessary.

'Uh-oh.'Bobby pursed his lips and waited for Ruby's response. 'They've nearly all fallen through the gaps,' Ruby said. 'They won't live, they can't fly.' Her voice was shaky as she carefully tried to pick up the contents that had fallen from the container. Bobby pressed his face to the openings between the floorboards, one eye closed, trying to spy any survivors of the fall. Ruby's voice took on the steadiness and authority of the Silkworm Club president. 'I'll pick these ones up. Can you please go down and see if you can find any on the ground?'

She scooped up the mulberry leaves scattered on the floor, a few silkworm moths gripping to their surface, their delicate wings flapping wildly, their eyebrows furrowed. 'It looks like there are about five here. That means twelve are missing. This morning there were seventeen.Hurry up, Bobby, they only live for a few days so we need to find them and put them back in the box. Then they can lay their eggs.'

As usual, Bobby followed her instructions. Even though he was older by three years, Ruby was the club president, and besides, she was good at organising everything and everybody. It was easier to just follow her directions and do what he was told.

He scrambled down the tree trunk, hanging onto the timber

steps and hand guides that wound their way down to the ground. The thought of looking for white moths that had probably drifted off on the wind made him smile. He knew that the heavy leaf litter and dense ferns growing wild under the tree would envelop and hide a free-falling silkworm moth that had no sense of surviving in the wild.

But he would try; he would do anything to please Ruby because she was, after all, his best friend.

CHAPTER 3

Dad says you've just got to get on with stuff,' Ruby said as she tidied the treehouse. 'Step forward and don't cry over spilt milk. I'll bring a mat up and put it over the gaps in the floor.'

The boxes on the table were now lined up straight. Everything had to be in its place and she cast her eyes over the timber boxes, squinted and then rolled her eyes when she noticed the ice-cream tin with a few large mouldy mulberries left in it. 'Got it.' Bobby tipped the few remaining mulberries out the window, replacing the container in its correct position on the shelf. Amused at how neat she had to have everything, he watched her move the crate chairs so they were even and straight.

They both ran their hands over the boxes that were full of cocoons. When the moths hatched, they would hopefully add to their now decreased tally.

'See you in the morning,' Ruby said to the silkworms.

Bobby held up the canvas for her as they made their way out of the treehouse and into the real world below.

When they reached the bottom of the tree they sat for a while, balancing on the huge protruding roots that were covered in the same rough bark as the trunk; sections of the roots smooth however, due to the continuous movement of bare feet across them over the years.

'I have to go in,' Ruby said eventually. 'It's nearly night.

Even Dad will go mad if I come in after dark.'

'I better go home, too. I still have to do all my jobs before Dad gets home. I'm sorry about the moths, Ruby Rose.'

'Best friends don't get mad with each other. It was sort of my fault, too.'

Emerging from the cover of the trees, they turned in the direction of their houses, both looking up at the horizon as the fading light threw an orange hue over the backyard. Ruby saw the light flick on over the back veranda and knew her dad would be starting to look at the clock, wondering if he should call her in to clean up before dinner.

'See you tomorrow.' Bobby sounded despondent, sad.

He never wants to go home, Ruby thought. He must really like the silkworms, and me, better than his own family.

The darkening light separated them, the clicking of the side gate indicating that Bobby was in his own yard.

Sure enough, Ruby's dad Francis was sitting out on the back steps, his work boots and socks kicked off to the side as he enjoyed a smoke in the balmy evening light. She ran towards him, her small legs going, as her dad would say at a million miles an hour. Placing his cigarette down on the brick stairs beside him, he held both arms out as she jumped onto him. Chubby arms wrapped around his neck, her kisses smothering his face.

'My Ruby Rose, my little mulberry fairy,' he said, squeezing her tightly, his face nuzzling into her blonde wavy hair.

'I'm never going to let go of you.' Ruby clung to him, her mulberry-stained face squashed into the hairs on his chest, her legs drawn up so she could nestle in, snug and secure.

' What have you been up to today, little one?' He moved her to one side so he could puff on his cigarette.

'Dad, Dad, you'll never believe what happ—'

Her mum's voice interrupted them. 'Right, you two, the pair of you, grubs. One covered in mulberry, the other in concrete dust. You need to clean up before you come in for dinner. Stop your story right now, Ruby. We'll listen while we have dinner and then I'll decide if you get dessert.'

Ruby recalled the earlier incident, when her mother was looking for her, calling out. It seemed so insignificant now. Wait until she told them about the moths, and how Bobby had rescued two of them, then surely she would get dessert.

Francis picked her up and she wrapped herself around the front of him, her arms around his neck and her legs wrapped around his waist. They looked at each other and laughed together.

Ruby's mum put on her cranky voice. 'Clean up, both of you, or else there'll be no dinner for either of you.'

Steam rose from the hot water as Ruby bathed, only her head above the water as she lay back in the old claw-foot bath. She loved the bathtub. It was deep enough for her to float in, and the warm water closed in over her, softening the mud and mulberry stains. Her dad would be in the outside shower now, scrubbing hard, removing the dried concrete and dust, the remnants of a day of hard work. She knew he would wait until she had run the bath water, letting her get the hot water first in case it ran out. After he finished, her mum would send him in to get Ruby moving.

She hated getting out of the tub. Instead, she always drew out her time, leaving it until the last moment to take the small scrubbing brush from the wire basket hanging on the wall. Then she would scrub as hard as she could, removing all of the dirt and stains from her hands and feet. She knew her mum would inspect her cleanliness, and if she had missed any marks, Ruby would have to use the bucket and cold water outside to finish off after dinner.

The door rattled as her dad banged on it. 'Hurry up, dinner's out.'

Ruby emerged scrubbed and refreshed. Her dad hugged her, one hand ruffling her hair, both revelling in the freshness of feeling clean.

The three of them sat around the small dining-room table and ate their evening meal, her mum smiling and relaxed now, her dad talking about his day. It was the usual steak and mash, carrots, and of course the greens—beans and peas. This was their favourite time of the day. It was quiet, just the family, all tucked up together, ready to chat and catch up with what each other had done during the day.

Her dad beamed at both of them. 'Righto, Ruby Rose, now tell us what exciting things you did today.'

~~~
~~~